BOBBI AND SOUL
A VALLEY VIEW ROMANCE

JB MARSDEN

SAPPHIRE BOOKS

SALINAS, CALIFORNIA

Editor - Kaycee Hawn
Book Design - LJ Reynolds
Cover Design - Fineline Cover Design

Sapphire Books Publishing, LLC
P.O. Box 8142
Salinas, CA 93912
www.sapphirebooks.com

Printed in the United States of America
First Edition – February 2019

This and other Sapphire Books titles can be found at
www.sapphirebooks.com

BOBBI AND SOUL
A VALLEY VIEW ROMANCE

Dedication

In memory of my brother, Ronald, R.N., M.S.N., LTC
(ret.) US Army Nurse Corps
1943-2008

Acknowledgments

No writer ever makes it on her own, least of all me, who needed many hands to midwife the birth of this novel. As usual, the crew at Sapphire Books made this book palatable for your reading. I thank especially my editor, Kaycee Hawn, publisher Chris Svendsen, graphic designer/ book layout LJ Reynolds, and cover designer Fineline Cover Design.

As I began writing about Dr. Bobbi Webster, I never intended her to have issues with her past relationship, but one day, while drafting the scene at the dinner with Erin, Yancy, Gen and others, she had a reaction to the conversation. It was then that the character "told" me she was a survivor of spouse abuse. I knew not a thing about this issue. So, first, I combed the research resources of the Burlington (Iowa) Public Library to understand spouse abuse and the potential responses of individuals to post-traumatic stress. Serendipity played the next role. I attended a panel on mental health at the Golden Crown Literary Society annual convention. There I met author and panelist, Rae D. Magdon, who offered to look at my material about Bobbi. She gave generously of her time to read Bobbi's reactions, both physical and emotional, and assisted in making those portions of the text more realistic and accurate, and I thank her profusely for her feedback. Her input gave me courage to continue with Bobbi's story. Nevertheless, any errors in interpreting Bobbi's reactions to spouse abuse are mine.

I took up writing as a fun thing in retirement from my job as an Episcopal priest. While some of my knowledge of the priesthood appears in the work the character Erin accomplishes in her parish, quite a bit of her character's ramblings on Christianity are totally mine. I love God and know that God loves me unconditionally, and does not make junk. Because so many of my beliefs are spoken in this novel as Erin's brand of Christianity, I hope you, the reader, realize the very personal nature of my Christianity. I do not claim to speak for other Christians, even though most of my clergy friends would agree with these beliefs.

Before being ordained to the priesthood, I held faculty positions in health systems organization and policy, focusing on rural health systems, from whence come the Valley View books about the people in a rural medical clinic. This is the second book set in that setting, and hopefully not the last. Some characters from the first novel, *Reclaiming Yancy*, have drifted into this novel, but the novel stands on its own.

I appreciate the relationship I have built with my local independent bookstore, Burlington by the Book, and its owner, Chris Murphy: for his support of local writers like me, for selling my books, and for inviting me to his fun activities for authors in our area of the country. I thank my sisters for their continuing support in this crazy idea to write, for being proud of me, and for giving me unconditional love. I am so grateful for my wife and love, Molly, for her steadfast encouragement, her willingness to watch me write into the night, even while worrying about my sleep, and for understanding when I half listen to her as I type away. She gives good feedback on drafts, too.

Notwithstanding all the above-mentioned education and the treasured relationships that have underpinnned this book about a priest and a doctor, I thank God for the gifts so richly bestowed upon me, and for the desire to write, which has, in surprising ways, drawn other queer people of faith to me.

Chapter One

*B*uzz, *buzz, buzz.* Bobbi downed the last dregs of her Hefeweizen, savoring the hints of citrus and clove, while trying to ignore the text coming through from the Babcock County Hospital's emergency department number. Damn, why did they *always* call her during a date?

"Sorry," she murmured to Amanda, an attractive woman who worked as a nurse at the hospital. Bobbi grabbed the phone and took the call. "Be right back." She winked and grinned at Amanda, then left their table for the door. "Dr. Webster."

"Hi, Dr. Webster." It was the ER nurse manager. "One of your patients just showed up with vomiting, diarrhea, and a fever. We've got him on a saline drip, but Dr. Manning is slammed tonight. A big wreck on the highway. Dr. Lambert already came in to help."

"I'll be there in twenty." Bobbi ended the call, sighed, and looked back at the cute brunette, who sipped her white wine while listening to the guitar guy playing some folk-Americana music here at the microbrewery. Bobbi had heard about this place and had been wanting to come, being a beer lover. Amanda was a fun person whom Bobbi had dated once before. No strings, no expectations, and no flashbacks to Stephanie—Bobbi's type of night.

When she made it back to their table, Amanda looked up with a slight frown. "Gotta run?"

"Sorry." Bobbi shrugged and slung her coat across her shoulder.

"I'll go too."

"No. No need." Bobbi stilled Amanda with a hand on her shoulder.

"No fun without you here." Amanda gave her a sexy smile.

Bobbi's libido ramped up. *Boy, what a waste of a night,* she thought. She helped Amanda on with her coat. They had driven separately, because Amanda said she liked her independence. It had proven to be true when she stayed overnight at Bobbi's last Saturday night. Bobbi smiled ruefully, sure her disappointment showed on her face.

But she was here in rural Colorado, not to meet up with women, but to get her skills honed in treating rural patients. Her goal was to open her own family medicine practice in her eastern Oregon hometown or join another one close by. So, breaking a date to take this patient was a no-brainer. Clinics and hospitals were short-staffed out here on the plains, just like home in the high desert of Oregon. Physicians could not be lured easily to places without amenities. Hell, this town didn't even have a good place to eat that wasn't fast food or fried food, barring the local diner that had a pretty good mutton stew occasionally. Thank God for this cute microbrewery, even though they'd had to drive to San Sebastian, a thirty-mile trip from Babcock.

She put her hand on the small of Amanda's back as they made their way together to the parking lot. Their breaths fogged as soon as they left the warm brewery. "Thanks for coming with me. I appreciate you making the effort, since you're not a beer lover." Bobbi pecked Amanda on the lips. "Can we have a rain check?"

Amanda returned the kiss and deepened it. "Sure thing, cutie." She chucked Bobbi under the chin and turned to get into her battered Ford Explorer.

"Drive carefully." Even though it was five years old, her own four-wheel drive Honda gave her confidence, but Bobbi was a little concerned about Amanda's older car making it back to town.

"Been driving these roads all my life. Don't worry about me," Amanda said with a small smile, as if she read Bobbi's concern over her beat-up car. She closed the door, and started the car. Bobbi watched her pull out onto the snow-packed road.

When Bobbi arrived at the hospital, the ER looked like a small tornado had swept through two patient treatment bays. Used plastic tubing, bloodied gauze, electrical connectors for the EKG, and surgical gloves littered the floor. A blue ER gown with a large rust-colored stain hung out of the linen bin in the corner. Although it was quiet, Bobbi felt a lingering sizzle in the air from the bustle and drama of the minutes before she arrived.

"Bobbi." She turned to the right. Dr. Lambert waved her over. "Our little ER got totally filled up tonight. Your patient is in bay four. We've stabilized him, but we've been taking care of three MVAs. We had to medevac one to Denver, barely hanging on with internal bleeding from her injuries. The other, her boyfriend, just went upstairs to the OR to have a reduction of a compound fracture of the left tibia. Jaime and I are working on the third victim in bay three. An older man who we think had a heart attack and may have sustained other trauma we're trying to detect right now."

Bobbi nodded. "Wow, you *have* been busy.

Thanks for taking care of my patient, Dr. Lambert."
Dr. Gen Lambert, the medical director of Valley
View Medical Care and their two clinics, was also her
fellowship director, someone she liked very much, so
far. She watched Gen go back into bay three and caught
the tail end of Dr. Jaime Garcia-Brown, the fellow on
call, talking. "...BP stable. Where's the x-ray?"

Bobbi passed their bay, walked down the hall,
and pushed open the doors to the staff changing room
to don scrubs and a lab coat from the hook at her place.
Coming out into the hall, she nearly collided with the
gurney whisking through the hall with patient number
three from the accident. She swerved and plastered
herself against the wall while Jaime and a nurse passed
her by. At the nurses' station, she grabbed a tablet
from a charging dock, ran her fingerprint ID across the
screen, and scrolled to find the vitals on her patient.
She then pushed aside the curtain and began her
assessment.

≈≈≈≈≈

Arriving back at her condo in a new development
on the outskirts of town around three a.m., Bobbi
pulled off her boots, shrugged out of the parka, and
tossed it onto the couch. Normal routine: dark house,
quiet, alone. The electronic thermostat had already
shifted to cooler temperatures for nighttime sleeping
and she rubbed her arms as she trudged into her small
bedroom. Wearily pulling off her faded jeans, wool
sweater, plaid shirt, and jog bra, she nabbed chilled
pajama pants and long-sleeved T-shirt from a hook on
the bathroom door. She pulled them on, immediately
feeling the goosebumps on her body. She stretched her

back, which had stiffened from being in the cold after standing some amount of time in the ER.

Feeling frozen to the bone, the instant cocoa warmed her and also helped her come down from the frisson of excitement. As she sipped her cocoa in bed, she flipped through social media on her phone, but decided it was much too late to send a text to Amanda.

She'd admitted her patient to Babcock, their local small rural hospital, for overnight observation. He reported eating sushi from a gas station a day ago. A gas station! She couldn't believe someone would buy uncooked fish at a truck stop on a Colorado highway. He was old enough to know better, but he reported drinking beer before stopping at the station on his way home from his job at a local ranch, which Bobbi reckoned fogged his better judgment. He, like many others she'd treated for food borne illnesses, must have thought, "Alcohol will kill anything bad."

She treated him for salmonella even though the labs would not be conclusive until Saturday some time. She sighed into her cocoa, wondering at peoples' thinking process. Or rather, their lack of thinking. Lots of non-thinking activities brought locals to the ER doors, even at small places like Babcock. Weekend nights especially plagued ERs across the country, as drinking and driving, fights, and other traumatic activities brought people for treatment. She wondered how the wreck on the highway had happened, resulting in three injured people, one very seriously, and hoped impaired driving hadn't been the culprit.

Amanda had been a trooper about the call interrupting their date. Bobbi was not on call last night, but in rural areas like this, she expected to have to show up even when she was off, certainly because patients stacked up in small local ERs, but also, her fellowship in rural medicine made demands on her learning that she did not want to treat lightly. Dr. Gen Lambert told the rural medicine fellows on their first day, three weeks ago, to expect unscheduled call-ins just like this.

As far as Bobbi saw at this early stage of her fellowship, Lambert exemplified the work ethic she expected from her rural medicine fellows. She came into the clinic an hour or more before it started and stayed until all the paperwork had been finished and the labs and other tests were reviewed for each patient. Especially, Dr. Lambert did not treat her rural medical trainees like residents, making them do all legwork for laboratory and medical tests.

More impressive to Bobbi, her boss's encounters with the other staff, whether doctors, nurses, or techs, were never anything but professional, and all her communications stayed respectful, even in the throes of an emergency. Dr. Lambert dealt with both physicians and other staff equally, regardless of their credentials.

Most astounding, Bobbi could not remember hearing her gossip about co-workers, a major accomplishment in the clinic's bubbling cauldron of cliques, stories, whispers, and innuendo. Bobbi hated gossip, especially since she'd been the focus of it during her earlier residency days in rural Oregon.

She shouldn't be surprised; Dr. Lambert's excellent credentials stood out, as the former director of rural training in the family medicine program at Kentucky. She'd been hired to create a training program for rural family medicine here in this well-funded clinic outpost in eastern Colorado. Bobbi wished she knew

Dr. Lambert better and hoped she would as her two fellowship years progressed. But she found her hard to get to know so far. While her boss dropped her own work in a second to consult with the resident fellows, she had a professional distance about her. Bobbi knew the doctor was engaged to Yancy Delaney, a prominent local rancher, but she shared no personal information about herself.

She had briefly met Dr. Lambert's fiancée, one of the benefactors of the non-profit that owned and operated two rural clinics, when the fellowship started January 2nd. Delaney, as board president, had formally greeted their group of three resident fellows who initiated the very first physician training program for Valley View Medical Center.

Bobbi smiled, thinking about the handsome board president and sophisticated Dr. Lambert. They seemed like opposites—Lambert, put-together medical authority, with never a hair out of place; Delaney, relaxed in her boots, jeans, and western shirt. Both good looking in their own way. Both crazy smart. Nice, Bobbi thought, to be around other women leaders.

Yawning, Bobbi tipped the cocoa cup to drain it, then put it on the nightstand. This fellowship would be just what she needed to continue her training and set up shop in her hometown. She felt proud and very happy to be here in Babcock County, Colorado.

Chapter Two

E rin grabbed everything she needed for her Tuesday clergy group—her travel mug full of her own coffee blend, her lectionary text, and her sermon notebook. No one ever arrived on time, so she dawdled along the snowy highway the twenty minutes it took to reach San Sebastian.

Her clergy group, composed of leaders of the progressive churches in the two counties, provided a small respite from dealing with the everyday issues of her priesthood. She could put aside her worry about the old furnace that made terrible noises during services, or her fears about the health of her favorite parishioner and lay leader, Charlotte Stephens.

Today, her mind pondered whether her own church, Holy Spirit, could make it another year with a part-time clergy, or whether she would either lose her job or be put on an even smaller part-time salary. They'd just passed a deficit budget, estimated to be five thousand dollars in the hole by the end of the year.

No church she knew had it easy these days, as Christianity had entered a new phase of its life in the world. Gone were the halcyon days of big congregations and big pledgers. Nowadays, most churches could barely keep their doors open. Several, teetering on the brink of demise in her home diocese of Chicago, had closed in the last ten years. She'd only been ordained five years, but her theology education prepared seminarians to expect to need other sources of income, even another job, because of the diminishing number of full-time clergy positions around the nation, and indeed, in most industrialized countries.

Some blamed the entrance of women and gay clergy as the death knell of Christianity, straying from its rootedness in "orthodoxy." But she, and others like her, felt that Christianity had taken a turn *toward* the gospel of love for all people, not away from it. The gospel, Jesus's love and compassion for the outcasts of society, did not agree with everyone's politics, either during Jesus's time in the first century or now.

With these big thoughts, she arrived at the snowy parking lot of St. Lucy's, where the vicar, James Latimer, met her at the door, dressed in jeans and red Converse sneakers, his hipster beard long and bushy.

"Morning, Erin." James smiled, while opening the door for her. "Came to make sure the door got unlocked." He rolled his brown eyes.

Erin smirked. James's office volunteer, Dwayne, who came only on Tuesdays, and whose duty was to unlock the door, was notoriously forgetful. Together, they intoned, "But he's free staff," then giggled like teens.

Erin scooched through the door with her full messenger bag, juggling her coffee mug. "Beautiful morning, if you like this sort of thing," she joked, because, while the sun shone brightly, the temperature would make it to only eight degrees today. They walked down the small corridor outside James's office, where he stopped at a sink to start the coffee brewing.

Erin tossed her bag on a chair in his cramped office. A laptop, several large biblical commentaries, and papers crammed the desk in the corner. Floor to ceiling bookshelves along the far wall groaned under the weight of too many books stuffed in any way possible along the shelves. She cringed again at the disorder but laughed inwardly. The smartest guy she knew, James's work area still looked a wreck. On the other hand, her work spaces, both at church and at the vicarage, held well-ordered tomes, arranged by topic. She neatly filed sermons away each week, so she could access old ones as the liturgical year cycled around. Whenever she carelessly tossed one on her shelf after a Sunday service, she became antsy until she had time to put it away.

Her mother called her a neatnik. Whatever.

The oldest of the clergy group, Mary Jane and Leon, already sat in their usual seats—Mary Jane on the right wall, in front of the low, shabby coffee table, Leon in front of the wall of books. They all greeted each other.

Mary Jane, in her skirt, tailored wool jacket, and clerical blouse, probably headed to some meeting after the clergy group, busied herself dragging out a file of sermon notes, her book of weekly bible texts, and her Greek bible from a large woven bag. Leon sat without any papers or books of any kind, one brown corduroy leg crossed at the ankle over the other one, his potbelly hanging low, sipping a jumbo iced drink from the local convenience store. Mary Jane was the putative leader of the group, but each week, a different clergy member led the discussion of the week's biblical texts assigned for the next Sunday, and which served as the fodder for their sermons.

Erin took the space next to Mary Jane on the second-hand love seat. Jeans-clad Erin felt underdressed next to her, but Mary Jane didn't seem to notice.

"How're the natives?" Mary Jane asked. Mary Jane had taken a proprietary interest in Erin since she'd arrived last May. Holy Spirit, Erin's church, was still coming to grips with hiring her as their very first gay clergyperson. A cadre of parishioners welcomed her with open arms, while a vocal few made their dissatisfaction with her known, often and to all and sundry. Once a week, Erin had met with Walter, an older parishioner, whose job, he decided, was to point out every small error Erin made. One week, he complained about the smallness of the print in the bulletins. She dutifully enlarged the font for the next Sunday, which increased the number of sheets of paper. So, the next week he claimed they were killing too many trees by using more paper.

"Oh, about the same. No one has tried to fire me this week, anyway." Erin wanted to laugh, but then decided it was true.

"My parishioner was found guilty. Maybe you all saw it in the county news." Mary Jane drank out of a Clergy Pension Group mug. She had deeper dark circles under her eyes this week. Erin wondered what else she was dealing with.

"Oh, man," Erin said. "The meth lab guy?"

Mary Jane nodded. "He and his girlfriend both."

"Got to have some income, you know?" Leon joked. "What about the death of the old man in Johnson County?"

Mary Jane frowned at Erin in concern.

"You mean the murder?" Erin clapped her hand over her mouth. "Damn. You didn't hear that." She felt her blush rise.

All eyes fell on Erin. "I can't say more. His

daughter came to talk to one of my parishioners. She shared it in confidence. But I did hear from other sources that four people have been arrested. Let me just say drugs were involved." Erin scrunched her face in remorse.

"Crap," Leon said.

The last members of the group, a pastor in Erin's county, her friend Julia, and Hugh, from this county, appeared in the doorway, casing the lone empty chair. James filed in behind them, lugging another folding chair in one hand and the coffee pot in another. He laid the chair up against the door frame and set the coffee pot on the coffee table. "We can put this one in the doorway," he said as he unfolded and placed the chair.

Mary Jane sighed. "When are we going to find a larger place to meet?"

Erin groaned inwardly. Every few months, they discussed finding another meeting spot. The local diner: too loud. The library: too quiet. Another church: too far to travel, especially in the winter. They always came back to meeting here at St. Lucy's, the most central location, despite it being, by far, the smallest of their collective churches. No one had an answer for Mary Jane.

After Julia sat on the chair James had clapped down, she held up her hand. She waited a minute until the clanking of the heat radiator stopped. "Before we start in on meeting places again, I have an announcement. Raymond started kidney dialysis yesterday. I'd like your prayers."

A silence overcame the group.

Erin's stomach dropped. She placed her hand on top of Julia's, her heart plummeting about the news of

Julia's husband, who'd been fighting kidney ailments the past year.

"I'm so sorry." James stopped his forward movement toward his desk chair, turned, and gave Julia a side hug. "What can we do?"

Tears threatened to run down her cheek. "Hugs are great," she said in a raspy voice.

James said, "We'll certainly have you and Raymond in our prayers." He made his way to his desk and finally all were seated. "Good to see everyone. Where's Gary?"

"Remember, he took a vacation right after Christmas, to see his in-laws in New York." Mary Jane had a memory to rival an elephant.

Hugh asked, "Who's leading today?"

"It's you, Leon," Mary Jane, the keeper of the group's schedule, said.

They all groaned aloud for Leon's sake. Erin smiled at their joking around.

"I am deeply hurt," Leon, the group's jokester said, mocking himself. "But did you hear about the priest, the minister, and the rabbi who wanted to see which one was best at their job?" Everyone grinned, anticipating Leon's story. "So, each one goes into the woods, finds a bear, and attempts to convert it. Later, they all get together to compare notes. The priest says, 'When I found the bear, I read to him from the Baltimore Catechism and sprinkled him with holy water. Next week is his First Communion.' The minister says, 'I found a bear by the stream and preached God's Holy Word. The bear was so mesmerized that he let me baptize him.' Then, both the priest and the minister look down expectantly at the rabbi, who is lying on a gurney in a body cast. 'Looking back,' the rabbi says, 'maybe I shouldn't have started with circumcision.'"

Groans all around. Laughing a little, Erin shook her head again. Leon could be trusted to make the worst jokes. But, what would she do without this group? It kept her balanced, laughing at herself, putting priestly difficulties in perspective.

"I could 'bearly' stand that one," James said. More laughter and groans.

"Very punny," Hugh added.

Erin laughed between sips from her travel mug, shaking her finger at Leon. Fortunately, she loved playing around with her clergy group, mainly because she so rarely got to with her parishioners. Oh, they entertained her, especially the antics of Mike and Carol Ellesby, the biggest donors and the most faithful in attendance, who just happened to be the most laid-back folks in the congregation. She often joked around with Mike as they stood at the back of the church before walking down the small aisle of Holy Spirit to begin the Sunday service.

But mostly, her parishioners were stoic ranchers, harried office workers, and a couple of overworked professionals, most of them in their fifties, sixties, or older, too tired to joke much. Two parishioners lived in the county home for the elderly. One, a widower in his nineties, still lived at home but could not make it to church on Sundays. Another older woman just told her last week she was moving to St. Louis to be near her daughter and her son-in-law.

Leon's joke led to others. The banter went on for a good ten minutes, before Mary Jane, ever on task, took an opportunity during a lull in the laughter to say, "Here we go," then she read aloud the first reading for the upcoming Sunday, while they shifted in their seats and settled back, smiles melting into the work at hand.

Hugh read the next reading appointed for the upcoming Sunday service in all their churches. It was an obscure passage of a letter from the apostle Paul to the newly formed church in Corinth. They all discussed St. Paul's context, and what Paul could possibly have meant by writing about the end times to his flock in Greece.

Then Erin read the gospel. Leon regaled them with his vast and detailed exegesis of the passage from the gospel of Mark designated for next Sunday, about Jesus calling two fishermen to follow him. Erin sighed under her breath.

Leon went on for some minutes "mansplaining," as Erin thought of it. He ended with, "Follow me and I will make you fishers of beer."

"Lutherans," Erin said, her brows raised to the heavens.

They laughed.

"What do Episcopalians drink?" Leon asked plaintively.

Without a pause, James stated in mock seriousness, "Where two or three are gathered, there is bound to be a fifth." James winked at Erin, who smiled at the old joke.

More laughter.

Then, they got serious again. A discussion ensued of some of the more esoteric aspects of the passage in the gospel and how to link it with other bible readings for the day.

Somehow, they got off the topic yet again. James told a story about prejudices against Hispanic people in his parish. Most of the group agreed they had the same problem. The discussion waned.

"Hey, are we going to pray?" Hugh said.

They forgot to pray unless Hugh reminded them. Erin smiled ruefully that clergy, people in the "God business," forgot to pray for themselves. Hugh led them in a closing prayer that mentioned Julia's husband Raymond, the man murdered in Johnson County, and all who suffered from drug addiction; he asked God's blessing on each of their parishes and for each of them as spiritual leaders. Hugh's prayer made her day. As a new vicar, she needed any help she could get.

Chapter Three

A manda took her coat off and Bobbi hung it in the front closet.

She turned around and Amanda slid her arms around her neck and kissed her softly. "Thanks for dinner tonight. I enjoy being with you."

"Mmm." Warmth spread from Bobbi's stomach further south and created want.

"Would you like a nightcap?" Bobbi turned, bent from the waist, and opened a cabinet door in the built-in bookshelves. Rummaging around in it for a minute, she said, "I have bourbon and some beer in the fridge." She stood and produced a bottle of red wine. "And some Chilean wine."

"No, thanks, nothing for me." Amanda wrapped her arms around Bobbi again.

"Would you like to go to my room?"

Amanda murmured between kisses, "Thought you'd never ask, Doc."

They stumbled into the bedroom, clothing flung on the floor in their wake. Bobbi backed Amanda onto the bed and levered herself on top. The warmth turned into an insistent pulse between her thighs. They kissed passionately, both groaning and breathing deeply. Bobbi thought her lungs would burst with the pent-up sexual tension.

She looked down at Amanda, whose eyes burned with lust, and knew she'd picked a good companion for a light fling. Amanda didn't make demands. She gave Bobbi great sex and expected nothing in return except to be treated with respect. The perfect friend with benefits.

On an impulse, Bobbi murmured, "Strap on?" into Amanda's ear.

"God, yes," Amanda said between gasps.

Her breath ramping up in anticipation, Bobbi shuffled around in her nightstand drawer. She stood and slipped on the leather strap with the purple dildo dangling from it. She leaned back onto Amanda and thrust toward her. Amanda grabbed the dildo and stroked it between their bodies a few times, firing Bobbi's want even more. Bobbi closed her eyes and moaned, then reached for the lube and applied it. She raised up then slid back down, while Amanda guided the dildo into her vagina. They both groaned. Bobbi was throbbing now.

God, Bobbi thought, *if this is half as good for Amanda as it is for me, we both won't last long.* They bucked together in a rhythm that beat louder and faster with the minutes.

Panting, Bobbi asked, "You okay?" She felt things building in her own groin.

"Just keep going, baby." Amanda gasped her answer.

After another few minutes of Bobbi's steady strokes into Amanda, she yelled out and spasmed, grabbing Bobbi's shoulders in a clinch that dug into the flesh. Bobbi responded with her own wet climax and collapsed on top of Amanda. They both breathed like fire engines.

Bobbi looked into Amanda's grinning face, her light brown hair spread across the pillow.

"Wow, that was worth waiting for," Amanda said

with a loud sigh.

Bobbi lifted off Amanda and took off the toy. She laid next to her, bringing her arm around Amanda's shoulder and her head into the crook of her arm. They lay there for some time, getting their breaths back and relaxing into each other.

Bobbi played with Amanda's blond highlights. After a few minutes, Amanda sat up in bed to look at Bobbi. "As much as I'm comfortably snuggled here, I really need to go. Thank you for a very sexy time." She kissed Bobbi's lips lightly, then got up from the bed to dress.

Bobbi stretched, then hopped out of bed and donned her robe. "I'll walk you out." At the door, she helped Amanda with her coat, and kissed her on the cheek and said, "I'll call you, okay?"

"Sure. Good night." Amanda smiled and walked out to her car.

Bobbi closed and locked the door and leaned against it, feeling the post-coital haze fade away. The apartment fell silent except for a ticking of her kitchen clock.

Her living room held only a small brown couch, a matching, tatty, overstuffed chair, and a scratched, dark-maple coffee table, all second hand. Nothing here felt particularly homelike or welcoming. From the time she'd had her own apartment in medical school, home décor didn't make her list of top ten priorities. Tonight, after the disconnectedness of sex with Amanda, a weight of sadness descended on her in the plain, echoing living room.

Amanda treated her well. They both wanted the same thing: no risk. How long could she go without having a deeper, more fulfilling relationship, though? She and Stephanie ended last year, badly, as she finished her second year of residency in Oregon. Remembering, she shivered, partly from fear. No, make that entirely from fear. She shrugged off the beginnings of remembrance, steeled herself, and breathed. Better. Definitely calmer.

❧ ❧ ❧ ❧

At the end of the next day, readying to take night call, Bobbi checked in with one of the other fellows, Dr. Joe Manning, and Dr. Lambert, in Dr. Lambert's office, around five-thirty. Joe reported a quiet night last night. Only one call, a child with an ear infection. He had met the child and her parents at the clinic and started treatment about two in the morning, then sent them home with meds and instructions.

Bobbi listened to her colleague's Arkansas twang closely. She liked both the other fellows, Joe and Jaime. She appreciated Joe's quiet way and understanding of rural farming life, his own background. Joe's wife Marty served as a nurse at the hospital and they had two small preschool-age girls. Marty had studied nursing at Iowa, and they met while Joe was a medical student at the University of Arkansas, where she had her first nursing job. Bobbi had yet to work with Marty at BCH, since she worked with pediatric patients, and Bobbi'd not admitted any children since coming to Valley View. She listened while Joe finished his summary of the little girl he had treated last night, wondering if he thought of his own girls when he had seen the patient.

The presenting medical problems of clients here echoed the problems she had seen on call as a family medicine resident in rural eastern Oregon— minor, acute issues or flair-ups of chronic diseases. An occasional life-threatening episode, like a heart attack or, too often, car crashes. Sometimes a woman in the throes of labor. She looked forward to giving patients her attention, no matter what the problem.

But, hardly anyone called their doctor in the middle of the night without something real needing attention. Rural adults barely called the doctor anyway. They needed coaxing to come for any preventive care. Yes, they took care of their children's vaccinations and showed up for their school physicals but parents didn't come in for their own problems.

Rural adults were not used to relying on others for health care. Her own father waited a day before he had her mother take him to the emergency room after he cut his arm on fencing. Her mom came home from teaching third grade, saw the five-inch gash on his arm, treated it with over-the-counter antibiotic cream, a gauze bandage, and a pain killer, and they went to bed. When the arm became red, swelled, and the cut oozed pus the next day, she had to take a day off from school to take him into the nearest medical clinic. Even then, he wouldn't let them stitch him up, after he found out it would cost more. No, rural patients would give her little worry tonight.

At home later that evening, sipping tea after dinner, Bobbi sat in the uncomfortable chair in the living room of her rented condo. She flicked through an issue of the *Journal of the American Medical Society* devoted entirely to articles on rural medicine. The articles spanned the gamut of topics, from electronic means of treatment and rural social medicine to rural health policy. Her eyes grew heavy, and she noted that it was after eleven. She'd read longer than she thought.

She went to bed after a long, hot shower,

yawning. Her condo tended to be on the cool side, so the shower warmed her hands and feet. Just as she lifted the sheets to get into bed, her phone buzzed with the number of the clinic's after-hours answering service. She answered, wrote down the patient's number, and phoned it.

"This is Dr. Webster."

"Doctor?" A woman's voice.

"Yes. Who is this?"

"This is Maria Sterling. My dad, Harold Mendes, is a patient at the Delaney Clinic. I'm here at our house and he isn't responding to me." Her voice became high; she sniffled. "He's breathing, but I can't wake him up."

In her head, Bobbi ran through the possible issues. "How old is he?"

"My dad's ninety-nine."

Could be anything at his advanced age, Bobbi reasoned to herself. "Okay. Call an ambulance and get him to Babcock County Hospital. I will meet you at the emergency room."

"Can you come here, please? The hospital's so sterile and impersonal. He would hate it, I know."

Bobbi closed her eyes for a minute to think. After she asked Maria some other information, she said, "Okay. What's the address?" Bobbi typed Maria's address into her phone. "I'll be there in ten minutes."

Bobbi quickly rose from the bed, pulled up her wool trousers, shrugged into a turtleneck, and threw a sweater over top, not noting whether it all matched or not. She opened the closet, checked her medical bag, got on her parka, hat, gloves, and scarf, and headed out the door to the private drive where her Honda was parked in the snow.

In less than ten minutes, the GPS led her to a

small bungalow on Rancho Delgado Street with the right number. Two cars filled the short gravel driveway, so she parked on the street. When the door opened, she met a petite woman with pixie-cut, brown hair and glowing, creamy skin. Her heart immediately beat faster. She's small, petite. Bobbi quickly took a deep breath. But, what a cutie.

"Maria?"

"No. Come in, Doctor. I'm Harold's priest. Maria called me first and I suggested she phone the clinic."

Bobbi nodded, glancing at the small, attractive woman who said she was a priest, and took off her winter outerwear before going farther into the overheated house.

"He's in the bedroom." The priest led her down a small hall. "I'm Erin, by the way."

Bobbi took her hand and stared at her face, complete with dimples and twinkling eyes. Not quite like Stephanie. Breathe, she told herself. *She looks like an elf*, Bobbi thought. "Dr. Bobbi Webster."

The bedroom was stifling hot. A very old man's pale, wrinkled face peeked out of a heavy, navy blue comforter.

"Hello, thank you for coming, Doctor." An older woman looked up at her for a moment and went back to stroking what little hair the old man had. "I'm Harold's daughter, Maria."

"I'm Dr. Webster. I'll do short assessment and see what's going on." Both women stood quietly to the side. Bobbi opened her medical bag and fished out her stethoscope, thermometer, and blood pressure cuff, but when she saw his face drooping to one side with drool dripping down, she asked, "How long has his face drooped?"

"Never before," Maria answered.

Bobbi checked the blood pressure, which was quite high. She tried to rouse him without any success. "Is he being treated for anything at all? High blood pressure? High cholesterol? Heart condition?"

Maria looked thoughtfully and said, "No. I've been taking him to his check-ups for the last year. They only said it was old age."

"Um-hmm." Bobbi took out her tablet. "Does he have Wifi?" She kicked herself as soon as the words were out of her mouth.

The priest raised her eyebrows with a quick, teasing grin. "No. No Wifi. No internet. No cell phone. He's ninety-nine years old."

"Sorry, dumb question," Bobbi mumbled, feeling herself blush. "I would like to get him to the hospital as soon as possible. He's had a cerebral vascular accident and we need to treat him as soon as possible. The sooner you treat a CVA, the better the outcome."

Maria looked at Erin. "What's a CVA?"

"Stroke."

Marie shook her head and said, "He would definitely not want to go to the hospital."

Erin stepped closer to Bobbi and produced a paper. "This is the DNR order and the living will I helped him fill out last summer. He does not wish to have any extraordinary measures."

"That's not what those documents mean." Bobbi eyed them briefly. "They mean that he wishes not to be put on life-saving equipment that would breathe for him. He's breathing on his own, so that's not the issue." Bobbi's eyes slanted into Erin's, trying to get her to understand what was happening here.

"We know that," Erin answered. "But Maria

and Harold and I all had a specific conversation a few months ago. He did not wish to be in a hospital in his last days. For anything. It's spelled out here." She held out the document again.

"Look here, er, Reverend," Bobbi said, her heart starting to beat in her ears. *I will make my opinions known. I will take control.* "My job is to make sure he makes it to another birthday. I won't be able to help him do that unless his daughter takes him where he can receive the proper treatment. First, we need to restore blood to his brain by giving him some anti-coagulants. Get an MRI, CT, check his carotid arteries. Then later, therapy—"

Maria's tears coursed down her cheeks. "No. No. You don't understand. He wants to die here at home. He's never been in a hospital. He wants to stay here. He asked that we help him stay home. I'll take some days off to take care of him."

Bobbi puffed out her cheeks while she took in the two stubborn women in front of her. "May we continue this conversation somewhere else?"

They gathered in the small living room. Erin and Maria sat together on a flowered couch. Bobbi sat on the matching, frayed chair. "Are you saying he wants end-of-life care? He wants no medical care to prolong his life?" Bobbi looked intensely at them each.

"Yes." Maria sat up and nodded. "That's it exactly." Erin put her hand on Maria's shoulder.

Bobbi rubbed her temple. A headache began pounding. "I'm not sure he's dying. He could recover quite nicely."

"Yes. But he could do that here at home."

"Maria, are you your father's power of attorney?"

Maria looked at Erin. "What's that?"

Erin answered, "She means, do you write his checks, make his decisions?"

"Oh. Yes, yes all of that. He hasn't been able to write checks since he fell last winter."

"Your father fell? Did he have a head injury? Did anyone, anyone medical that is, look at him?"

"No, Doctor. You don't understand. He didn't go unless I took him. He said he was fine after he fell. But I noticed he was a little slower. Moved slower. Lost some memory, maybe."

Bobbi nodded slowly. She tried hard not to groan. "Reverend, is this all correct?" Bobbi decided to get all the information. This was becoming one killer headache.

"I've lived in Colorado only since last May, over in Johnson County. I've visited with him and Maria several times when I brought communion. Maria lives with her father, provides his meals, and takes care of getting him to his check-ups. She is very competent. His cognitive abilities have been very good up until tonight and he made these decisions with a clear mind. He knows what he wants, and that's not to go to any hospital. To die in any hospital." The Elf raised her head and straightened her narrow shoulders.

Bobbi sighed deeply. "I'm sorry. I'm not used to this kind of problem. He may not be approved for hospice care if he has some rehabilitation capability. Also, if he wanted to die at home, why did you call the clinic tonight?"

Maria let out a small, "Oh."

Erin said, "I had Maria call so that we could get his condition checked out, maybe get the right kinds of medication for him. We did not call expecting him to be hospitalized."

"I am beginning to see," Bobbi said wearily. "Do you have his medications? I would like to see what he has been taking."

Maria rushed into the bathroom and returned with four medication bottles.

Bobbi took them from her and studied them. "Let's see. We do have a blood pressure medication. An arthritis medication—"

"He had terrible arthritis in his hands," Maria piped up, worry lines deep in her face.

"A blood thinner. And an iron pill. Is this all? You're sure no heart medication?" Bobbi handed them all back to Maria.

"That's it."

"So, where are we?" Bobbi had written the meds and the doses into her tablet. "I could give you a prescription for a larger dose of the blood pressure medication, which is certainly indicated." She handed Maria a prescription. "Tomorrow I could call hospice and get someone over to assess him as a candidate for care."

"Yes," Erin said. "Very appropriate. Hospice would bring comfort for both Maria and her brothers. And it's Harold's wishes."

"I must be honest with you both. My training prepares me to treat and heal. Only after all other treatment is no longer indicated do I bring in hospice. It's the last-ditch effort, palliative care, that is. Care for comfort only. I'm going against my own instincts not to bring Mr. Mendes into the hospital. But, on the other hand, I understand a man of his age not wanting to leave home. My dilemma is that I haven't made an effort to make him as functional as I can with my skills, as I have taken an oath to do. Do you understand where

I'm coming from?"

Maria and Erin looked at each other. Maria looked directly at Bobbi and said, "You're a healer. My dad doesn't want healing; he wants to go peacefully."

Bobbi nearly whimpered. "You've said that, yes. But I don't believe he *is* dying. My expert opinion is that he may be capable of recovery. His stroke is new. With quick intervention, he may be fully functional again."

Erin eyed the doctor. "Do you really believe he'd talk, walk, and eat like he has been, without any disability at all?"

Bobbi stammered, "He may, yes." This elf wanted to be the boss, Bobbi realized. Breathe, just breathe.

"But, a ninety-nine-year-old man also needs his dignity and independence. Chances are quite low that he'd retain any of those skills after a very severe stroke. You can't argue with a person's needs, Doctor." The priest's face turned cold.

Bobbi pulled her hand through her short hair and rubbed her eyes. "Dignity and independence."

"Yes." Erin stared at her.

Bobbi met her stare. "I'll call hospice tomorrow." She went into Mr. Mendes's bedroom to retrieve her medical kit items. She checked his pulse. It was steady but barely perceptible. Perhaps he wanted to die.

Maria and Erin stood as Bobbi stepped back into the living room to go to the front door. "Good night, Dr. Webster. I hope we haven't called you out for nothing. But you now know what my father wants."

"Yes. It's abundantly clear to me. Good night to both of you." Bobbi strove to keep a neutral face. She nodded to Erin and Maria, put on her cold weather gear, and Maria opened the door for her.

Chapter Four

A nd you say he may have some rehabilitation potential? In your opinion, he may not be actively dying?" Dr. Gen Lambert drilled her eyes into Bobbi with her best clinical demeanor. Not challenging her exactly, but helping her think through Mr. Mendes's issues.

Bobbi ran her hand through her disheveled brown hair, a little intimidated by Gen's stare. "It was hard to gauge. His pulse," she looked down at the patient's file on her tablet, scrolling to find the vitals she had recorded last night, "was very low." She detailed the high blood pressure reading and other findings from her assessment.

"I see," Gen said. "We can't go against the living will he signed."

Bobbi puffed out her cheeks. "I hate this."

Joe Manning put in, "I had a patient in this limbo once in Arkansas the first year of residency. She died very quickly, even though my assessment showed she was not in bad shape. She'd had a successful surgery for a benign brain tumor but developed a brain bleed and went into a coma. Anyway, similar problem. I fought with the family, but they were adamant she wanted to die peacefully."

The third fellow, Jaime Garcia-Brown, chimed in, "I grew up here. Coloradans are a stubborn, independent bunch. I knew Mr. Mendes in his heyday, when he ranched for sixty years before he retired. Proud. But a good man. He's the kind of independent guy who wouldn't want to lie around a hospital with tubes coming out of him, surrounded by beeping machines." Jamie steepled his hands beneath his chin.

Bobbi relaxed the squint in her eyes. "I agree. The rural folks I've treated are more self-sufficient, sometimes stubbornly so, as far as medical care goes."

Gen nodded, shuffling papers around her. "You all know how our rural patients can be. Add to that the system issues and you have a perfect storm. I am not saying that Mr. Mendes has no right to refuse reasonable treatment, but lack of insurance and long drives to the medical facility also keep folks out here from even considering getting care." Gen rested her hands on her papers and gazed at Bobbi. "Your patient, your call."

Bobbi couldn't read her expression. Dr. Lambert gave off neutral vibes about the decision, leaving it all to Bobbi. "I'll try to get out to see him again later this week. I'll call first and talk with his daughter and see if she at least wants some home nursing help with him." Bobbi blew out a breath.

Gen asked, "Have you called hospice?"

"Yes, this morning. They'll call Maria, his daughter, and go out later today for a nursing assessment. It, of course, means I've signed off that he will receive no more treatment for stroke other than the blood pressure medicine and any palliative meds for comfort here on out."

Everyone around the table nodded, but Bobbi shifted uncomfortably in her chair, still uneasy about the whole affair. The daughter and her priest had ganged up on her. The priest even looked happy when she whipped out the papers. What was it about spiritual types? In her experience, death did not daunt them. While the old man couldn't speak for himself, she supposed the priest and his daughter had brought up the issues of treatment versus death with him before his stroke. She wondered if this was really what he had in mind—not to receive treatment for a treatable condition. On the other hand, he'd lived a full life, at age ninety-nine. She wished Mr. Mendes's condition were more clear-cut. The decision still nagged at her.

Chapter Five

Yes, Mrs. Barrington, that's right…No, please don't do that, I'll take care of it. We don't need you to fall and break something…Thank you for calling. Bye and God bless." Erin rubbed her head, rolled her stiff shoulders, and got back to composing her sermon with a deep sigh. Another Saturday afternoon rush.

Invariably, something like this complaint would come in while she feverishly worked to finish her sermon. She hated when she had to complete her sermon well into Saturday afternoon. Some priest friends from Chicago did that every week, even writing into the wee hours of Sunday morning. It would drive her mad. Early on, she had set her goal to finish sermon-writing on Thursday, to take a day off on Friday, and to do small tasks in the office on Saturday to prepare for Sunday. Fat chance of that working this week.

As the cold weather settled in, icy patches formed around the church's sidewalks. Thank God, they didn't have the added hassle of a parking lot to take care of. Her older ladies got in a tizzy about salting and shoveling clear paths for them on Sunday morning.

As soon as Erin typed the last word in her sermon, she saved it to her hard drive, with the idea of printing it out later, so she could shovel and salt right now before she forgot and some parishioner broke something. Unfortunately, all the most physically capable of the retired parishioners went to Arizona for two or three months every January, so she figured it was up to her to do the shoveling.

She straightened her shoulders. Why would a Chicago girl have trouble putting some salt on a few frozen, icy patches? In the mechanical room downstairs, she found the de-icer bag covered with cobwebs, sitting on the concrete floor next to the large red snow shovel. She grabbed the bag, tugged to get it unstuck from the floor, and grunted, dragging it up the five stairs to the side door of the church. She sweated already.

Try as she might, she had little effect on the icy, packed snow with the red shovel's puny aluminum edge and plastic body. Because the temperature would dip below ten tonight, the de-icer might work while the sun still shone for a short while this afternoon, but not overnight. The whole task may be a waste of time; nevertheless, she sprinkled as much of the gritty stuff on the ice as possible, then turned to drag the heavy bag back to the door and down the stairs. As she turned, her foot caught the ice and skidded out from under her.

Seemingly in slow motion, she felt herself fall toward her left side. She immediately put out her left hand to catch herself and her wrist bent back painfully. Her face hit the pavement with a whack. She thought her head may even have bounced, the impact was so rough.

It took a minute for the pain in her wrist and forehead and a bunch of other places to begin to register. Then bells rang in her ears. Her knees burned from meeting the pavement. Someone had socked her in the jaw, or so it felt. The left wrist looked okay under her cardigan, but the pain sparked a double "fuck" under her breath.

Gaining her bearings, she tried to gauge whether she could stand and get back into the church without doing more damage. She'd be damned if she would let a little Colorado ice show her up. She was a Chi-town native, "tougher than Grabowski." She could do this.

She sat gingerly on the sidewalk to get her bearings and breathe, as cars passed by without stopping. This wasn't the busiest street in town, but because the church sat one block from State Street, it got its share of Saturday traffic. Another car went by. Protecting her left wrist near to her torso, she put her right hand on the pavement and thrust her ass into the air to boost her body to an erect posture. Someone, if they even noticed while driving by, would get a butt show.

She slightly bumped her wrist, cried out loudly, "Shit, fuck, and damnation!" and immediately regretted her outburst. Parishioners could swear till the cows came home but let one expletive leave her mouth and it was doomsday. Another of those unhealthy double standards between clergy and laity.

No one seemed to hear her, so, humped over, she slid slowly and carefully on the icy walkway toward the church door, got close enough to grab the latch, and yanked with a grunt at the solid oak door, swinging her whole body around. Why did churches have these humongous oak doors that no one could open?

The door creaked outward and she stepped into the warm vestibule, now realizing how cold she had been without her coat. She should have known better than to make a foray onto ice without her parka. Dumb move, O'Rourke.

Several parts of her body started to throb in her heated office. After she called her church secretary without any answer, hoping to get some help, since she lived only two blocks away, Erin waffled on calling an ambulance. Finally putting aside that idea, she decided to call the clinic. Her damned wrist felt bad but she didn't think she had broken it. Nevertheless, she needed an x-ray. If she thought she had a headache before, now her head pounded like a herd of rabbits were using tiny jackhammers inside her skull. She touched her forehead and her hand came back bloody. She let out another "shit, fuck, and damnation" in the privacy of her office. While the cursing made her feel a little better, she began to worry whether she would be able to do tomorrow's service.

Erin drove herself to the clinic in Babcock County, the closest medical facility, a twenty-minute drive on good roads. But the roads were ice and snow covered, so it became a thirty-minute trip instead.

Finally, she reached the clinic. For a moment, she relaxed back against the driver's side headrest, then got out into the cold wind to hurry to the door. She checked in at the receptionist's desk and sat on a blue vinyl-covered chair, holding a hanky to her forehead and cradling her wrist against her stomach. She closed her eyes and tried to steady her breathing. "Dumb. Dumb," she huffed to herself.

After only a few blessed minutes, a medical assistant called her back and situated her on the exam table, immediately giving her a gauze bandage to staunch the blood. She then took her vital signs, wrote down Erin's recounting of her injury, and left quietly, saying the doctor would appear shortly. She had hardly relaxed on the table, when she looked up, and there she was coming through the door, Dr. Take Charge, the good-looking physician who had given her and Maria trouble with Harold. The doctor's hazel eyes looked even better in the light of day. Her physique seemed muscular but not particularly slim. *Probably a gym type,* she thought.

"Reverend, how are you today?" Dr. Wester looked down at her tablet. She looked up at Erin with a small smile.

Erin frowned. "Um, just so you know, Reverend is not a title, it's an adjective. The Reverend Erin O'Rourke. You may call me 'Erin', or 'Mother Erin', or just 'hey you', but not 'Reverend.'"

Dr. Webster smirked. "Sorry. I didn't know. Not much for churches myself."

"S'okay," Erin said. She shook her head slightly.

The doctor looked at her with concern, getting closer and peering at her forehead. "What happened? You fell on ice?" She pulled a lamp over to observe the damage. "Looks like you hit your head pretty well. You will need a few stitches. Any fuzziness in your vision? Headache?"

"Head hurts, but no blackout or dizziness. My wrist got bunged up too." Erin pushed up the sleeve of her navy cardigan to show Bobbi the purpling knot on the outside of her left wrist.

Bobbi took it gently in her hands and palpated tenderly all around the injury. "Tell me where—"

Erin sucked in a breath. "Right there."

"I want to get a picture of your wrist. Do you need something for the pain?"

"I'm good." Erin looked up into the doctor's clear eyes and blinked with their intensity. "Listen, Dr. Webster, I need to be able to lead my ten o'clock service tomorrow, okay?"

"I'll do my best to fix you up so you shouldn't have a problem," Bobbi said. "Let's see about your head first." Bobbi took a small flashlight from her lab coat pocket. "Please follow my right hand with your eyes."

She shone the flashlight in each of Erin's eyes, then moved it up, down, left, and right.

"You didn't sustain a head injury. I don't think we need an MRI or CT scan." Bobbi smiled.

Erin nodded. "Good."

"Be back shortly to do those stitches. Don't go anywhere." Bobbi laid a hand on Erin's arm, smiled again, and turned to the door.

Erin exhaled and laid back on the exam table. The touch on her arm felt good, as if the doctor cared. Well, she seemed competent enough, but Erin wasn't sure she trusted her. Why did that doctor have to be working today?

The next thing she knew, the doctor and an assistant surrounded her, one on each side of the exam table. Dr. Webster told her to look at the assistant, a short, gray-haired nurse, with a nametag that said, "Doris."

"Hi, Doris," Erin said.

"Hey there." Doris smiled widely at her. "Here ya go, Doctor." She handed the doctor something out of Erin's eyesight.

"The lidocaine will sting a little; make sure to keep your eyes on Doris. We'll let you lie still a short while to make sure everything is nice and numb."

An intense, but short, pain streaked through her forehead down her cheek. "Wow." Erin gulped. "You weren't kidding. That stung, definitely." In a minute, she tongued a numb cheek.

Doris and Dr. Webster were talking in low voices at the counter, opening up a package and laying out items on a tray on wheels covered by a green cloth. Dr. Webster had already discarded her first pair of latex gloves and put on a fresh pair.

"Ready for this?" Bobbi prodded Erin's forehead with a silver stick. "Can you feel this?"

Erin looked at her and shook her head, not quite sure she liked getting stitches. "I've never had stitches before."

Bobbi looked tenderly on her. "We'll make it as painless as possible. You won't feel a thing."

Doris swabbed her cut and put something on it. Dr. Webster bent over, dragged the overhead light more directly onto her face. Erin blinked several times. Doris laid green cotton cloths over Erin's face below the cut and another one above the cut, or at least Erin imagined that's where it was, since her eyes were now covered. Occasionally, the doctor asked Doris for an item.

Erin felt some pressure around her head, but otherwise felt nothing. After a few minutes, the doctor said, "I think that'll do it, Doris. Will you take care of the bandage for me?"

"Sure thing."

Erin heard the door shut, then Doris's kind face appeared after Erin's eyes and head were uncovered.

"You had four stitches, Ms. O'Rourke. I will get this bandaged. I don't want you to touch it tonight. Leave the bandage on tomorrow. You can stop by on Monday so we can check it over and rebandage it then. No water near it, please, which means no shower, unless you put your head in a plastic bag." Doris let out a quick laugh, then sobered. "Just kidding. No shower, understand?"

"Got it," Erin said. *All I need, a nurse with a weird sense of humor*, she thought.

"Okay, we're done. I have some instructions for you here." She handed Erin a printed sheet on wound care. "Now we're going to get you down to x-ray."

Her head spun a little when she tried to sit up.

"Stay down until I get back, please."

With that, Doris was out the door and reentered pushing a wheelchair.

"You can sit up slowly now. Don't want you falling over." She took Erin's right arm and helped her off the table and into the chair.

After the x-ray, Doris wheeled Erin back into the exam room. "Dr. Webster will come in after she's read the picture of your wrist. Just relax here on the table."

Erin laid back, shut her eyes, and wondered what time it was. She needed to get the church ready for Sunday yet and print out her sermon. And check the stupid sidewalks again before it got much darker. Her anxiety ramped up, hoping this was about over.

Amidst her mind's wanderings, Dr. Webster knocked and came in.

"You've got good bones, Ms. O'Rourke. No breaks, just a bad bruise and a minor sprain. How is your head feeling? Still no blurry vision?"

"Vision good. Head feels pretty good, although it was pounding when I got here."

Dr. Webster took her right hand, surprising her a little. Nobody'd held her hand for a long time and Erin thought it felt really good. She felt like a basket case, if she were this hard up for physical contact.

"As I said after your exam, I don't think you sustained a concussion. But if you get nauseous, your vision gets blurry, or you feel faint, give me a call ASAP. Got it?"

Erin nodded. The feel of the doctor's fingers on her hand sent a wave of warmth through her. Dr. Webster patted her hand and turned to write a prescription. "You can sit up if you feel well enough."

Erin carefully sat, dangling her legs over the edge of the table. The doctor's short, dark blond hair, curling messily around her high cheekbones, gave her an informal look. Her eyes warmed Erin, then Erin caught herself. No, she couldn't like Dr. Take Charge, despite her handsome self being kind to her.

Dr. Webster handed her the prescription. "This is for pain. You may also take ibuprofen with it, but not acetaminophen. We don't want to ramp up your analgesics. This is enough to get you through a few days. If you need more, call. Also, try not to use your wrist for anything more strenuous than eating, okay? It needs time to heal. I don't think you'll have any problems with doing what you need to do tomorrow at church." Dr. Webster paused and gave Erin a pointed gaze. "Do you have any questions?"

Erin was caught deep in the doctor's gaze when she registered that the doctor had asked a question. "What? Sorry."

"Can I do anything else for you?"

"How is Mr. Mendes?" Erin focused in on Dr. Take Charge.

The doctor raised her eyebrows. "Can't talk with you about another patient, sorry. HIPAA rules, you know."

Erin frowned. "Really? As a priest, I have always talked with medical staff about my parishioners' health. I consider it part of clerical confidentiality.

You know, information that's held under the collar." Despite her warm demeanor through the treatment this morning, was the exasperating physician going to cite her rulebook again?

"I would love to discuss confidentiality some time with you, but I have other patients to tend to right now." Erin picked up annoyance from the doctor. "Anything else, any questions about your injuries?"

Erin, put off again by the doctor's attitude, just shook her head and glared at her. "Thank you."

"See you in two weeks to take out those stitches." The doctor was out the door like an L train in the Loop. Just when you thought you had one, it was gone.

Chapter Six

Erin made her way home during a setting sun and collapsed on her sofa. As the numbing wore off, her cut started to throb, so she took one of the pain pills Dr. Webster had prescribed, having filled the prescription on the way home. She heated up canned tomato soup, cut up Colby cheese, and picked out five wheat crackers from the pantry, then took it all into the living room on a tray. She still had to go over to the church next door to finish getting things ready for Sunday. She moaned aloud, refusing to swear again.

The hot soup and drugs put her in a sleepy, warm place. She pulled up the afghan slung over the back of the sofa and covered herself, while she watched an old Katherine Hepburn movie on the classic movie channel. She got through the first hour, fighting sleep. She closed her eyes for just a minute and immediately dropped off.

Erin woke to a throbbing in her wrist, the sun sending striped rays through her blinds onto the hardwood floor. Her whole body felt stiff from the uncomfortable couch.

Her heart lurched when she realized it was Sunday morning. She threw the afghan on the floor and hurried into the kitchen. It was only 6:22, but she had to run over to church to set up for Holy Communion, print out her sermon, put salt on the sidewalks, and Lord knew what else she would find.

She shook the fuzzy feeling from her head, grabbed the ibuprofen from the kitchen cabinet, and sloshed it down with half a glass of water. She looked down at her outfit and decided it would do to check the church.

Breathing heavily from anxiety and jogging from the vicarage, when she got into the church, she turned up the thermostat to get the heat started. It immediately clanked through the ancient radiators. She turned on lights all down the hall, opened the sacristy door, and quickly got out the items to set up for communion. Going over the order of Holy Communion in her mind, she grabbed things from cupboards. She took the silver chalice and other items out of a locked cabinet, then carried them into the back of the church to a table next to the altar, panting lightly all the while.

After setting up the rest of the altar cloths and getting her vestments laid out, she scurried into her office to print out her sermon. Finally, with those tasks completed, she felt she could now salt the sidewalks on the way to home next door. Thankfully, no one had taken off with the bag of salt where it still lay on the sidewalk. She sprinkled all the pavement on both sides of the church, then, one-handed, lugged the heavy bag back to the side door, which she locked after herself.

By the time she arrived home at seven-thirty, her heart beat loudly with the subsiding panicky feelings. Coffee would help center her. After she got it started, she ran upstairs to have a shower. Just as she reached the bedroom, she cursed under her breath when she remembered she couldn't take one. Blowing out her cheeks in frustration, she instead cleaned up the best she could, got her clerical clothes on, and made it back to church by nine.

This hurry and chaos on Sunday morning made her crazy. Definitely not her style. Things ready by Saturday afternoon was her style, so she could spend Sunday morning in more silence and centeredness. She regretted falling asleep in front of the TV last night, but yesterday had worn her out.

A certain doctor had also populated her thoughts since the clinic encounter. She couldn't decide whether Dr. Webster was a jerk or not. Her bedside manner had been warm and attentive. She certainly wasn't hard on the eyes, either. Large hazel eyes and short, dark blond curls, a winning combination in Erin's mind, especially, with a body that Erin was sure saw plenty of exercise.

But Dr. Webster's need to put rules over patients annoyed Erin no end. Didn't they teach anything but procedures and treatment in medical school? Her mom, a nurse, used to complain about certain doctors she worked with who only wanted to do their specialty procedures and had little time for conversation with patients. Did Dr. Webster always toe the line instead of listening to patients?

Erin prided herself on being a people person, not a rule person. She studied psychology at Northwestern, then did a master's degree in pastoral care at Loyola of Chicago. While at Loyola, she was shocked when she felt she was being called to the priesthood. By the time she had jumped through all the hoops—committees, meetings with the bishop, and theological schooling— she was thirty years old. That was five years ago.

Here at Holy Spirit, Erin met her goal to be in charge of a parish, where she chose the weekly hymns and music and the liturgical prayers. But she really was drawn to the pastoral aspects of the priesthood. She gave succor to those in need, and especially liked visiting the shut-ins at home, the nursing home, and the hospital. Her mind and heart went to pastoral concerns automatically, to helping folks deal with the spiritual side of illness. She thrived on helping people with questions about God's presence or absence in pain and suffering, about whether God cared. Her job, as she saw it, was to represent God's care in her healing presence with them.

But this morning, Erin did the other, more routine, rote administrative priestly work. However out of kilter she felt, she trudged single-mindedly through the bitter cold over to church an hour before the service started, to set out the bulletins, turn on the lights in the nave, unlock the front doors, and pick up random items left around from the week.

These tasks often pulled her down. Last week, she'd had to call a plumber when she found a plugged-up toilet in the men's room downstairs. This week it was the ice on the sidewalk, and, earlier in the week, a downspout that had blown off in the high wind of a winter storm. Winter in old buildings like Holy Spirit's wreaked havoc with her need for tidy schedules and routine. On top of all this, the congregation's attendance would probably be minimal because of the bitter cold.

Even with all the uninteresting priestly duties that piled up this morning, Erin gave a prayer of thanks when she put on her stole after the duties had been discharged. While sometimes the nitpicking problems of being a vicar buried her, she never lost hope or faith that her priestly vocation was God's way of allowing her to reach people in need.

At Ryan Delaney Clinic on Monday, Bobbi finished her last patient of the day and sped through the paperwork in record time, then sprinted to the conference room to be briefed on last night's on-call experience. She looked forward to a slow Monday night, as most patients had taken care of medical issues from the weekend by coming to the clinic. But rural folks didn't abide by suburban- or city-dwellers' rules. Because they needed to put in a full day's work, ranchers, farmers, and blue-collar workers might wait until evening to notice an injury or illness. Doctors Lambert and Jaime Garcia-Brown were already discussing last night's call when Bobbi arrived.

Jaime hailed from eastern Colorado, a hometown boy who had made good in his Hispanic-American family. His energy pulsed around him like electricity. Bobbi wondered how much of his energy arose from his wife being eight months pregnant with their first child.

As she entered, Jaime was speaking. "...two flu and some colds called in early evening. Nothing after that."

"Any questions, Doctor?" Gen looked at Bobbi.

Bobbi shook her head. "I think I'm good to go." Dr. Lambert's auburn hair shone in the light of the conference room. Bobbi noted intelligence in her keen eyes. Yancy Delaney was very lucky to be engaged to this sharp woman.

"You may want to stop the pre-call conferences, Dr. Lambert." Jaime nodded his head of black, straight hair in agreement. "I think the three of us rural fellows can handle the call situation now after nearly a month. Except for the air evac last week, none of us have run into anything out of our experience."

"You may be right. But, please be sure you call me if any unusual cases arise, or any strange issues, like the air evac."

Both the junior doctors nodded their heads.

Bobbi said good night to the two others.

She went home to get some supper, however meager the contents of her kitchen. Ever since she had been a medical student in an apartment on her own, she had yet to master the adult skills of shopping and cooking for herself, a quirk Stephanie seemed to especially criticize. Her fridge held a few leftovers from local fast food places, which, in this small town, didn't give her many choices. She sighed and grabbed last night's Tex-Mex leftovers, warmed them in the microwave, and sat on the couch, watching the national news to rest before her night on call. Around ten-thirty, she went to bed with her phone on the nightstand.

At 2:47, the shrill beep of the phone woke her from a sound sleep. Instantly, her training kicked in and she picked up her cell phone. "Yes. Dr. Webster."

The service gave her a phone number that looked familiar to her. With the light of the phone, she punched in the numbers.

"Doctor, this is Maria, Harold Mendes's daughter. The hospice nurse is here. My father just died."

Bobbi squinted in the light of her phone. "What? I'm not sure I heard you. You said your father just died?"

"Yes. Since you are his doctor, the hospice nurse wanted me to inform you."

Bobbi shook her head and rubbed her brow. "But he just began hospice. I'm so sorry."

Marie sniffled. "Thank you. Dad was ready to go.

He was ninety-nine; his body was failing him. He went the way he wanted to go." She heard muffled voices over the phone. "Wait, please, Mother Erin wants to speak to you."

"Hello, Dr. Webster. I want to thank you for understanding Harold's wishes. He died peacefully without regaining consciousness. I came when Maria called me about an hour ago, to anoint and pray for him."

Bobbi sat up in bed. "Is there anything you need me to do right now, Rev...er, Mother Erin?"

"Nothing, but thank you, Doctor. I need to go help Maria with some things. Thank you again."

"You're welcome," Bobbi answered with a questioning hesitation in her voice. She ended the call and shook her head. "What was that all about?" she mumbled to herself as she rose to go to the bathroom.

Why did they call her? There was no emergency. Nothing for a doctor to do. It could have waited until the morning. And, Bobbi felt more coerced than really acceding to Mr. Mendes's wishes. Oh well, chalk that one up to another clinical experience. Bobbi's mind went over the weird phone call.

Then the cute face of Erin O'Rourke came into view. Very cute. Why did she have to be a bible thumper?

Although, from what Bobbi had heard, churches that ordained women were on the liberal side of Christianity. So, maybe she wasn't one of *those* Christians—the ones who judged her and her "lifestyle." What the hell did that even mean? Her lifestyle consisted of eating take-out food and working her ass off for the good of other people. She paid her taxes and tried to live a simple life without undue luxury. Her biggest splurge last year was for camping gear, since, when she left Oregon, she also left her brother Matt's tent and other equipment.

Back to Erin. She'd also picked up an interesting gaydar ping on Erin. She probably worked in a super-liberal church. Why an out lesbian chose to work in a patriarchal structure like the Christian church gave her pause. The whole idea gave Bobbi shivers, as she turned off her light and wrestled the covers over her weary body. That petite body. Her aggressiveness that night at Mr. Mendes's house. Bobbi blew out a deep breath. Breathe, in, out, in, out.

Chapter Seven

"Come on in," Erin said to Dr. Genevieve Lambert and Yancy Delaney, at two o'clock on a Wednesday afternoon in February. She indicated the two old armchairs in her office as she rolled her office chair from behind the desk to join them in a triangle for conversation. "Can I get you anything?"

"Nothing, thank you, Mother Erin," Yancy said, surveying the small, shabby office. The walls needed paint. The bookshelves were inadequate for the books overflowing onto the floor. The armchairs looked worse for wear. A thin, faded oriental rug completed the shabby-chic design.

Incense had burned in the air recently. Colorful icons drew Yancy's attention, and she brought herself back to the present. "As you know, my mother, Nina Delaney, recommended you for our upcoming marriage."

"Yes. I met her at Diocesan Council at my first meeting last month. She's a real go-getter."

Yancy grinned. "She's got a lot of spunk for a sixty-nine-year-old. Keeps pretty busy with several groups."

Erin looked intently at Yancy and Gen. "Before we start with paperwork and calendars, tell me about you two."

Gen smiled. "I moved here last year to take the medical director position at Valley View, and met

Yancy, who until last week was the president of the board. We started dating, and well..." Gen caught Yancy's eyes while squeezing her hand. "Anyway, here we are."

"I can tell you are devoted to each other." Erin smiled warmly. "So, any previous marriages?"

Yancy took a deep breath and spoke first. "I had a two-year committed relationship. Trish died five years ago."

"I'm so sorry." Erin peered at Yancy, but gave her a look of understanding, not one of pity, which Yancy found difficult to bear.

Yancy glanced down at Gen and linked their hands in her lap. "Yeah, cancer. She was only forty-one. I had to get over my grief before I could be in another serious relationship."

"Understandably." Erin paused, but Yancy kept silent, looking down at their clasped hands. "And what about you, Gen?"

"I am officially divorced for four years now. We were married nine years. She was unfaithful, causing us to have a crisis that we couldn't overcome."

Erin nodded. "I see. This was where?"

"We lived in Kentucky. She was a pathologist and I led the Rural Health Initiative for family medicine. We were both at the University."

Erin nodded while riffling some documents on the desk, then gathered them and a yellow legal pad. "It's great to meet you two. Before we are done with our weeks together in pre-nuptial counseling, I'll come to know you fairly well. But, first things first. Do you have an idea of the dates we're considering?"

Yancy and Gen talked with Erin to set up their date. They then jumped into the discussion of Gen's

Roman Catholic background. Erin explained that the divorce would cause extra paperwork for the bishop's approval.

"Will there be a problem?" Gen asked.

"No. The bishop deals with divorced people asking for second marriage all the time. And being Roman Catholic doesn't matter at all." She smiled warmly.

She's just like a little pixie, Yancy thought, smiling, taking in Erin's short, dark brown hair and her petite frame. The whimsical items on her clean desk—a bobble-head Jesus, a Moses finger puppet, and several types of stuffed toy sheep—added to Erin's charm. She looked like a teenager. How old was she?

After filling out the forms for the bishop's approval, Yancy and Gen left Erin's office with a website password to take their online, prenuptial-counseling questionnaire.

"I think this counseling will be fun." Gen threaded her arm through Yancy's on the way to the Rover. "And she is the perfect minister to do our wedding."

"I like her." Yancy glanced at Gen to gauge her reaction.

"She's cute. And she's single. I should set her up with Dr. Webster." Gen smiled wickedly at Yancy.

"Oh, geez." Yancy shook her head as she helped Gen into the tall, truck-like car. "Dr. Webster doesn't strike me as the type to date a priest."

"You never know until you try," Gen answered with a twinkle in her eye.

Yancy groaned, but smiled at her fiancée, who, just like her friend Roxie, yearned to see all the single people around her matched up.

Chapter Eight

After her prenuptial appointment, Erin drove over to the hospital to see her favorite parishioner, Charlotte, who'd been admitted with pneumonia. Charlotte Stephens, a sprightly eighty-seven-year-old, kept her on her toes with her wit and biting humor, so she looked forward to seeing her today. Erin had lucked out to have such a grounded, practical woman to work with as her vestry's senior warden.

As she walked toward Charlotte's room, she saw the usual postings for an isolation room, requiring her to don a paper gown and latex gloves to enter. Erin stopped and did as directed, then entered to find Charlotte hooked up to an oxygen cannula, looking pale.

"Well, if it isn't the lady priest." Charlotte used her pet name for Erin. "Good to see you, Mother."

"Hi, Charlotte. Thought I would bring communion for you, since you missed Sunday."

"Didn't need to go all out for me, kid." Charlotte patted the bed.

Erin grinned. She bent down and hugged Charlotte lightly. They discussed Charlotte's pneumonia while Erin took items from her communion kit and laid them out on Charlotte's rolling table.

"What do you think you're doing?"

Erin whirled around to meet the angry eyes of

Dr. Webster.

"She's giving me communion, you heathen," Charlotte shot back.

"Those items are not allowed in here. This room has restrictions." Bobbi pointed to the communion set on the table.

"Well, suck it up, buttercup, 'cause I'm having communion with my priest." Charlotte glared at the doctor, breathing hard.

Dr. Webster took two steps and was at Charlotte's bedside, taking her pulse. "You're getting riled up, Mrs. Stephens."

"Damn right I am. I don't care what that sign says outside my door, my priest is here and all I want is some time to pray and take communion."

Bobbi pursed her lips and looked daggers between Mrs. Stephens and Erin. Finally, she spoke, pointing to the communion vessels. "Are those items clean?"

"Silver communion vessels are put in boiling water to clean them after each use, Doctor," Erin replied in an even voice, standing tall at five foot even, and giving her a steady glare. "I would appreciate it if we could have some time together for spiritual care."

Bobbi spun away and called on her way out, "Don't overtax the patient. You have ten minutes."

Erin had detected Bobbi's ashen look when she approached Mrs. Stephens. Erin smelled a fragrant perfume Charlotte wore. Was it a trigger for the doctor? Erin became intrigued about Dr. Webster's quick departure.

An hour later, when Erin got home after seeing Mrs. Stephens, she threw her parka on the couch and went immediately to the fridge for a glass of wine. She was madder than a Bears fan after a loss to the Green

Bay Packers. That damn doctor. What the hell was wrong with her? And why did she push Erin's buttons so much? Usually, Erin let the antics of annoying people roll over her.

Erin relived the encounter in Charlotte's hospital room several times while she sipped her Pinot Noir. Finally, realizing she needed to vent, she rang Julia Wachtmann, her colleague and friend in town, hoping she wasn't tied up with an evening meeting. Erin was grateful when she answered on the third ring.

"Hey, Julia. It's Erin. Do you have a minute?"

"Hi. Ray's making dinner, so I'm good. What's up?"

"Wow. Ray sounds like he's doing better."

"The nephrologist said it was a miracle. They thought his kidneys were shutting down, but after the dialysis, all the blood work started to get back to normal last week, and he bounced back as good as new. The doctor said he'd had a stubborn kidney infection. We're both a little giddy." Julia breathed deeply and continued, "So enough about us. What did you need, kiddo?"

"I'm calling to bitch. Do you know Dr. Webster at the clinic? A new resident or something over in Babcock County."

"Hmm. Don't know if I've run into a Webster. In my hospital visits, I see Dr. Lambert, and that one guy, the cardio guy who has treated one of my people, can't remember his name. Dr. Lambert's great. Very personable. Kinda cute, too, don't you think?"

"She's marrying the clinic board's president. Why do straight people try to fix up gay people with the first gay person they meet?"

Julia chuckled. "Sorry. My bad. Who's this other

doctor you're talking about?"

"That's why I need an ear to listen to me rant and rave. For one thing, she's a real stickler for protocol. I had a ninety-nine-year old who had a stroke at home, whom she wanted to hospitalize against his wishes. His daughter and I had to rally on his behalf before she would back down, even though he had a DNR order. Then today, I visited a sweet lady who's in isolation. I put on the stupid gown and stuff and got ready to give her communion when Dr. Take Charge nearly threw me out of her room, claiming my communion kit was dirty."

"Sheesh."

"Yeah. That's what I said." Erin sipped her wine. "That M.D. after her name has overpowered her understanding of patients' needs. She sure needs to be in charge."

"No ministers are like that, for heaven's sake." Julia snickered.

"Oh, shut up. She's a pain in my backside, that's for sure."

Julia waited a beat. "Not to sound too pastoral, but why are you taking this personally?"

"What? I'm not taking it personally. What are you talking about? Wait a minute, you think just 'cause she's good looking and a lesbian I have a thing for her!"

"Hold it. How would I know if she's a good-looking lesbian? You didn't tell me that." Julia softly giggled into the phone. "Wow, now I know what's going on. You told on yourself, my friend."

Erin held the phone away from the loud laughter hitting her ear and groaned. She *had* given herself away. Damn. "Okay, smart ass. She is very attractive. But also, she is arrogant. I don't think she's my type.

Got it?"

"Sure. Sure, whatever you say." More laughter.

⚜⚜⚜⚜

Bobbi ran another circuit around the gym before collapsing on a bench, sweat dripping down her T-shirt. All afternoon, she fumed about that annoying elf, Mother Erin. Twice now, the minister had messed with her patients. Today, she had compromised the isolation room with her stuff. Maybe Mr. Mendes would still be alive and well had she not interfered in his treatment.

She was a pain in the butt. Should Bobbi report her to hospital administration? What would she say? That she, Dr. Roberta Webster, couldn't handle an irritating imp, all five feet of her? Just the thought made her ashamed she'd let Erin get to her.

And why couldn't she get that cute face out of her mind? Big brown, chocolate-drop eyes, an adorable haircut, everything about her petite and feminine, in contrast to Bobbi's own muscular, five-foot-eight body. Next to her, Bobbi felt like a clumsy oaf. Just like she did with Stephanie. Damn.

And Mrs. Stephens' perfume didn't help. Her heart ramped up. The therapist had told her that small things could set her off, making memories return. She hadn't expected something like that, and with a patient, too.

But why should any of this matter? She had a dinner date tonight with Amanda from the hospital. Just her style. No ties to bind her. Amanda didn't remind her of last year. She was safe. Nothing to keep her from her single-minded focus on her work. Amanda, like the few, casual friends with benefits during her residency, didn't get in the way of her pursuing her goals. Bobbi needed low-maintenance relationships, especially after Stephanie. Nothing, least of all love and its messy consequences, could stand in her way to becoming an excellent rural, family medicine doctor.

No matter how cute, this vexing elf Erin was off the relationship table.

※ ※ ※ ※

As Yancy stepped into the back door of the ranch house, her cell rang. "Hey," Yancy answered. "Just thinking about you."

"Are we still on for tomorrow night?" Roxie, Yancy's best friend, asked.

"Sure. You're making chili and we're bringing dessert. I think Gen's making a raw apple cake."

"Wow. I love apple cake. Make sure you bring some ice cream. Haven't had apple cake since my Granny made it when I was a kid." Roxie waited a beat, then continued. "I've asked some other folks to come too."

Yancy recognized Roxie's "sneaky voice". "Okay, let's hear it, dork."

"It's not bad. It's, uh, kind of a civic service project."

"Who are you fixing up now? Is this a surprise attack, like you arranged with Gen and me? That night didn't turn out so well, if you recall." Yancy sighed, remembering Gen slapping her after she'd grabbed ass.

"Don't be too grateful. I hear a wedding is coming up," Roxie answered dryly. "You guys got over it, and I was right-on with my matchmaking."

"Okay, okay. But who're the victims this time?

"Gen's hunky rural medical fellow, Dr. Webster, and the pastoral counselor that's an Episcopal priest, Erin O'Rourke. She's cute as a button. I think they'll hit it right off."

"Where did you meet Erin O'Rourke? We just met her a couple of weeks ago to begin our prenuptial counseling."

"In February, she started doing pastoral counseling with my office one day a week. She's only part-time at her parish in Johnson County, so the arrangement helps both me with my client load and her with her income."

"You must like her to invite her for dinner and throw one of Gen's rural fellows at her."

Roxie grinned. "Yes, I do. And I like Dr. Webster too. She's got spunk. Add to that the dearth of lesbians in eastern Colorado, and you've got a match."

"If you say so. See you tomorrow then."

Gen called from the couch, where the Kentucky basketball game played without sound on the TV, "Did Roxie want anything else than the cake?"

"Ice cream."

"Of course." Gen laughed.

"Did you know about the blind date?"

"It's not exactly blind. I think each of them knows another person will be there."

Chapter Nine

B obbi entered her condo around three a.m. on Sunday morning, and tossed her coat on the second-hand brown sofa. She went into the kitchen and poured a cup of milk, which she then heated in the microwave. She rubbed her tired eyes. When the milk had warmed, she stirred in hot-chocolate powder and took it into her bedroom, where she got ready for bed.

She made sure to turn off the alarm on her phone and fell asleep nearly as soon as she finished the warm drink.

The phone chirped at nine that morning with a call. Bobbi sighed and reached for it, noting Roxie's number.

"Morning," she replied with a raspy voice.

"Oh my God, did I wake you?" Roxie asked.

"No problem. I had a call last night, but I got some sleep and should be getting up anyway." Bobbi sat up in the bed and took a deep breath to wake herself up.

"Just a quick call to make sure you're still coming tonight at six for dinner. We're having chili."

"What can I bring? Some beer?"

Roxie answered, "Heavens no, don't bring a thing. You're a guest. Gen is making dessert and I'm making some corn bread to go with the chili. We're all set. Also, my wife, Kate, usually has enough beer on hand for a rugby team."

Bobbi could hear the smile in Roxie's voice.

"Okay. I'll take you at your word."

"And I know we talked about it on Wednesday when I stopped by the clinic to ask you and Gen, but I have also invited another person. It will be an all-lesbian gathering."

"Great, I'd like to meet other women." Bobbi hoped this wasn't a set-up. "Just casual, right?"

"Casual, yes. No need to worry. Just wear comfy clothes. We may play some poker or something. Kate also got a new board game for Christmas we're interested in trying out."

"Uh, do I know the other people that will be there?"

"I think so. You certainly know Gen and you've met her fiancée Yancy. You'll meet my wife, Kate. And I've invited the new pastoral counselor at my office, Erin O'Rourke."

Bobbi scrunched her eyes and frowned, breathing in deeply.

"Are you still there?" Roxie asked.

"Yeah, sorry, I just needed to...uh, reposition the phone so it wouldn't drop. I met Erin with two of my patients who are her parishioners."

"Good. She won't be a stranger, then. Well, I'll let you go. See you at six?"

"See you then." Bobbi ended the call and dropped back onto the bed. "Why me? Why Erin O'Rourke, of all the lesbians in Colorado? The Elf."

❧ ❧ ❧ ❧

"A medical fellow, she said." Erin picked out a top to go with her black jeans. "Casual, Roxie said." She placed a cherry red sweater up to her chin, threw it on the bed, then modeled the indigo blue one. "Much better." She pulled it over her head. "I wonder if there is more than one woman doctor in Gen's fellowship program?" she asked herself in the mirror. She blew out the breath she had been holding. "You're in for it, O'Rourke. I just know it's her. Dr. Take Charge."

≈≈≈≈

Nearly simultaneously, Bobbi and Erin parked on the street in front of Roxie and Kate's house in town. Bobbi stepped out of her car and noticed that Erin tiptoed along an icy patch on the sidewalk leading to the front door. She caught her arm gently. "Let me help you," she mumbled. "We don't want a repeat of your fall."

"Thanks," Erin said.

Bobbi quickly glimpsed Erin's small round face and rosy cheeks, framed by the fake fur of her winter coat, then led them both to the door.

The door opened before they could ring the bell, and Roxie brought them in with a warm smile and a hug. "Hi, kids. Get in here where it's warm."

Bobbi liked Roxie. She had given a talk to the new fellows in their first week at Valley View on local mental health resources, meager as they were. Roxie had peppered her talk with plenty of anecdotes and examples of local issues, making the time pass quickly. Bobbi imagined Roxie to be a very good psychologist. Today, she was dressed in a red and purple wool shawl that she had probably knitted herself. Bobbi remembered her clothes matched her bright personality.

"My wife, Kate." Roxie had her arm around a taciturn, taller woman, whose tanned, wrinkled face spoke of time outdoors. Kate shook both their hands, saying a quiet "hello and welcome." Roxie took their coats, then she swept them into a living area, where Yancy was watching basketball.

Yancy stood and shook hands with Bobbi and Erin. "Good to see you both again. Did you drive together?"

Erin spit out, "Oh, no," while Bobbi shook her head quickly. *Never with The Elf,* she thought.

Yancy looked puzzled, glancing at each of them, then brightened and showed them some seats. "Gen and Roxie are cooking, so get ready for good food, y'all."

"It smells terrific," Erin said.

"Yes," Bobbi agreed. She still stood, feeling at a loss for words with these two women. Yancy she had met only twice—at her initial interview for the fellowship and again for a reception for the new fellows in January with the board of Valley View. The open-concept great room held warm colors. Very inviting.

Erin. Well, that was better left unsaid. She only hoped to get through the evening without arguing with her.

Gen walked into the living area, wiping her hands on a towel. "Hi, Erin. Bobbi." She hugged each of them, smiling.

Bobbi noted her auburn hair shining in the light of a standing lamp, her large green eyes twinkling, her peaches and cream skin glowing, and her overall demeanor both warm and bright. She hoped Yancy knew she'd won the lesbian lottery being engaged to such a beautiful woman. Gen's reception of Erin surprised her. "How do you know Mother Erin?"

"She knows Nina, Yancy's mom. Erin's officiating

at our wedding, so we're doing prenuptial counseling with her now." Gen sat next to Yancy on the couch and motioned for them to sit. "It's been eye opening and fun so far."

Erin grinned widely. "You guys. You're a couple of sweeties. I'm enjoying talking with you and getting to know you. I wish all my prenuptial counseling went this well."

"What do you mean? Had some ringers?" Bobbi had no idea what prenuptial counseling entailed.

"Well, let's just say some couples are not meant to wed."

How can The Elf order people not to wed? "You mean, you forbid them to get married?" Bobbi asked, her eyes big with indignity.

"No, no. Nothing like that. But it becomes apparent at some time during counseling sessions when a couple doesn't know each other, or, worse, that they are overlooking some major red flags."

Bobbi was intrigued now. "What kind of red flags?"

All eyes trained on Erin. "Sexual incompatibility is always a big one. And money is the other. Those two can wreck a relationship faster than a speeding bullet." Erin sighed. "Then there's my favorite, abusive behavior. You know, bullying, controlling, demands, insults, and emotional cruelty. All these symptoms predict violence in the relationship, either physical or emotional or both. And sometimes, the relationship has already devolved into physical violence."

Bobbi blinked. "Oh."

Images flashed before her. A small angry woman. Being pushed into the wall while warding off the rush of fists. Lying on the floor being kicked. Yelling. Police arriving, saying neighbors had complained. Bruises that Bobbi would try to hide under long sleeves. An ER visit for cuts that needed stitches.

Fear gripped her insides, her stomach roiled, as she pursed her lips and closed her eyes against the images.

Erin's voice, "Hey, you okay, Dr. Webster?" She lightly grasped her forearm.

Bobbi internally shook herself out of her memories. She tried for a smile. "Sure. I'm sorry, what did you say?"

Erin looked at her with sincere, kind, brown eyes. Bobbi realized how well Erin's short hair fit her. The Elf kept smiling at her. "What?" Bobbi asked, panicky about missing some important conversation.

"I asked, have you ever been married?" Erin's eyes remained trained on Bobbi's face, a shadow of concern darkening her face.

Gen said, "You look a little pale, Bobbi."

Bobbi gulped. "Will you excuse me?" She leapt up from her chair. "Bathroom," she murmured.

She tossed water on her face with trembling hands after seeing her ashen skin in the mirror. Her heart pounded in her ears, her hands were clammy, and she struggled to breathe. She recognized the anxiety attack. She closed her eyes and counted to ten to slow her rapid breathing and heartbeat.

It had been a while since the last one of these. She sighed, her head hanging between her shoulders for several minutes. Finally, she checked her pulse and decided she could return to the dinner party as a normal person.

At dinner, Bobbi noted that Erin was looking at her whenever Bobbi's eyes looked in her direction.

Bobbi smiled weakly at The Elf and attempted to attend to the conversation swirling around her. As Erin regaled them with pastoral counseling anecdotes, all were laughing. Bobbi, not having caught the whole story, thought she should laugh too, but couldn't rustle up the appropriate amount of mirth.

As soon as the dessert had been consumed, Bobbi said her goodnights to the group.

"You're not going to have some coffee with us?" Roxie asked, disappointment strewn across her face. "We thought we'd play some group game."

"I'm kind of beat. Sorry, I hope I don't break up your fun," Bobbi answered, not precisely telling a lie about being tired, but not telling the whole truth either. She'd been battling the demons of her past since Erin's talk about abusive relationships. She needed to get home.

"I understand." Roxie brought her coat and led her to the door, after Bobbi had thanked them all for the evening. "Are you sure you're all right?" Roxie peered knowingly into Bobbi's eyes. "I noticed you checked out during dinner. Did we do or say something?"

Bobbi quickly replied, "Nothing. No. Y'all were very gracious. The food tasted great. I apologize for my appalling social skills. After a long night on call, I can be in another world."

Roxie nodded, seeming to take in that rationale. "Well, go home and get some rest. I hope to see you again soon." She smiled.

Chapter Ten

As soon as Bobbi closed the door at her condo, she breathed deeply and relaxed her tight shoulders. She'd not felt her heart rate ramp up like this for at least three months. She hadn't drunk any alcohol at Roxie and Kate's, but now just wanted to check out from all the memories she'd shut away last year. First, Erin, then Mrs. Stephens's perfume, and now relationship talk. Too much all together.

She grabbed the bourbon from her living area cabinet, poured two fingers, got ice from the fridge, and plopped on her couch to sip. It was only eight-fifteen. She hoped she hadn't been rude to leave so early. But hell, it hurt, even after a year.

The devils of memory swirled around her brain. Stephanie, so kind that first day of her residency, helped her get the lay of the land at Oregon State's rural residency program. Then Stephanie flirted openly with her. Bobbi liked her very much and asked her out on a few dates. Stephanie's behavior, always coquettish and feminine, was a magnet to Bobbi.

Bobbi never had time for seriousness in her previous dating life. Always too much studying in medical school, too many body systems to memorize, drug actions and reactions to learn, and disease symptoms and treatments to understand. But with Stephanie, things had transpired differently. She felt herself falling for her. Her smile, her intelligence, her petite figure, and her perky personality—all held Bobbi in thrall those three months of dating. Finally, Bobbi gathered up her courage and asked Stephanie to move into her apartment in Bend.

Stephanie moved in on a Saturday and they made love nearly the whole, beautiful night. Bobbi felt on cloud nine. Sunday, they relaxed, catching up on their medical journal reading, feeding each other pizza, and kissing. It felt so good to have someone in the house with her.

On Monday, Stephanie came home late.

Her voice held a tone Bobbi hadn't heard before. A tinny, cutting tone. "What are the dishes still doing in the sink?"

Bobbi looked up, shocked to hear the disapproval lacing Stephanie's statement, and mumbled, "Sorry. I'll get right on it."

Stephanie threw her briefcase on the couch roughly. Bobbi jumped, startled. "Did you have a bad day?" She couldn't comprehend Stephanie's mood. She only wanted it gone and strove to fix it the rest of the night.

The next week went fairly well, but that weekend, they had a fight about what to have for dinner. Bobbi apparently had forgotten to get chicken for a recipe Stephanie planned to cook. Stephanie threw a kitchen towel in Bobbi's face.

Bobbi again felt stunned. She didn't grow up in a household where yelling and throwing things had ever occurred. Her parents had their squabbles, mostly about the lack of money. They raised their voices, but the fights were always short-lived and afterward, included kisses, hugs, and apologies. As a younger person, she would tense for a bit during their loudest exchanges, but they never scared her or made her feel her parents didn't care for or respect each other. Bobbi started to wonder where she was going wrong with Stephanie.

Stephanie's behavior the next week amplified. She found something wanting every day about Bobbi's clothes and hair. Or the house never was clean enough. Or she'd forgotten to clean the cat litter.

The atmosphere in the apartment took on a tension that caused Bobbi to stay at the clinic longer after seeing patients. She would find reasons to look up diagnoses in the library or consult with an attending on a patient's treatment.

This had been the wrong thing to do.

Stephanie became outraged when Bobbi walked in very late one night. She grabbed Bobbi by the collar and asked where she'd been. Bobbi's heart rate skyrocketed, her hands became clammy, and she stuttered her answer, "I…I was at the library checking on the latest treatment for congestive heart failure." She gave a pleading look into Stephanie's squinting eyes. "Remember? I'm giving a presentation at rounds tomorrow."

Stephanie dug into her shoulders painfully.

"You'd better be calling me when you're late. How do I know you weren't out with that nurse from the med-surg floor?"

Bobbi looked wildly at her, trying her best to remember any nurse. "What nurse?"

That's when Stephanie shoved her into the dining table, causing the crockery pot with a small plant on it to hit the floor in pieces. Bobbi rubbed the spot on her hip that had caught the edge of the table. She gulped.

"You know damn well which nurse. The redhead who keeps flirting with you."

"She's not flirting. I swear. We shared a joke a couple of days ago. You came by just when she hit the punch line." Bobbi's voice felt small and afraid. How could she fear this tiny woman whom she thought she loved?

Stephanie grabbed her by the shirt again, then flung her toward the bedroom. "Get out of my sight. I don't want to see you again tonight. Do you hear me?"

Bobbi was so flummoxed she didn't even know how to argue back or defend herself. She spent the night in her bedroom, trying, without much success, to read for her presentation, her breathing rapid with uncontrolled fear.

The next few days continued in this vein. Bobbi tried mightily to do everything Stephanie wanted, but it seemed impossible. Anything was fair game for being criticized: how she did the laundry, the lackadaisical housework, her bad cooking. Bobbi knew she wasn't the neatest housekeeper, but Stephanie would point out the most insignificant, minor problem, from not taking out the trash to leaving her shoes in the living room.

Stephanie also began to harp on the amount of time Bobbi was away from the apartment. She didn't like Bobbi's friends, her colleagues, or her family, and insisted that Bobbi do everything with her. She required Bobbi to check in through the day so she knew where she was and what she was doing.

And when Bobbi didn't respond to Stephanie's satisfaction, the physical abuse escalated as well. In a rage over spilled coffee on the kitchen floor, Stephanie pushed Bobbi against a wall. She punched Bobbi in a fit of anger over Bobbi leaving the mail in the mailbox.

Bobbi could feel again the pushes, slaps, kicks, cuffs, and the constant criticism of the smallest failures. Always, in a half hour, Stephanie cried and begged. She was always so sorry, so apologetic. It wouldn't happen again.

Bobbi forgave her each time.

Bobbi had bruises on her arms, her legs, and, one day, a black eye. She was having a hard time keeping these from the people at the clinic, so she had to come up with rational explanations for her "clumsy behavior."

But Bobbi felt worst about being hit by a woman several inches shorter and some pounds lighter than she was. Why couldn't she hit back? Why did she let Stephanie control her like this? She only knew she felt out of her depth with Stephanie and could only try to love her the best way she knew how. By acceding to her every whim and wish.

Bobbi began to feel more and more ashamed of her actions, of her choice of a girlfriend, of her weakness in not standing up to Stephanie.

Finally, the breaking point arrived.

"Why didn't I hear from you until two this afternoon? Where the hell were you? What were you doing that you couldn't think about me, worrying about you?"

Bobbi took a deep breath. "Surgery. I told you I was assisting in a minor plastic surgery case this morning with Dr.—"

Slap. Stephanie hit Bobbi across the face, hard.

Bobbi reeled back, cupping her cheek and temple. Her head rang. Stephanie wore a ring on her right hand and it must have cut into Bobbi's face, because her fingers came back dripping in sticky blood. She breathed rapidly and cowered from Stephanie, stepping away from her toward the living room wall.

Stephanie looked at Bobbi's cheek. She gasped. "Oh, honey. I'm so sorry. But you really need to let me know what's going on during the day. See what you made me do?"

Bobbi had heard this too many times before.

"Let me stitch you up." Stephanie turned toward the bathroom to get the first aid kit.

"No." Bobbi grabbed her coat and keys. She ran out the door before Stephanie could return. She raced over to the ER. All the way, she decided how she would explain the latest of her "clumsy accidents."

After the ER visit, the same nurse, Monica, who had questioned her before about the bruises, questioned Bobbi in the clinic.

They were both in the break room at the end of the lunch hour.

"I need you to listen to me, Dr. Webster."

Bobbi tried to run out of the room, but Monica blocked the way. "I have a patient."

"You don't; I checked. Your schedule is free for the next forty-five minutes, and I am telling you to sit down."

Monica was in her late fifties, her mom's age. Reluctantly, Bobbi sat down. "What do you want?"

"Dr. Webster, I have seen the way you look when I ask about your bruises and other injuries. Your latest, when you needed stitches in your cheek, makes me need to act. Did your girlfriend do this? You need to be honest."

Bobbi looked around the room for an escape.

Monica went on, "As clinicians, it's our job to notice abuse when we suspect it. Your life is not safe."

At that, Bobbi's eyes teared up. She gulped, not able to look at Monica.

Monica put her hand on Bobbi's shoulder. "It's all right," she said tenderly.

Bobbi whispered, "No. She's…She's sorry. I'm screwing up all the time. I didn't—"

"You and I know that's one of the symptoms of abusers. They are always sorry and it won't happen again. Am I right?"

Bobbi said through tears, "Yes." She was mortified.

"Just because you can bench press someone's bodyweight doesn't mean they don't have the power to put you in the hospital."

They talked for at least an hour that day in the break room. Miraculously, no other staff came in the door for all that time. Had they all known but Bobbi? How dumb could she be? She felt ashamed.

"Don't you dare take this on yourself. You know that too. They always make it seem that it's your fault. Don't buy that shit, Dr. Webster. Use your training on yourself. Diagnose your own problem and then take action to heal yourself."

Monica was a bulldog that day, setting Bobbi straight, and Bobbi finally admitted she lived with a charming, beautiful abuser, five inches and twenty pounds smaller than she was. Humiliating.

Bobbi heeded Monica's advice and began to take charge. As difficult as it was for Bobbi, she confronted Stephanie. Stephanie denied any abuse, accusing Bobbi of making her be the way she was, because she was always fucking up. Bobbi refused to waiver, remembering Monica's words, "Your life is not safe."

Stephanie was out of her apartment by the end of the month. Bobbi retained a 'no-contact' order from the police in Bend. While Bobbi still ran into her on rounds and in the clinic, she was rid of the daily mental and physical beating she had been enduring because she thought Stephanie loved her. And, she thought she loved Stephanie.

Chapter Eleven

"Hi, Mom."

"Hi, sweetie. How are things in Colorado?" Erin's mom often video-called on Friday nights if Erin was free.

"Good. Cold but good. No parishioners dying or marrying. About to start Lent, so lots of planning for that."

"And how's your snarky doctor?"

Erin quirked her lips in a surprised smile. She shrugged. "I don't know. I saw her for dinner with friends last Sunday. She seemed not quite her snarky self. Said she'd been on call, so I imagine she was operating on minimal sleep. And, just to set the record straight, she's not *my* anything. I saw her professionally, and have run into her with my parishioners, but she and I have only a passing relationship."

"That so, huh?"

Her mom could be stubborn with her matchmaking. "Yes. She's too much...something for me."

"Attractive?"

"Well, she might be if she got off her pedestal and stopped trying to be God."

"That's quite an indictment. Not your usual loving self."

"But it's true. I told you about poor Mr. Mendes. She was going to keep him suffering when he just wanted to let go." Erin puffed out an exasperated breath at the memory. "Thank God, he died the way he wanted, but not without his daughter and I going to bat for him."

"Too bad she's a good doctor. Isn't that what they do? Treat people?"

"Funny, Mom. You medical types always stand up for each other. But, she took it one step too far that night."

"If you say so." Margaret O'Rourke kept a skeptical tone.

Erin's parish, winter weather, in both Colorado and Chicago, and other, less hot topics finished their conversation.

Afterwards, Erin watched a video program she hoped to use during the Lenten study program at her church, but had a hard time concentrating.

Dr. Webster had seemed more than tired on Sunday after they had started talking about wedding counseling. Distracted was a better description. Sad. Yes, sad. What was going on for the usually in-charge doctor? Had something happened in her network of family and friends? Did she just have a bad night on call? More than a minor mishap led to the doctor's withdrawal, Erin was certain of it.

Erin worried she'd done or said something wrong. While she didn't always understand the doctor, or like her, she respected her professionalism and commitment to her career. In fact, she found her competence and forthrightness quite attractive. If nothing else, Dr. Webster didn't pull any punches. Erin usually could trust her to say what was on her mind, except for Sunday night. A niggling feeling told her that the doctor was holding back and it was hurting her. Erin wanted to know, and wanted to help her, instinctively. And Bobbi could use some pastoral attention, according to Erin's assessment of her sadness.

But Erin couldn't solve this problem tonight. She shut down the video and prepared for her prenuptial meeting tomorrow.

❧❧❧❧

The next morning, Yancy and Gen arrived for their third Saturday session. In the first two sessions, Erin had led them in a discussion of the results of their online couples' questionnaire on the two sticklers for most couples—money and sex. Their responses showed they held similar opinions on both topics and that they felt very satisfied by both areas of their relationship. And in the sessions, Yancy and Gen said they experienced few problems.

Today, family dynamics were on the docket.

After they were settled, Erin shared with them the results of their set of questions on children, household management, chores, and other domestic issues.

Gen looked at Yancy, and said, her voice strained, "You don't want children? I didn't know that."

"I didn't know you *wanted* them." Yancy blinked and gazed back at Gen.

Erin smiled to herself. Aha, the first chink in the relationship armor. "Let's explore your answers. Who wants to go first?"

Gen and Yancy both continued to stare blankly at each other. Gen took a large, cleansing breath. "I'll start." She looked directly at Yancy. "In a nutshell, my body clock is ticking. I'll be thirty-nine in July and would like to try to conceive sooner rather than later."

Yancy gulped. "Geez, Gen." She cleared her throat. "It never crossed my mind. It's not that I'm opposed to having kids, er, a kid. But who would take care of it? My schedule is crazy, especially in the summer. Yours is crazy all year."

"I know, darling. But first, I would take some months of maternity leave. Then, I hope we can get some young person to come out to be a nanny for us the rest of the first year. At least during the day. You know they train nannies at the community college. Then, after the baby's a year old, we can use day care. By then, my rotation of rural fellows will be stabilized, their work more predictable, and I'll be able to take fewer calls. I'll be freer at night."

Yancy shook her head and raised her brows. "Holy cow. You seem to have thought through a lot of details. I didn't know half this stuff."

"I've thought about it a lot; I was on the verge of starting the process on my own before we met. In Kentucky, the university provided excellent childcare services for employees. My friend Stacy used them for her toddlers. It seemed like a good time for me to try, but then I moved."

Erin quietly watched the two, thinking they were being quite attentive to each other. A good sign for couples.

"I feel blindsided," Yancy said. "It's not that I don't like kids, I do. It's just…Hell, I don't know if I'm parent material."

"You'd be a great mom. I saw you with the riding therapy kids back in September. You were very patient and caring with that little boy."

"Yeah, but I was teaching around horses, a place

where I'm comfortable. It was a no brainer. But, night feedings? Diapers? Screaming toddlers? Hold your horses, baby."

"Don't be so dramatic." Gen patted Yancy's arm.

"Why didn't we discuss this before?"

"I don't know. We've been pretty busy talking about other things. Me moving to the ranch. The house and Connie's change in schedule. Christmas. Our schedules and planning the wedding."

"My mind's spinning here. This scares the shi— crap out of me. Can you really see me being a mother?"

"Sure, darling. I can see you cuddling a baby. Teaching a toddler how to ride Honey. How to play baseball. You'd be a wonderful daddy." Gen grinned.

"Ha, ha."

Erin interposed, "Sorry, guys, but our time is up. You did good work today. We have our last session next week. In the meantime, I want you to continue this discussion and report to me how it goes. You may not agree on everything, but you should be able to listen and understand where each other's coming from. I don't need to tell you that having kids is a choice you both should agree on." Erin smiled knowingly at them and directed them out of the church.

❧❧❧❧

Erin walked into Murphy's Diner, saw Roxie, in her usual colorful outfit, at a table in the back, and wended her way through the tightly placed chairs.

"Good to see you. I was shocked you were free for lunch." Roxie smiled, watching cutie-pie Erin slide into the chair.

Erin sighed. "I know. I was too." She picked up

the laminated menu. "What's good here? I've only been one other time."

"I'm having my staple cold-weather food, chili and grilled cheese."

"Ooh, boy. Not sure I can eat all of that. Maybe I'll have the chicken soup. Is it good?"

Roxie nodded enthusiastically. "Unfortunately for my figure, everything at Murphy's tastes great." She laughed.

"You're in great shape." Erin admired Roxie's full figure.

"Thanks, but you must need new glasses." Roxie rolled her eyes.

After they ordered, Roxie started the conversation. "I'm happy you're working with me at my clinic. I thought we'd check in to see how things're going." Roxie took a drink of her water. "Any problems, any questions?"

Erin played with her knife and fork on the table, shaking her head. "Not a thing. I'm enjoying the work. It's different from the church, more controllable, nothing unexpected. I like the routine and I enjoy one-on-one time with clients."

Roxie nodded. "Super. I thought things were going well. I am so slammed with clients these days, your one day a week really helps my load." Roxie looked down at her bowl of chili as the server placed it on the table.

Erin smiled. "Glad to help. Anything else you wanted to bring up?"

Roxie grinned. "As a matter of fact, yeah." She looked up sheepishly from taking a bite from her chili. "I was wondering what you thought of Dr. Webster. She's not hard to look at, huh?"

Erin shook her head. "You. I've known you less than a year, and you have me pegged. Yes, okay? She's good looking. Better than that, actually. But, I don't like her. There, I said it out loud."

"Don't like her? Oh, cutie-pie, you can't mean that. What's not to like?" Roxie grabbed Erin's left wrist and shook it.

"Have you ever had to work with her? She's bossy. She takes charge for her own means and doesn't listen to her patients. She's—"

"Exasperating?"

"I see your little smirk there. You won't play matchmaker with me. I know you invited her to your house. You and Gen got together."

"Why, I'm shocked you would think such a thing." Roxie put her hand over her heart, mockingly.

"Yeah, whatever." Erin slurped a spoonful of her chicken soup. "Mmm, this is good."

"Don't change the subject, munchkin."

"Munchkin? Now I'm offended." Erin's mouth went wide.

"Well, what are you, all of five feet tall? Even that?" Then Roxie gazed at Erin. "I've seen how the good doctor looks at you. And it's not like a sister, let me tell you."

"Oh, come on. Now, you're delusional."

"No, really. At the dinner at our house, before she pooped out on us, she could hardly keep her eyes off you."

"That may be, but we've had two run-ins about my parishioners who're her patients, and I don't want to have another, thank you very much." Erin pouted at the memory of Mr. Mendes.

"Don't be a killjoy. You're lonely, and she's in

her white doctor coat, looking all brilliant and sexy. Don't lose this chance at having a life. You may regret it."

"Let's change the subject, Dr. Campbell." Erin frowned. Despite her bossiness, she thought how sexy Bobbi Webster was in that white coat and stethoscope.

Chapter Twelve

The monthly clinical conference started exactly at seven a.m. All the fellows and attendings from Valley View sat around the conference table with coffee. Some had picked up a donut from the side credenza. Bobbi let out a big yawn, having been on call the night before, hospitalizing a child with the flu and a high fever. Bobbi had checked in at four this morning to find her fever under control, but the child's mother needed the most care. She had nearly screamed into the phone the night before with anxiety. Bobbi had calmed her when she met them in the ER at BCH at one a.m.

Gen introduced Dr. Roxanne Campbell again with the topic of today's conference. Bobbi noted Roxie's dark blond plait of hair. Even though Roxie was in her forties, she looked bright and energetic, more like a teen in her bright outfits. Today, she had on a multicolor sweater, jeans, and Birkenstocks with wool, rainbow socks. Bobbi liked her open smile and sparkling blue eyes, as she began the presentation to the doctors on mental health issues in primary care and the clinic's systems for assessment, a topic she knew little about. She took notes from Roxie's PowerPoint presentation. She was surprised that the clinic offered an online screening program for the diagnoses she saw most often. Most small, rural medical centers didn't have that luxury.

"Will we discuss the latest treatment options?" Bobbi asked, as Roxie wrapped up the presentation.

"Yes. I have an up-to-date list of psychotropic drugs, their dosages, and major side effects." Dr. Campbell grabbed a stack of papers and began to distribute them on both sides of the table to the doctors.

Bobbi skimmed through the ten-page packet of information in small print and noted she would need to study these drugs in more detail.

"I am a psychologist, not a psychiatrist, so, as you know, I can't prescribe. That's where you at the clinic come in. A prescription would help some of my clients. I may contact you with a recommendation for specific patients of yours. As their primary care physician, I would rather you prescribe than a psychiatrist. As you also know, Babcock and the two contiguous counties have no psychiatrists. I don't want my clients to have to go to Denver to see one, just for a prescription."

Gen said, "I think we all can get behind Roxie's plan for assisting each other with patients who present with a mental health issue. I have here a sheet with all the mental health practitioners in the three-county area." She passed out a single page.

"There are only three names here," the clinic's pediatrician commented.

"Yep," Roxie replied. "There's me, a clinical social worker over in San Sebastian, and the Rev. Erin O'Rourke. Mother Erin is an Episcopal priest who has a master's in pastoral counseling. She works out of my office one day a week. As some of you know, she's only part-time due to her part-time church work."

"So, we have two-and-a-half mental health professionals in total for the three counties." Gen summed up the situation.

"You can imagine we all work crazy hours. My office is on Main Street, in a multi-use office complex. Rural mental health clients generally balk at going to a freestanding building to see a mental health professional. There's still a lot of stigma about mental illness out here."

The doctors around the table murmured about this problem.

Jaime said, "I've had a problem getting one rancher to go. He's adamantly against getting help. I've prescribed anti-depressants, but he would be a good candidate for grief counseling."

The group discussed these issues until eight o'clock, when patients began arriving for scheduled appointments. Bobbi packed up her notes and handouts and placed them in a file folder, grabbed some more coffee, and was about to leave the room, when Gen came up to her.

"Dr. Webster, can I have a second with you?"

Bobbi turned to her. Given Gen's smile, it must not be bad news, anyway, she thought. "What can I do for you?"

"In looking over your fellowship application, I saw that you had a rotation at a hospice in eastern Oregon during your residency."

"Yes. It was not much of a challenge, medically. Signing off on palliative care protocols primarily. The nurses and social workers did most of the patient work."

"Can we talk after clinic today? I have a proposition for you."

"Okay," Bobbi answered, wondering what Gen could be offering.

Bobbi worked hard that day, struggling to keep

focused after a night of little sleep. Later, after she signed the last patient chart, she leaned back in her chair at the counter outside the patient rooms, sighed, and stretched. She glanced at the clock behind her on the wall and noted it was after six, hoping Dr. Lambert was still in the clinic. Bobbi walked down the hall to the medical director's office. The door was ajar and light spilled out into the hallway in a thin strip.

"Knock, knock."

Gen looked up from paperwork at her desk. "Come on in, Bobbi."

Bobbi stifled a yawn and sat in the comfy chair across from where Gen sat behind her desk.

"You look tired, Doctor."

"Long night."

"Ah. I won't keep you long. Dr. Manning is on tonight I think." Gen came around the desk, straightening her pencil skirt, and Bobbi tried not to stare at her shapely legs. "I wanted to talk with you about an opportunity that has come up with the Tri-County Hospice."

Bobbi nodded.

Gen continued. "Their in-house medical director, Michaela Lopez, wants to add more local doctors to their consultant list. I thought, because of your hospice experience, you might be interested."

"What do they want consultants to do?"

"She, as medical director, can handle the day-to-day patient supervision with nurses, but she needs someone to answer questions during evening hours. You know, of course, there are no emergencies in hospice, so it's mostly routine stuff from nurses about prescription adjustments for palliative care. You're familiar with how hospice nurses do most of the care on their own, using the hospice protocols signed off by Dr. Lopez."

"How many evenings a month?"

"How about you direct your questions to Dr. Lopez? Here's her card with the contact information. She would like someone to start in March, I believe."

Bobbi took the card, nodded, and said good night to Dr. Lambert.

On the way home, she pondered doing some hospice work. Gen had been right; it would entail no emergencies. Hospice aimed to give patients a good death, which medically, was about providing comfort care. Occasionally, weird things might happen. A patient may ask to go off morphine. She remembered a case when a daughter of an older man requested she help him die. Of course, she refused. She raised his dosage, reducing both his pain and the daughter's anxiety. But such calls from hospice nurses were rare. She would call Dr. Lopez tomorrow.

⚖⚖⚖⚖

Two days later, Bobbi finished rounds on four Ryan Delaney Clinic patients who were hospitalized. Everything looked good on the heart patient and a patient with a flare up of cellulitis. The rancher with a compound fracture of the tibia was resting comfortably and would be released later that morning. However, a mother and her newborn were both recovering from a difficult delivery. She called in a neonatologist from Denver for the baby. The mother had received blood transfusions, but seemed to be getting her strength back. When she finished around noon, she decided to pick up some quick lunch at the hospital's small cafeteria before heading to the clinic, where her first patient wasn't expected until two p.m. As she walked in, she noted that Erin, The Elf, sat at a far window table overlooking snow-covered plains. Bobbi went to the counter, ordered her BLT and a coffee, and stood to the side until the counter worker called her.

After she paid for her lunch, she balanced it all on a tray and walked uncertainly over to Erin's table, not knowing what welcome she might receive. Erin's attention intently focused on the horizon. She didn't notice Bobbi until Bobbi spoke. Erin's head snapped up. "Oh. Dr. Webster. What a nice surprise."

Bobbi hoped Erin truly felt it was nice. She'd been grumpy around her since they met, so Bobbi wouldn't begrudge her being less than welcoming. Bobbi inhaled when she realized Erin wore a green sweater over her clerical shirt that was the same color as one Stephanie used to wear. She admonished herself that she would look past the sweater. "Do you mind if I join you?"

"No, please do." Erin swept her hand to the open chair. "I was checking my email, then got caught up in the scenery. I stopped for some coffee after I visited a client of the mental health clinic who was admitted last night."

"Hospitalized for mental health issues?"

"Sorry, Doctor, I can't talk about my patient." Erin sat back, crossed her arms over her chest, and slapped a smug look on her cute face.

Bobbi grinned lopsidedly. "Touché." She held her coffee up in a salute to Erin.

They looked at each other for a moment with laughter in their eyes.

"Sorry. I shouldn't have asked that. I know better." Bobbi began eating her sandwich.

Erin took a moment, seeming to ponder something, then spoke. "I don't want to pry, Doctor, but I noticed at our Sunday dinner that you checked out of the conversation. I wondered if you were okay. I hope none of us offended you or spoke out of turn."

Bobbi chewed thoughtfully, wondering how to respond. "I, uh...I'm fine, more or less. You talking about problems in relationships hit a sore spot with me, unfortunately. It's certainly not your fault. It took me down a rabbit hole. I'm sorry it came across so rudely—"

"Not rude. No, we didn't think it rude. We were concerned about you, is all. You seemed far away and, well...sad."

Bobbi looked on Erin and her astute assessment of the situation. "You could say that, yes. But I'm good now. No harm, no foul."

Erin didn't look convinced. "Did we call up something from your past?"

"Yes." Bobbi took a big bite of her BLT.

Erin waited for her.

"Yes," Bobbi repeated, inhaling deeply before she added, "I don't want to talk about it today. I hope you understand."

Erin waited, her eyes softly watching Bobbi, a small frown crinkling her forehead. "I don't want to push, Doctor."

Bobbi swallowed. "You're not pushing. And, could we get to first names? We've run into each other quite a bit lately. I hope you'll call me Bobbi. Doctor sounds a bit off-putting."

"Sure, no problem, Bobbi." Erin smirked. "You can drop the Mother, too. Just plain Erin."

"Okay, plain Erin." Bobbi smirked in kind, while

she finished the last of her sandwich. She gathered her leftover wrappers and napkin onto the tray. "I need to run. Good to see you, Erin."

"Likewise, Bobbi."

Bobbi nodded in Erin's direction, then left. Erin had been pleasant and seemed concerned about her. Nice. Despite the stupid sweater.

Chapter Thirteen

That afternoon, during a lull between patients, Bobbi talked with Dr. Lopez at the hospice office, agreeing to be a consultant for one year.

Three days later, after having agreed with Dr. Lopez's request for medical help, Bobbi had a message from her to come to a patient conference today at five-thirty.

She grabbed her diet coke and headed out into the cold winter wind with her hood up and gloves on.

When she arrived at the hospice office, the receptionist guided her to the correct room. She walked in to see three people—two women she didn't know, and The Elf. Was the woman stalking her?

Bobbi stood in the doorway briefly to gird her loins, then nonchalantly made her way to the remaining empty seat around the small round table.

The two women quickly shook her hand and introduced themselves as the social worker and nurse on her patient's case.

"Hi," Erin said quietly. "Good to see you, Doctor...er, Bobbi."

Bobbi just nodded at Erin, noting she wore another sweater today, totally okay.

The nurse, a pudgy woman with gray streaks in her short, dark chestnut hair, began. "Thanks everyone for coming out in the cold this afternoon. This should be fairly short. We need to finalize the treatment plan for Mrs. Meredith, whom we admitted yesterday." She passed out a one-page summary and began to read it.

No slouch, this nurse, Bobbi thought. One to get to business.

"She's a ninety-five-year-old widow with end stage renal failure. She also has COPD and diabetes. She's no longer ambulatory, completely bed-ridden, with a catheter. Her daughter—"

"Annabelle," Erin added.

The nurse nodded to Erin, then hurried back to the patient's information. "Yes. Annabelle has been the primary caregiver and Mrs. Meredith is at her home. We delivered a hospital bed late yesterday. When I did my full admission assessment, her blood pressure was steady but low, pulse low, other vitals okay. Jane, do you want to fill us in on her situation?"

The nurse's speech had clipped along very fast. Bobbi hoped she'd caught all the important data.

The social worker nodded, and spoke in a much slower cadence. "As you indicated, her daughter Annabelle takes care of her. She is a retired teacher in her early seventies, living in a modest two-bedroom house on one floor, so no stairs to negotiate. Her husband, Pete, supports all this, but is not much help except physically helping to move his mother-in-law. A grown son, Gavin, comes around occasionally and brings his two elementary-school-age daughters. Gavin lost his construction job some weeks ago when he broke his foot and is waiting for disability payments. In the meantime, he's getting help from his parents. I have applied for medical assistance for Mrs. Meredith, since she's not got any savings to speak of. That should help in paying for hospice care."

"My church has been aiding this family for

some time. We bring food once a month and help with the heating bill when we can. Several people from the parish visit once or twice a month to bring communion and the day's altar flowers. The family doesn't come to church because of the burden of caregiving." Erin sighed. Bobbi thought she looked sad at this information.

Bobbi looked down at the notes she'd brought from her patient's clinic chart. "Medically, she's holding her own. I expect her not to last more than a week, given her kidneys' functioning. She probably won't suffer."

Nurse Hurry-Up answered Bobbi, "I agree; she probably won't. In the kidney deaths I've seen, the patient doesn't suffer because they often go into a coma until death."

All around the table nodded with this assessment.

"What can I do?" Bobbi asked.

The nurse produced a typed list. "I have a list of medications she's currently taking, as I'm sure you do. If we could cut it down to only those with palliative purposes, to keep her comfortable. "

Bobbi took the prescription list and looked it over. She took the pen out of her pocket and began marking the sheet with notes, then, after a few moments, handed it back to the nurse. "This should be sufficient. I am not writing any scripts for pain. Does that sound right to you?"

"Yes, Dr. Webster. If we need anything, we can call you and one of us can run to the clinic for a script, but I don't think it will be necessary."

Erin frowned at the nurse then at Bobbi. "No morphine, then?"

Bobbi looked at her. "No. Unless she becomes

agitated from the effects of the kidney failure, she will probably be comatose, so she'll not be feeling pain. But the hospice staff will let me know ASAP if things change, then I'll write a script."

"Yes, I understand now. Thank you." Erin smiled at Bobbi, surprising her.

The social worker asked, "Reverend, will you be visiting the family soon?"

Bobbi inwardly smirked hearing the social worker call Erin the hated title, "Reverend."

"I'm going over tomorrow. I called and they were happy to have me visit for prayer. I'll give the family and Mrs. Meredith pastoral care, and I hope to discuss Mrs. Meredith's funeral arrangements. It's what I'd do for any parishioner with such a short time left. In other visits with them, Annabelle and Pete seemed somewhat relieved that things were winding down for her mother. She's been ailing for several years and unable to take care of herself or do the things she enjoyed doing. But in the last weeks, her health has been rapidly going downhill, putting a tremendous burden on Annabelle, both physically and emotionally."

"Not unusual at all," the social worker added. "Hospice can provide a volunteer to go out and help Annabelle with household chores, maybe sit with her and chat."

"Sounds great," Erin answered, smiling at the social worker.

After a short, quiet moment, the nurse said, "I think that wraps up what we needed to discuss today. Anyone have anything else to add?" She looked around the table. "Thank you again for coming. Dr. Webster. Mother Erin." She shook each of their hands and they all left the room.

Bobbi helped Erin on with her coat. "What's in the water over at your church?" she teased. "I keep running into your parishioners as my patients."

Erin quirked her eyebrow. "I know. I didn't know you worked with hospice."

"I'm starting a year-long consultation, helping out the medical director. In fact, this is my first case with them. It just worked out that Mrs. Meredith is one of my own patients."

"Same here. I've never had a Holy Spirit parishioner in hospice before, well, except for Mr. Mendes those two days." Erin blushed. "They knew I was Annabelle and Pete's priest, so they invited me to the conference."

Bobbi looked out the front door of the hospice office. "Looks like snow. You going to be okay getting home?"

"Oh, sure. I'm from Chicago, you know." Erin laughed.

Bobbi thought Erin's laugh sounded like tinkling music. She wished she heard Erin laugh more. "I didn't know. Excuse me." She laughed, bowing slightly. "Then you know more about driving in snow than most, I assume."

"You got that right," Erin said. "Well, I'd better get going. I've got a whole evening to myself. What a treat. No meetings. My sermon's done, and tomorrow's my day off. Hallelujah."

Bobbi watched Erin's face brighten and thought for a moment. She wanted to get her past out of her system, despite Erin triggering some anxiety. She certainly felt attracted to her. "Er, if you've got no plans, would you like to catch some dinner or something? I'm done at the clinic for today, and thankfully am not on call tonight." Bobbi went on, deciding to tell the tale of her woeful household. "My fridge is virtually empty, as well."

"Doctor." Erin shook her head and wagged her finger playfully. "Bad on you." Erin's pink face drew Bobbi in. "But, another soul sprung from the daily drudge. Good for you." Erin clapped her on the back, while she seemed to ponder Bobbi's offer. "Sure. Let's get something to eat. Where did you have in mind?"

Chapter Fourteen

They decided on a bar and grill that Bobbi had seen from the road only, situated not far from the hospice office's location. Erin knew the owner, the sister of her hairstylist.

Bobbi followed Erin in her green four-wheel drive without too much sledding around on the snow-packed road. As they arrived at the destination, Kenny's Tavern looked worse for wear. The "Tav" letters were not lit on the neon sign and the tinted front windows hadn't seen a cleaner in a while. Dirt stained the white clapboard walls and the roof sank on the left side.

Pickup trucks filled most of the parking lot. When she entered, country music from the jukebox and the smell of greasy fried food assaulted her senses. Cowboys, construction workers, farmers, ranchers, and other blue-collar types stood shoulder to shoulder at the thirty-foot-long bar. Two men in flannel shirts and baseball caps played pool in the area behind the tables, and she noted they were the only women in the place. A couple of the men in denim turned to peer briefly at them, then returned disinterestedly to their desultory beer sipping.

Erin indicated one of the few small, round tables that stood empty between the bar and the pool table. They sat in the one furthest from the jukebox. Erin waved at the bartender. "Hey, Milly."

"Be right there." Milly nodded her head amidst

filling up mugs from the tap. "Beer?"

Erin looked at Bobbi.

"High Country, if you've got one," Bobbi answered.

"Same for me," Erin told Milly. "Milly, this is Dr. Webster."

Milly nodded to Bobbi from behind the bar. "Good to meet ya, Doc."

Bobbi raised her eyebrows. "They got good food?"

"Don't you trust me, Doctor?" Erin grinned coquettishly.

Bobbi felt herself redden. "Sorry. I just..." Bobbi's eyes swept the bar.

Milly appeared with two frosty mugs. "Here ya go, ladies. What'll ya have tonight? It's chili night. We got some good mutton stew, too."

Bobbi looked at Erin, then said, "Mutton stew for me."

"Chili, please, extra jalapenos on the side." Erin grinned, swept Bobbi's menu up, and gave Milly both menus.

"You like it hot, eh?" Bobbi asked. She regretted her flirty statement as soon as it left her mouth. What a thing to say to a priest! "Sorry. Didn't mean—"

Erin laughed. "You're so adorable when you're flustered. Please don't filter your words for me. I'm from a blue-collar neighborhood, where a bar like this sits on every corner, filled with guys just like this. And, yes, for the record, I like it hot. Chili, that is."

Erin's flirting back. Now what do I do? "I'm glad you like it hot, Mother Erin," Bobbi said. She fiddled with her utensils. "It appears I don't know much about you, other than you came from a blue-collar neighborhood in Chicago."

Milly plunked two bowls and a basket filled with crackers in front of them, asked if they needed anything else, then headed back behind the bar. They both began to eat.

Between bites, Erin said, "Well, let's see. I've got three sisters. All live in the Chicago area. My dad's a retired priest, which means he travels around to fill in for priests who go on vacation or are ill. My mom is a nurse who just retired last year. They stay in Chicago all year, as opposed to a lot of their friends, who are snowbirds in either Arizona or Florida. They like their winter-season activities, like the symphony, theater, the Christmas festivities. New Year's Eve in Evanston. The restaurants and music. All the good Chi-town stuff."

"Do you miss the city?"

"Sometimes I do. But I'm so busy trying to make a go of this tiny parish and doing other jobs to shore up my income, I don't have time to miss it. The food and music, sure. But not the traffic on the Kennedy Expressway or the jam of tourists on Michigan Avenue all summer. How about you? What do you miss in Oregon?"

"That's easy. I miss my mom's cooking. Although, truth be told, I've not had it on a regular basis since college. I'm thirty; you'd think I'd have learned how to be an adult by now." Both of them laughed lightly.

"There's something to be said for holding off on adulting if you can. Maybe you just aren't a cook." Erin looked with compassion on Bobbi.

Bobbi inexplicably liked the look she was being given. "You're being too nice. I'm too lazy to shop for groceries."

"Bad nutrition, Doc."

"Yeah. I know. Whatever."

As they finished up their suppers, talking about home, a ruckus began at the bar. Two men shouted at each other.

One, a man in work overalls, his face scarlet, slurred, "You're a damn liar." He shoved the other man, smaller than him by a head.

Milly flew out from behind the bar in a whirl. "Get the hell outta here, Jake. You too, Wes." She walked toward them, just as Wes took a broad swing toward Jake, the man in overalls. Jake swerved; Wes's arm swung wide, came around, and connected with Milly's jaw.

Bobbi stood up, knocking her chair over, breathing hard and shaking.

Milly shook her head from the blow. Two other men looking on from their perches at the bar quickly grabbed Jake and Wes and hauled them out the front door.

Erin ran over to Milly. "Somebody get some ice, please."

A cowboy stepped behind the bar and filled a rag with ice from the cooler. After he handed it to Erin, she placed it on Milly's jaw, and led her over to a chair.

Milly sat, feeling her bump. "I'm all right. Just a bruise. Those damn rowdies. I told them not to come in here with their squabbles. Like two old ladies."

Bobbi stepped over to Milly to check out her injury. Her cold, clammy hands shook while she felt along her left jaw. Milly would have a large contusion, but the bone didn't feel broken.

Bobbi's head felt light and her breathing erratic. Another damn anxiety attack.

Erin glanced at her. "Are you all right?" she whispered and grabbed at Bobbi's forearm to lead her to a seat.

Bobbi resisted Erin's hand, pulled away, and went back to get her coat. "Milly, keep ice on that for a day or so, twenty minutes off and on."

"You gotta be kiddin', Doc. I'm serving people in here. It'll be okay. It ain't the first time I been clocked by some stupid drunk." Milly got up with the ice pack on her jaw and took her place back behind the bar. "Well, boys, that's all the excitement for tonight." She laughed heartily and the men ordered up again.

The talk in the tavern resumed as if nothing had happened.

Bobbi tried to sneak to the door to escape Erin's questions, but Erin turned and caught her. "Wait a damn minute. You're in no condition to be driving. You look like you're going to faint. You're as pale as a ghost." Erin stood in front of Bobbi. "Sit down, Doctor, or I'll push you down."

Bobbi raised her brows. She believed Erin would push her down. She was small but gutsy. An image of Stephanie filled her vision for a moment.

To quell her anxiety, she sat, breathing deeply to calm herself. After a minute, when that didn't work, she brought to mind the grounding routine her counselor had taught her.

First, breathe deeply for ten seconds. Feeling Erin's eyes on her, she counted down from ten. Then, she went through the list, internally, her eyes unfocused on her surroundings:

Five things I can see. *Table, chair, beer sign, jukebox, bar.*

Breathe.

Four things I can touch. *Table, coat, button, shirt.*
Breathe.

Three things I can hear. *Country music, Erin talking, clump of boots of man walking by.*
Breathe.

Two things I can smell. *Chili on Erin's breath, her perfume.*
Breathe.

One emotion I feel. *Embarrassed.*
Breathe.

Erin sat in the opposite seat at the table. "Where did you go just now?"

Bobbi thought for a moment and then decided to lay it on the line. "I was grounding myself."

Erin nodded thoughtfully, put her hand on Bobbi's forearm. "Anxiety attack. I'm sorry. Do you know what triggered it? I hope it wasn't something I said or did."

Bobbi shook her head. "Fight," was all she could get out of her mouth. The images of Wes's fist coming through space and punching Milly's head came again to her, and she gulped in air.

"I'm going to drive you home," Erin announced decidedly.

"No," Bobbi said, raising a hand in protest. "Give me a minute more."

After another minute of Erin watching her closely, she got up. Her breathing had gotten under control. Her head felt better; her hands quit their shaking. "Really. I'm recovered."

Erin quirked a brow. "Not sure I believe you. You still look peaked."

Bobbi put a reassuring hand on Erin's shoulder. "Please, don't bother yourself. I'm good to go."

Erin put her coat on. "Well, I'm walking with you to your car. If you don't look steady, I'm taking your keys." They left the bar for the snowy parking lot.

"You're a feisty elf, aren't you?" It came out of Bobbi's mouth before she could stop it. She smirked.

"Elf? Elf?" Erin gasped in faux horror.

Bobbi looked into her dark eyes, glowing in the lot's lights. She breathed deeply.

Erin moved toward Bobbi, lightly grasped the lapels of her coat, and looked deeply into her eyes.

Bobbi felt her warmth, a tingling, and breathed in Erin's smell of soap and light perfume. Their breath mingled in fog. Was Erin about to kiss her? This was unexpected!

Erin took a deep breath at the same time Bobbi came to herself. They each stepped away. Bobbi whispered, "We'd better get out of this weather."

Erin looked at Bobbi with tenderness. "Yes. Definitely. You sure you're all right?" Her hands traced down the front placket of Bobbi's jacket.

"Yes. Thanks for your concern." Bobbi took a step toward her car. "Well, I'll see you around."

"Yeah. Until another sick parishioner, eh?" Erin smiled.

Bobbi nodded absent-mindedly. "Right. Be sure to get your church's water checked," she teased. "Good night."

From the inside of her warming Honda, Bobbi watched Erin drive away. What did she think she was doing with The Elf? A priest, for God's sake. Didn't she know Erin wasn't her type? Didn't Erin probably want something more than a fling? Bobbi shook her head to erase the image of them standing close and nearly kissing.

Chapter Fifteen

Yancy fidgeted with her bow tie. "How the hell do people tie these things?"

Roxie stood in front of her. "Let me, baby cakes. You're just nervous." She expertly retied the red bow tie, pulling on it to make it span out just right. "There you go, Studly DoRight. All set."

Yancy took a deep breath and blew it out slowly. "Is it time yet? I hear the music starting."

"Calm down, will you?" Roxie smoothed Yancy's lapels and straightened the matching red boutonniere. "We have twenty minutes."

"Why did we decide to have classical guitar music twenty minutes before the ceremony? I'm crawling out of my skin."

"Will you quit mussing with your hair?" Roxie slapped Yancy's hand away from her head. "Geez, you're like a ten-year-old. I should have brought you some whiskey or something."

"Oh, hell, no. I would just be buzzed and still nervous. I'd have probably fallen on my ass getting to the altar."

"Why are you so anxious? You've been in front of groups before. Are you backing out? Cause if you are, I'll kick that ass."

"I'm not backing out." Yancy paced. "I'm nervous 'cause I've never said these things to anyone before. Especially in front of an audience. It's…not my thing."

"Oh, news flash."

Finally, the guitar changed to Pachelbel's Canon, cuing their entrance. Erin walked up behind Yancy and Roxie in the vestry room leading to the back of the church. She wore her white alb with a white tapestry stole. "Time to rock and roll, girls." She placed her hand on Yancy's shoulder.

Yancy took another deep breath, looked directly at her, and nodded. "I'm ready." She and Roxie walked behind Erin, out to the steps in front of the altar. They took their places and stood. The scent of the baskets of red and white roses on either side of the altar filled Yancy's head as she breathed deeply to calm her nerves.

Her brother and his wife sat in the first pew on her left, while Gen's friends from Kentucky were to the right of the aisle. The usher had just seated her mom and she smiled widely at her, with watery eyes. Yancy's brother did his best attempt at a jaunty wink, but he was not a winker, so Yancy shook her head slightly at him. She smiled and relaxed a little.

The guitar music stopped for a moment, then resumed with the processional, as Stacy, Gen's friend from Kentucky, entered the back of the church, wearing a knee-length, off-white dress with a red sash. She carried a small rose bouquet. When she reached the altar, Yancy saw Gen, accompanied by both her parents, standing at the head of the church aisle. She wore a beautiful white dress that just brushed the floor, with satin and lace trimming. Her auburn hair had been styled up and held pieces of baby's breath on one side.

Yancy drew in her breath in awe. *This woman is marrying me!* She smiled at them all the way, as Gen and her parents made their way to the altar. Her father placed Gen's hand in Yancy's and she gazed at Gen. Both of Gen's parents smiled and kissed Gen on the cheek. Gen's mom brushed her hand lightly over Yancy's cheek and mouthed, "We love you."

"I love you, too," Yancy whispered to them. She then faced Gen, her smile nearly breaking her whole face open. Her knees ceased their trembling. Her heart filled with joy at being here with the love of her life. Gen had captured her nearly from the first day they met, when Yancy interviewed Gen for her job as medical director of her family's rural medical clinics. They'd had their rough spots, one being Yancy's own depression and acting-out behavior that nearly drove Gen away completely. But after getting her issues under control, she charmed Gen and Gen charmed her in return. They worked well together to improve the medical facilities available in her ranch community. Gen was her soulmate and her best friend, her touchstone, and in a few minutes, would be her wife.

Yancy came to the present as Erin began the opening sentences of the service.

The service passed quickly from vows, to rings, to prayers, and to the final kiss. Yancy took Gen into her arms and gave her a passionate kiss that lasted longer than she realized, when the congregation started to laugh, and Roxie tapped her on the shoulder and whispered, "Okay, tiger. Leave it for the honeymoon."

Yancy could hardly contain her happiness. Grasping Gen's hand, they nearly skipped down the aisle in a whirl of applause surrounding them from the congregation.

Later, they greeted people at the reception hall, with their parents in line with them. Then it was time for dinner and dancing. Toasts preceded the first dances.

Yancy danced with her brother while Gen danced with her dad, Paul. They then switched partners.

"You look radiant," Paul told Yancy as they whirled around the dance floor to a waltz.

"Thank you. I feel pretty damn good. Gen looks gorgeous."

"Yes. She looked much happier than at her wedding to Rachel, I must say. You bring out her inner beauty, Yancy."

Paul looked on Yancy with great affection. She felt her heart swell. She had no answer to his remark.

The dancing started in earnest then, with the DJ playing faster music, including oldies from the sixties and seventies for the parent generation. Yancy and Gen danced them all, whispering endearments and laughing. As the evening waned, the DJ played more recent music. Yancy noticed Erin dancing with Dr. Webster and nodded in their direction so that Gen could see.

"Oh, they're dancing. That's a sight I was hoping to see." Gen grinned. Yancy swung her around on the dance floor.

Roxie and Kate stopped them mid-dance. Roxie leaned into Gen's ear. Yancy heard her say, "I'd say our matchmaking is making headway at last."

"You guys better back off. Those two may not be the best match, you know." Yancy hated it when people tried to get couples together.

Roxie punched her arm lightly. "What do you know about it? You're as clueless as Kate most of the time."

Kate, standing next to her, shrugged her

shoulders. "I try to mind my own business."

"Yeah, whatever happened to minding one's own business?" Yancy lightly punched Roxie's arm back.

Roxie moved out of range of Yancy's arm. "What fun is that? Most people need a little shove."

"Gen and I didn't need any shoves."

Roxie and Gen laughed. "Are you kidding? You needed professional counseling and prescription drugs to get your act together. What a dork."

Yancy's family met her and Gen as they stood on the edge of the dance floor.

"Darling." Her mom, Nina, hugged Yancy and kissed her cheek, then took Gen by the shoulders and brushed her lips across her cheek. "You two look stunning. I am so happy for you both." She looked Gen in the eye, tears running down her cheek. "You finally tamed our Mary Ann."

Yancy's brother hugged them both. "Who knew our wild Yancy would be a married woman?" He tugged on Yancy's tie. She grinned as she shrugged off his hand. His wife hugged Yancy and Gen and said, "May your marriage be as happy as Phil and mine."

"I love you," Yancy whispered into Nina's ear while giving her a goodbye hug.

Yancy's family all left together for Denver.

The party was breaking up. Bobbi and Erin came together to wish the couple well.

Gen smiled at them. She took one of Erin's hands in both of hers. "Thank you, Erin. The service went so well. You made it beautiful."

Erin hugged Gen. "You two looked stunning together. I loved doing your wedding."

Bobbi shook their hands. "Congratulations, Yancy, Gen. It was a lovely service. And, a very fine reception. I loved your DJ. Great dance music."

Yancy said to her, "Are you a dancer? You had some good moves out there."

"Oh, yes, not a good one, but I enjoy moving to music. My family all plays some instrument and loves to square dance."

Gen said, "What do you play?"

Bobbi ducked her head and blushed slightly. "I play fiddle and banjo. I'm not great, but I can play well enough for family."

Erin looked at Bobbi. "I play violin too, but not for dancing. I'm classically trained. Played in the orchestra in high school and in college, before I went to grad school. I haven't picked up my violin in some time."

"Then we must have a music night sometime after we get back from our honeymoon." Gen grinned at Roxie, who grinned in return.

"Sounds like a plan. I'll tune up my piano. I haven't played much either." Roxie smirked. "We'll have a trio."

Yancy shook her head. "You two," she said aside to them.

Roxie and Kate said their good nights, and they all left the hall. A few stragglers kept dancing.

Yancy looked into Gen's eyes, "Well, Ms. Lambert, shall we go?"

"Ms. Lambert? Don't you mean Ms. Delaney?" She smoothed Yancy's lapels, leaning into her body, and gave her a lingering kiss.

❧❧❧❧

Bobbi found herself and Erin walking to their

cars at the same time, so she let Erin catch up to her. It was only polite, especially in the dimly lit parking lot of the reception hall.

"How are you doing? You had to work hard this afternoon." Bobbi thought some small talk to be in order, since they'd not conversed at all while dancing a fast dance in the loud music of the hall.

"Oh, I'm good. I have someone else doing my Sunday service tomorrow, so I get to go home and put my feet up."

"Would you like to get some coffee, or a drink or something?" Bobbi inwardly groaned. How the hell had that invitation come out of her mouth? She liked Erin on some level, but still had not come to grips with seeing her as a romantic prospect. She was a priest. She got in her way with patients. She was...something Bobbi couldn't quite identify. But that something irked Bobbi. Pushed her buttons. On the other hand, Erin's eyes and bright smile faced her right now, and she couldn't look away.

Erin looked a little surprised, but she then smiled. "That would be nice."

"How about the new microbrewery out on the highway?"

"Great. I love craft beer. Good Irish, Chicago South Siders, we O'Rourke's would never turn down beer."

Bobbi caught herself mesmerized by Erin's pert lips turned up in a dazzling smile. "I can drive, then bring you back for your car, if you want."

"To get home, I need to drive back past San Sebastian, which is not far from the brewery. No need to bring me all the way back here."

"I'll see you there in about fifteen minutes?"

Bobbi reluctantly turned from Erin's smile and toward her Honda.

At the microbrewery, after they got comfortable at a table, they both ordered Hefeweizens. "So, you're a wheat beer drinker," Bobbi said.

"Oh, yes. Chicago has great wheat beers. I grew up on them." Erin busied herself checking her phone. "Sorry, just in case of a pastoral emergency."

"I don't know much about Chicago. I've been there a few times for medical conferences, but I fly in and out in forty-eight hours and don't have time to take in the city. I like what I've seen of it."

"I love it. Jazz and blues music. Chicago hot dogs, deep-dish pizza, and, of course, Goose Island beer. The Cubs. Music at Millennial Park in the summer and ice skating in the winter. The neighborhood festivals and Gay Pride Weekend. Great restaurants of all types. I love going by L anywhere. I used to bike to grad school from my apartment in Rogers Park. I love to people watch down at the Lake." Erin eyed Bobbi intently. "What about where you're from?"

"Eastern Oregon? Not much there, but beautiful mountains and high desert. We have some great beer, too."

"I know, I know. I love some of the Oregon beer. Deshutes comes to mind. And you're from a farm, then?" Erin asked.

"Ranch, not farm."

"Oops, my Midwest showing." Erin laughed lightly.

"Dad's a rancher. Mom's a third-grade teacher. My brothers are both back there. Matt ranches with Dad. He's married with two kids. Little brother Mike's a barista in Portland, plays bass in a band. A new-age hippie."

Erin listened attentively, nodding. "I'm the third daughter of four. All my sisters are service types. Two are nurses, one a social worker."

"That's pretty interesting. Why do you think y'all are into human services?"

"Not hard to figure out. Dad's an Episcopal priest. Mom's a retired nurse. We were surrounded." Erin huffed a small laugh.

Bobbi sipped her Hefeweizen and absorbed Erin's graciousness and witty conversation. She smiled back at The Elf, who became more and more attractive.

"And coming out? How was that?"

Erin inhaled deeply. "Gee. Not that bad. I think Mom was more upset when I told her I was being called to the priesthood." She grinned at the memory. "One of Mom's sisters is a lesbian, so it didn't faze my folks. My sisters all have gay friends, especially the two who are nurses. Why do there seem to be so many gay medical types?"

Bobbi raised her brows. "Darned if I know. I think you're right, though, now that I remember the number of gays and lesbians in medical school and my residency."

"Did you have a girlfriend before coming out to Colorado?"

Bobbi studied the condensation dripping on her beer mug and cleared her throat. "Yeah. Short term. We lasted six months during my residency."

"Sorry."

"No, no. Not like that. I, um..." Bobbi cleared her throat again. "It's good it's over. We didn't make the best couple, let's say."

Erin gazed at Bobbi, not responding.

She's in her pastoral counseling mode, Bobbi thought. "Did you have a girlfriend in Illinois?"

"No. I dated a few women in grad school. But since seminary, I haven't dated much. The work of seminary contained both emotional and intellectual challenges, not to mention challenges to your faith. I had a pretty intense time of it, so didn't feel very much like dating, although I bonded with seminary friends through the experience. I imagine in the same way you may have bonded with medical school friends."

"The competitiveness of medical school makes bonding and being friends hard. Everyone's trying to outdo the other person, so no. I didn't bond with people then. In my residency, I felt closer to friends. We had an emotional component to our training but nothing like seminary, I'll bet."

"In seminary, they challenge you to explore your emotional reactions to situations and people. You know, birth, death, and every family emergency parishioners go through. You're trained to have a neutral response, to keep yourself well-balanced, and to respond, not react, to people. I'd already had that training in pastoral counseling. That was a no-brainer for me. I actually like doing funerals, where I can be pastorally present for families. And I enjoy Sunday worship. I talk to people and catch up on their lives. It's what I do best, what I enjoy best."

"Not weddings?" Bobbi was intrigued.

"Oh, no. Many—thankfully not Gen and Yancy's wedding—but many weddings are filled with family angst. Mother and mother-in-law dynamics and what-all. Weddings seem to bring out the dysfunction in families. It drives me a little crazy. And don't get me started on photographers and videographers who want to stand up on the altar to get their best shots."

"On the altar?" Bobbi asked incredulously.

"Well, I may have exaggerated a little. But, yeah, they want to get right in the action. I have to remind them that the wedding is a ritual of the church, a solemn occasion, and that I'm in charge of the choreography, not them. I've had a few run-ins in my short time as a priest."

Bobbi grinned and shook her head. "I like that, your 'short time.' Erin, you certainly make up for your lack of height with a powerful presence. I can see you now, bossing around some hulking guy as he lugs his video equipment."

"Hey," Erin huffed. "You're disparaging a priest of the church here."

Bobbi laughed outright. Between chuckles, she said, "Sorry...Mother Erin."

"Since we're being brutally honest, you don't hesitate to throw your medical degree around, Doctor." Erin eyed Bobbi with a smirk.

"Touché," Bobbi, still laughing, said, then added cheekily, "Elf."

They both drank their beer, chuckling.

"Gosh, what time is it?" Bobbi took her phone out of her breast pocket. "Wow, nearly midnight."

"I need to get home before I turn into a pumpkin. I'm never out this late on a Saturday. I'd be a wreck on Sunday, and the sermon would sound like it was coming from aliens." Erin stood. Bobbi helped her with her coat.

In the vestibule of the brewery, Erin turned to Bobbi, beaming. "Thank you, Doctor. I had fun getting to know you tonight. No matter how insulting you were towards the clergy."

"Sorry. It was meant with the utmost respect for the clergy." Bobbi shuffled her feet. She pondered her next move, but sailed full speed ahead. "Yeah, I had a good time, too. Would you like to go out to dinner some time? I, um, know you're busy, but if—"

"I'd love that. Do you have my number?"

They exchanged phone numbers and said goodnight in the parking lot.

On the twenty-minute drive home, Bobbi smiled to herself. The Elf had been pleasant company, engaging even. She found herself charmed by her laugh and easy manner. Was it only Chicago friendliness or did she treat everyone like this? She was a priest after all, and acceptance of everyone was in her toolkit...er, the Bible. Something like that, surely.

Ah, crap. What difference did it make? She'd call to schedule a time for dinner. They'd go out to eat, converse politely, then Bobbi would dutifully take her home. Erin, probably a goody-two shoes priest, was not likely to have casual sex, like Amanda. Erin was not the friends-with-benefits type.

Chapter Sixteen

It was Ash Wednesday.

Erin entered the church at five-thirty to finish readying for the six o'clock service. The liturgy lasted only a little longer than a normal Sunday, but always profoundly affected her, as well as those who came to participate. How could it not, when someone placed ashes in the shape of a cross on your forehead, and intoned the words, "Remember you are dust and to dust you shall return"?

Reminders of mortality bombarded parishioners all the time, as the news of death, whether someone close, or a catastrophe across the globe, found its way onto smart phones in a millisecond of its occurrence. Mass shootings, bombings, war, drug-overdose deaths of celebrities. Erin suspected that the over-exposure to death created a ho-hum reaction, an immunity from its reality, since death happened "over there," to "them."

Erin lamented that, in modern society, people handled death, even personal deaths of nearby loved ones, with a hands-off distance. They never really touched the body of their loved one; they didn't dress it for viewing or spend a night vigil with it, in prayer. These old traditions died out with the rise of the embalming of bodies after the Civil War. When Erin's grandmother, Bridget, died five years ago, the funeral home staff refused to let her dress her. Erin so wanted merely to have a last contact, a last bit of service she could do for Bridget, who had suffered so much in her final months from multiple problems and unrelenting pain. After seeing Bridget die such a death, Erin knew that hospice held the key to helping families and their loved ones go down the path toward death together, and she supported their work whenever she could.

She performed Mrs. Meredith's funeral last week, about ten days after her hospice admission. She'd talked with the family about their wishes for the service. And, even though Mrs. Meredith couldn't participate by speaking her wishes, the family had talked at length about these things with her before she entered into her coma. It was a good death, Erin thought.

These images of Mrs. Meredith's death and funeral flowed through her memory this evening as people gathered in the nave. Later, as she marked each of their foreheads and said the words reminding them of their mortality, she felt she was doing her bit to assist her parishioners to treasure life because they understood their own eventual death.

❦❦❦❦

That same evening, Bobbi took a call from the Cordero family with an eighteen-month-old child, Addison, who had contracted the flu. She admitted her to BCH with a very high fever and dehydration. The parents stayed in the girl's room, while Bobbi waited on lab work.

Suddenly, Marty, Joe Manning's wife, and one of tonight's pediatric night nurses, found Bobbi in the doctor's cubby around the corner from the nurses' station. "Child convulsing in room 121." She hurried off.

Bobbi leapt up from her chair and trailed the

nurse to 121. "Mr. and Mrs. Cordero, we need you to exit please, so we can do our work with Addy. We'll do everything we can to get her better," Bobbi reassured them.

The mother and father, whose eyes were wild, clutched each other and left the room.

Bobbi called out for an anti-seizure medication, which Marty had brought with her. She injected Addy, whose little body continued to thrash in the bed. Marty held her softly to keep her from harming herself, while Bobbi placed a small safety guard in her mouth.

After five minutes, the seizures waned and the Addy's body stilled. Too still. Bobbi took her stethoscope quickly to Addy's tiny chest. No heartbeat.

Bobbi called out for cardiac stimulation drugs and Marty rushed out of the room. Meanwhile, Bobbi performed CPR on Addy, counting out the rhythmic downward pumps of her hand on her little chest.

Marty handed Bobbi the syringe and she quickly stabbed the needle into Addy's heart. Bobbi checked the heart beat again. Nothing. She continued CPR.

"You can bag her, Marty," Bobbi rasped.

Marty began to artificially pump air into Addy's small body.

Bobbi and Marty continued the CPR for a long thirty minutes. Addy still did not breathe on her own.

With perspiration running down her forehead, Bobbi looked up at Marty and shook her head. Tears formed in the corner of Marty's eyes.

"Time of death, one-forty-seven a.m. Will you clean her up? I'll go talk with the Corderos." Bobbi took off her gloves and tossed them into the bin, her heart steeling itself for her job.

The young couple stood huddled together down

the hall. Bobbi gathered herself, breathed deeply, and led them into one of the consultation rooms, where they all sat around a small round table.

Bobbi looked intently at them, a smallish woman and her taller, but thin, husband, both in their late twenties. Too young, Bobbi thought. What a crappy thing.

Bobbi took a moment to steady herself. "Mr. and Mrs. Cordero, I am very sorry to tell you that Addy did not make it."

Both the mother and father gasped. The mother paled and began to breathe rapidly. Bobbi carefully put her hand on top of Mrs. Cordero's hand.

"I think she may have had some previous heart damage. The fever had been going on several days, you say?"

Mr. Cordero nodded, his face a pale mask of shock. "She began to have a fever about three days ago. We didn't think anything was very wrong, just a cold, you know?"

Mrs. Cordero let out a small wail. "Oh, my God. My God. This can't be happening." She clung to her husband's shirt and buried her head, sobbing. "This can't be. My little Addy," she said in a voice muffled by his shirt. "I need to see her. Be with her."

After Bobbi had comforted the Corderos and seen them off into the night with their grief, then taken care of the paperwork on baby Addy, she walked down the stairs into the clear, cold night in a fog of emotional and physical exhaustion. Her first pediatric death.

Bobbi drove home into a rising sun. She didn't have time to think or to feel. She quickly hopped in the shower in a daze, got dressed, and got on her way to the clinic. Her day began all over again.

Chapter Seventeen

She wasn't on call the next night but answered a call from Dr. Garcia-Brown on one of her own patients. At seven, Jaime admitted seventy-four-year-old Mr. Nelson for cardiac telemetry when he complained of chest pain. His enzymes showed he'd had a minor heart attack. Bobbi worried about him, a long-time smoker with high cholesterol and high blood pressure, so she drove over to BCH at nine that night to check him out.

Jaime was glad to see her, as he was busy admitting another patient for pneumonia. Bobbi waited until more blood work results arrived, looked over the EKG, checked the patient's vitals again, his meds, and talked with his wife briefly. Bobbi went home around two-thirty Friday morning.

Bobbi saw her full complement of patients on the clinic roster for Friday. She felt as if she was sleepwalking through the day. Her mind was sluggish, her reactions dulled. Several times, she asked patients the same question. No one complained. Maybe they thought the doctor checked on their answers by repeating the same question. Late Friday afternoon, Bobbi remembered she was to have dinner that night with The Elf.

A text came in just as she finished with her next to last patient. Erin wanted her to come to her house for dinner instead of going out. Bobbi didn't know what she thought of that plan. It struck her as less safe than being together in a restaurant, where she wouldn't be tempted to kiss her. But she was too tired to really care, and texted back that she would arrive at Erin's at the appointed time. Erin answered her query about what to bring with the word, "Nothing."

It was well after clinic closing hours when Bobbi finished her chart work. She rushed to the liquor department of the local grocery to buy a bottle of wine, then let the GPS guide her to Johnson County and Erin's house. The road had cleared with the warmer temperatures, but the March weather had yet to become spring-like. Bobbi easily found the brick, two-story house next to a small white clapboard church.

❧❧❧❧❧

Erin answered her door. Bobbi looked a wreck. Deep purple ringed her eyes. Her blue oxford button-down sported wrinkles and white stains graced the right lower hem of her navy cardigan. Even her normally in-place short hair stood up in the back. Erin's heart went out to her, but she held back her instinct to gather her into her arms for comfort. The good doctor, a grown woman, certainly could take care of herself.

"Hi," Erin said. "Come on in out of the cold."

Bobbi stood rooted to the doorway. "Here's a bottle of wine."

Erin guided Bobbi by taking her forearm and pulling slightly. Bobbi shook her head, seeming to come out of a trance. "Sorry. I'm a little slow on the uptake tonight."

Erin took her coat and pointed to a very warm and cozy living room. "Let me check on dinner. I thought it might be nice to eat here and not have to go out in the March weather. I hope you like Moroccan flavors. It's a vegetable stew," she called over her shoulder as she walked into the kitchen.

She stirred the stew, made the last preparations for a salad, then grabbed some cheese and crackers from the counter and reentered the living room. Erin placed the cheese plate on the coffee table, then brought some napkins from a sideboard on the opposite wall.

Bobbi walked the perimeter of the room, peering at Erin's artwork. "You're an impressionist lover," she said, pointing to one of the prints.

"Yeah. The Art Institute of Chicago has a lot of impressionist art, and as a member, I've gone to several lectures there. I pick up prints here and there. Are you an art fan?"

"Me? Nope, can't say I know anything about it. Oh, I like to look at classics sometimes. That one painted in Iowa. The gothic whatever, that one with the farmer and his wife. It tickles me."

"You mean American Gothic by Grant Wood, painted in 1930. I love it. I try to see it any time I'm at AIC."

Bobbi smirked at Erin.

"What? Can't I like art? You think I'm too blue collar to be cultured?" Erin crossed her arms over her chest.

"No. No. You just amuse me. Classical violin. Art lover. Is there anything else I'm missing from your résumé?"

Erin smiled; pretending to think, she said, "Let me get back to you on that one. I may have some other tricks up my sleeve." She turned to sit on the couch. "Come and have some cheese before I bring out the stew." She patted the seat next to her on the coach.

Bobbi plopped down and took a piece of the cheese. "I reckon this is gourmet cheese?"

"No, smartass. It's good old goat cheese from one of the local farms." Erin lightly punched Bobbi's upper arm.

"Hey." Bobbi faked hurt. Her heart did a quick uptick, but that's all. The punch hadn't registered as a Stephanie moment, thankfully.

Erin shook her head and laughed. Then she became more serious. "So, Doctor, tell me how your week was. You look a little worn out."

Bobbi looked down at her wrinkles and stains. "Oh, shit. I knew I forgot something. I didn't change clothes. My last patient ran over time, so I just skedaddled out of the clinic over here. Sorry, I'm a mess."

"Well, I don't care about your clothes. But you look very tired. Are you all right?"

Bobbi brushed a hand through her hair, a habit Erin recognized as a tactic when Bobbi felt out of control. "I'm fine. A couple of long nights, is all. Not something I haven't had before." With that, she let out a large yawn. "God. I'm sorry, that was rude."

Erin laughed again. She could tell Bobbi was underplaying her tiredness, but she let it go. *Doctors and their egos*, she thought.

After eating a few pieces of cheese and talking, Erin decided to get the dinner on the table.

Bobbi looked at the stew. "This looks interesting."

"It's got middle eastern spices, with chick peas, tomatoes, and few other goodies. I hope you'll like it."

Bobbi had her spoon in the stew, when Erin said, "I usually say a short prayer, if that's okay."

Bobbi quickly returned the spoon to the bowl. Erin prayed three lines of thanks, and they ate.

"I didn't know you were a vegetarian," Bobbi said.

Erin contemplated her answer. "I'm not, normally, but during Lent I like to cut back on meat."

"Lent. What does that mean, exactly? I saw people at the hospital Wednesday with stuff on their foreheads, which I understand as ashes. And I know it comes after Fat Tuesday and Mardi Gras. In other words, you party and then you repent?"

Erin's mouth lifted in a small grin. She relaxed back into her chair. "Something like that. Lent used to be a much more solemn and painful time for parishioners in the past. People would give up something important. But then Lent began to be very superficial. My friends at Loyola one year decided to give up broccoli." She huffed in laughter and shook her head. "But I tell my parishioners that Lent is a time of repentance in preparation for the resurrection of Christ. Not a time of beating your chest with how awful you are, but of really contemplating how you mess things up. Then you contemplate taking action to make your behavior more in line with your faith."

"You mean, like I can be arrogant. So, during Lent, I would think about that and try to make better decisions when I feel I need to defend myself. When someone or some event threatens me, and I tend to be huffy and self-important."

Erin looked at Bobbi with understanding. "Yes. You gave a good example. Prayer is important in this Lenten process too, though. You just don't think about your sins, you pray about them. God answers with love and grace."

"Love and grace. That sounds nice." Bobbi's eyes looked into the middle distance.

Erin smiled at this. "God's love causes us to strive to be our best selves. God doesn't make junk."

"God doesn't make junk. Yeah...Huh. I never heard that before." Bobbi smiled at Erin and continued to eat her stew.

"You never went to church?" Erin hated to tread into these religious waters, but she felt Bobbi could handle it.

"Nope. Mom and Dad said religion was a bunch of bunk. They were forced to go to church as children. Both Roman Catholic. They fell away from church in college and never went back. When they met, they both hated their upbringing and the strictures they'd lived under at home. So, our family never went to any church, and we didn't celebrate stuff either. Well, except for Christmas, when we gave presents, had parties and such."

"You're not alone in our generation. Hardly any of my college friends went to church, and many of them grew up in the church. Although, like you, some of our generation never have been in a church. Those who do often never return. But, religion is irrelevant to most Americans."

"Then why...How did you become a priest?" Bobbi looked up from her bowl. "If you don't mind me asking."

Erin placed her spoon into her bowl. "Hoo boy, I've had to answer that question about a million times. Between my ordination process, parishioners, and sermons, I've told that story every few months since my days at Loyola." Erin remembered the hardest of those times, from committees with the power to veto her ordination. "It's simple, my story, really. I never rejected God or church, even though my father is a priest, and many clergy kids get out of religion altogether. But I did resist the sense that God was asking more of me. I got my pastoral counseling degree right out of undergrad in psychology. I thought that was the answer. But as I was finishing that program, I still felt I hadn't done enough. That God still had something more for me. And one day, in chapel, alone, God told me I belonged in the priesthood."

"God told you?" Bobbi raised her eyebrows.

"I know you might not believe me. But, yeah. I heard an internal voice, not my own, but one very close to me, a very loving voice. It said, 'I ask you to be my priest.'" Erin looked down at her plate. Telling the story always took her breath away. She shrugged. "That's it."

Bobbi looked silently at Erin. "Wow," she said quietly. They sat without speaking for some moments. "You know, it was like that for me too, in a way. No voice of God. But one day, helping my dad with a lamb who had broken its leg, I knew I was meant to be a doctor. I was twelve or thirteen at the time. From that time on, I wanted nothing else. It's as if an angel or something had touched me. And I don't believe in angels."

"You don't have to believe in supernatural forces to be touched by them."

Bobbi and Erin sat quietly, finishing their meal. Erin felt the silence matched the gravity of their conversation.

Erin looked over at Bobbi and resolved to see what was going on. "You know, you look really beat. Did something happen this week?" Erin gazed tenderly at her.

"A pediatric patient died on me Wednesday night. My first baby. It was hard to see that little girl leave life without having lived it." Bobbi stated matter of factly, but Erin could see that Bobbi's eyes were haunted.

Erin nodded and sat silently. She'd never seen Bobbi claim vulnerability before, doubting that it happened very often.

Erin watched Bobbi fiddle with her napkin. "I've never wanted my own children. I figured I wasn't a good candidate for being a parent, given my schedule. Although I grew up in a loving home and know what good parenting is about. How they are there for you through thick and thin. You know, the unconditional love they give us. But when I saw that mom and dad at the hospital Wednesday night, I couldn't conceive of the pain they were going through."

"Mmm," Erin said. She didn't want to break into Bobbi's story.

"I just...That baby's death was so meaningless," Bobbi said in a choked voice.

Erin could see her eyes swimming with unshed tears.

Bobbi sniffed and sat back. "Can I help you with dishes?"

Erin could tell the emotional moment had affected Bobbi and now she reverted back to Take Charge mode. "No way. Mine is a one-butt kitchen, so go sit and relax." She began to stack their bowls. "I have a little light dessert, and tea or coffee. There's not much to do."

"Tea for me, thanks," Bobbi said.

Erin took her time stacking the dishwasher,

hoping to give Bobbi some moments on her own to deal with her emotions. She then prepared tea, while arranging a plate with cookies.

By the time she entered the living room, Bobbi's head was canted against the back of the couch. Erin leaned over and peered into her face, watching her chest rise and fall in a steady, deep rhythm, her eyes closed. "Bobbi?" she said quietly. When Bobbi didn't stir, Erin removed her shoes, then laid a throw from another chair across Bobbi's lap. She smoothed Bobbi's hair from her forehead and whispered, "Sleep well, sweetie."

She must trust me if she fell asleep here, Erin thought. Her angular face looked handsome in the light, but her gray complexion spoke of needing rest and rejuvenation. The arrogant doctor was giving way to a real person, with weaknesses like anyone else. Erin felt her heart open to this more real Bobbi.

Chapter Eighteen

By weekend standards, the Valley Pub held fewer people on Sunday nights. Erin walked into the fairly quiet microbrewery, excited to be hosting the first Beer and Bible group. Her church invited all young-adult parishioners, and Erin had added some of her friends from other churches, through her contacts in her clergy group. She expected a light attendance on this blustery March night, though.

She arrived right on time, entered the dark, yeasty-smelling place, and found the table reserved for them in a quiet corner in the back, away from the acoustic guitar player.

No one else had arrived yet, so she ordered a wheat beer, and sat back to watch for her people entering, when the server plunked it down in front of her. The guitarist played and sang country and folk music, which was fine. At least it wasn't loud, and she sounded pretty good.

Bobbi and another woman suddenly appeared at the door. It must be a date, because Bobbi's hand guided the woman on the small of her back. Erin didn't know the woman, but she seemed familiar. She had light brown hair pulled into a ponytail and wore casual jeans and a blue frilly shirt under a long, slinky sweater. Bobbi was dressed similarly, except her shirt was plaid and her sweater a conservative cardigan. She carried herself with a powerful walk and upright posture, towering over the other woman by three or so inches.

Erin had last seen Bobbi Friday night when she woke with a start in Erin's living room, around ten p.m., embarrassed at having fallen asleep. Erin had been glad to give her the safety of some rest. After Bobbi left, Erin felt surprised that the haughty doctor no longer held her contempt. In fact, Bobbi's vulnerabilities, her gentleness, and her ethics grabbed at Erin's heart. The anxiety attack she'd witnessed over dinner at Kenny's Tavern worried Erin, though.

And here Bobbi was, with a date. Erin didn't have a chance of getting to know her better tonight unless she made a move.

Bobbi scanned the room when she saw Erin, lifted her hand in recognition, and briefly smiled. They walked up to Erin's table.

"Are you alone?" Bobbi asked.

"No. At least I hope not. I'm hosting a Beer and Bible group tonight. Our first night and I'm the first one here."

Over Bobbi's shoulder, Erin caught the eye of three people whom she'd invited. She waved them over to the table.

They all greeted Erin. Erin introduced them to Dr. Roberta Webster. Bobbi shook their hands, and then caught the disappointed look on her date's face. "Oh, sorry. Everyone, this is Amanda. She's a nurse at BCH. Whenever we're both off, we like to come over for a beer. Well, more accurately, I have a beer. Amanda's more of a wine drinker."

Amanda's smile didn't reach her eyes, Erin noted, as she greeted each of the others.

Three more people walked to the table and all

began to sit, after greeting Erin, Bobbi, and Amanda. A couple of the young adults didn't know each other and Erin did the introductions.

Bobbi stood next to Erin's table, watching the group gather, now numbering nine, when two more joined the table and brought chairs with them from other nearby tables. The group laughed together. Bobbi smiled, not moving, while Amanda stood with her arms crossed at her chest, definitely not smiling.

After the commotion of the last people arriving had died down, Bobbi asked Erin, "What is Beer and Bible?"

Erin looked at her group of young adults. "We don't know yet, do we, gang?"

They all laughed.

"We don't have a schedule or plan. The general idea is for someone to name a topic from the news or another source and we talk about it from the standpoint of our faith." Erin looked around the ring of people at the table to nodding heads. "Yeah?"

"Sounds good," one thirty-something man with tats covering his neck answered. "I'm ready."

Bobbi looked intrigued. Erin asked, "Would you two like to join us?"

Grinning widely, and without glancing at Amanda and noticing her slight frown, Bobbi answered, "Sure." She then also missed Amanda's slight eye roll. Bobbi grabbed chairs for them and they all ordered their drinks. Erin wondered what their relationship entailed.

Erin looked at her group and tried to make sure everyone felt comfortable by asking each person first to share their name and occupation. She knew most of them by name except those whom others had brought tonight. But she didn't know them well enough to know what they did for a living, since most of them were only occasional churchgoers. Two of the young adults worked at technical companies, in Denver and Colorado Springs, but those living closer, in Johnson or Babcock Counties, worked in local insurance agencies, construction, or banking. One had a salon. The other three were health care professionals. When Bobbi introduced herself as a physician, many of them widened their eyes. The health care types among them looked on her with awe, and she blushed adorably.

Erin then asked them each to share why they came tonight. The reasons varied greatly. Some wanted time with others their age that didn't include singles clubs in Denver and drinking. The "meat market," one of the young women called it. Several nodded their heads. Others wanted to learn more about Christianity, or to be better Christians in their daily life. All agreed that church on Sunday didn't appeal to them as a way to accomplish this.

Then Bobbi answered, "I don't know why I'm here. Christianity intrigues me but I'm not really religious. I've never thought of religion. I've never attended church except for a couple of funerals and some weddings. Even most of the weddings haven't been in churches."

One woman put in, "Most of my friends wouldn't be caught dead in church." Several people nodded and laughed.

Erin said, "Go on, Bobbi. You don't have a relationship with church, but do you have a relationship with God?"

Bobbi stared at the table for a long moment. "Of course, I can't be a doctor without believing there's a higher being out there. I'm so privileged to be present at the beginnings and endings of the miracles of life.

And healing. I don't presume to take all the credit for someone's healing." She sighed. "Although I can't say I understand prayer or why people pray."

At that statement, several heads nodded. The banker added, "Yeah. I don't know what prayer is. How to pray, what to pray for. And if God knows us inside and out, why do we have to pray? Doesn't God already know what we need?"

Erin smiled inside. This was exactly the kind of meaty topic she had hoped would engage her new group. She rubbed her hands together. "Okay, let's discuss this. Why do you all think prayer is important?"

Bobbi frowned. "Wait, aren't you supposed to answer our questions? Aren't you the resident expert at the table?"

"No way. I'm a baptized person just like you guys, just trying to make my way along a path. Just because I've got book learning doesn't mean I understand all the mysteries of God."

Bobbi slowly nodded. "Well, just for the record, I'm not baptized." She gazed directly into Erin's eyes. "And, why aren't you the expert? You're a priest; how can you struggle with God?"

The physician assistant in the group said, "But she's a normal human being, too. Being ordained doesn't give you an inside track on God. At least *I* don't think it does. And I agree with Dr. Webster. Having a patient's life in your hands gives you lots of power that I don't want. I want to know that God's presence also guides me and accompanies the patient in their suffering."

Erin beamed. The group began to discuss prayer and healing and other topics related to faith. Her first group started with a bang.

Chapter Nineteen

"Oh, look." Gen showed Yancy the picture on her phone. "It's Erin's first Beer and Bible group at the brewery."

Yancy peered over Gen's shoulder while Gen flipped through three more photos. "Whoa. Go back to the last one."

"Oh, my God. It's Bobbi Webster." Gen gazed closely at Bobbi's unmistakable face.

"What the hell do you think she was doing there?"

"Well, darling, I have no idea. But it is surprising." Gen grinned, looking at the picture. "She's so professionally focused, I'd never predicted her being involved in Erin's church."

"Me neither." Yancy yawned. "Are you about packed?"

"Hmm," Gen answered, still thinking about Bobbi being in the picture. "Are you tired?"

"Didn't sleep the best. I never seem to the night before flying. I'm always afraid I'll miss my flight. Stupid, I know." Yancy sidled up to Gen and took her in her arms. "What an amazing honeymoon. Are you as happy as I am?"

Gen squirmed out of Yancy's arms. "Now, don't start." She chuckled. "Yes, Normandy was a dream. I loved every minute of it."

"Did you wish we'd had more time in Paris?"

Gen sighed. "I don't know. The peace of the

countryside was so nice. The walks along the beach and the cheese tasting. I loved the farm we visited to see the apple cider process."

"The Calvados wasn't bad either."

"Mmm. I'm glad we're bringing some home to remember. I hope we get a good price at the shops in the airport." Gen finished squeezing the last item into her suitcase and zipped it up. "There. All ready. When's the taxi coming?"

Yancy grabbed both their suitcases. "About five minutes."

Gen took her arm before she could open the door. Yancy put the bags on the floor again. "Hang on. Our lesbian kiss." She kissed Yancy and nestled in her arms. "The kiss all lesbians grab before going into public."

Yancy looked deeply into Gen's eyes. "I love you so much, my wife."

"Not as much as I love you, my wife."

Yancy grinned devilishly. "I thought I was your 'butchusband.'"

"You goof."

"Not dork?"

"You know, I don't really like that name. It's vulgar slang for penis. Doesn't quite fit you, darling."

Yancy's brows went up. "Geez. I'll give Roxie hell when we get back. She's been calling me dork since high school." They both laughed. "Hey, another kiss. The first one's worn off by now," Yancy said.

They kissed again then Yancy picked up their bags. Gen punched the elevator button and they began their journey back to the states.

⚘⚘⚘⚘

Bobbi finished up her patient at the clinic on this quiet Sunday evening. The sunset came later each day and she was glad not to have to go home in the dark. Just as she rose from her desk at the nurse's station, her phone went off. Another patient was expected into the clinic within the next ten to fifteen minutes.

She took the opportunity to get another diet drink from the machine and found a piece of cold pizza in the break-room fridge from a birthday party a few days ago. It tasted like cardboard, even after she warmed it in the microwave, but she figured she'd live. At least it staved off the hunger pangs.

The family, a woman in her twenties and her husband, arrived. Stan, the clinic guard who worked on weekends, let them into the building and led the young couple to Bobbi, who took them into an exam room. The wife's shirt was torn. A bruise bloomed on her cheekbone that dripped with a bloody cut. The husband looked wary.

"Ms. Myers, right?" Bobbi looked at her chart. Bobbi noted she'd been seen in the ER about three weeks ago for stitches.

The young woman nodded, not looking at Bobbi. "Shylah."

"What happened?"

Before the woman could open her mouth, the husband answered, "She's pretty clumsy. She fell against the kitchen counter."

Bobbi began her physical assessment, asking the husband to leave the exam room. She suddenly recognized him as one of the men from the tavern fight.

"I'm not budging. I have a right to be present." He crossed his arms.

"I don't care about your rights; I care about making a thorough exam of Ms. Myers, so I ask you again, please leave so I can do my work." Bobbi straightened up and stood between the woman on the exam table and her husband.

Wes eyed his wife, then turned and left.

"Now," Bobbi said, quietly to her, "tell me what happened."

"Just like he said, I guess I'm pretty clumsy. I fell against the kitchen counter this afternoon."

"What were you doing in the kitchen?" Bobbi needed this young woman to open up and trust her.

"Getting Wes a beer. He watches sports all day on Sunday. I try to keep out of his way, but I couldn't get the beer fast enough. I tripped on the rug."

Bobbi sighed at the recalcitrant Shylah sticking to her story of tripping on a rug. "Is Wes right handed?" Bobbi noted that the bruise was on Shylah's left cheek.

"What? Yeah, he's right handed."

"Shylah, you need to be straight with me. Did Wes hit you?"

Shylah looked down at her feet.

"I saw Wes punch a guy at Kenny's Tavern a few weeks ago. Did he do this?"

"Oh, Doc. I can't tell on him. He'll get in trouble and then when he gets out of jail, he'll really give it to me worse than before. Just please put a stitch or whatever you need to do and get me outta here." Shylah's eyes pleaded with Bobbi.

Wes knocked on the door. "What're you doing in there? You've had your time. I'm coming in." He burst into the exam room.

"Mr. Myers, please leave. I have to stitch your wife's cheek."

Wes grabbed Shylah by her wrist and dragged her off the exam table. "We're done here."

Shylah let out a small squeal as she stumbled off the table.

Bobbi, despite her breathing ramping skyward, gathered up her courage to stand between Wes and his wife. "Mr. Myers, she can't go anywhere until I treat her. She has asked for treatment and you have no authority to override that."

Wes let go of Shylah's wrist and pushed her away, where she fell with a loud bang into a metal and plastic chair in the corner of the room. He gripped Bobbi's upper arm painfully with his left hand while his right swung into a roundhouse punch aimed for her stomach. She quickly turned her body to the side to dislodge his grip. He swung wide of her body. She used her hip to leverage his body across her own and down to the floor.

He rushed up from the floor swinging, while Shylah yelled at him to stop. Bobbi caught a fist across the left side of her neck, as his intended punch missed her cheek. She kneed him in the groin just as he raised his arm to punch her again. He crumpled to the floor.

While Wes groaned on the floor, Bobbi lightly pushed Shylah out the exam room door. "Go. Get to the front door where the guard is and tell him to come," she rasped, breathing heavily.

Wes moaned and rocked on the floor, clutching himself.

Bobbi listened for the guard's footsteps down the hall, and when she heard someone rushing, she yelled, "In here, Stan."

Stan looked from the doorway at Wes on the floor and Bobbi standing over him, panting hard.

"Better call the cops. He assaulted me."

Stan stood off to the side, put in the 911 call, and suggested that Bobbi continue to treat her patient in another exam room. Bobbi nodded while she rubbed her left biceps and the area along her neck where his fists had met her flesh.

Bobbi sutured Shylah's forehead, trying to keep her shaky hands under control.

Deputy Rick and a woman officer, Rosa, arrived shortly at the clinic. While the woman questioned Shylah, Rick cuffed Wes, sat him out in the clinic waiting room, and took Bobbi's statement. They charged Wes and dragged him into the squad car. Rick left with Wes, while Bobbi clued Rosa in on the suspected spouse abuse. Rosa counseled Shylah about a no-contact order and about getting into a local shelter. Rosa suggested Bobbi call Roxie for information about the shelter.

Rosa offered to transport Shylah there, then ordered another squad car. When it arrived in five minutes, she and Shylah left. After both police cars had left the parking lot, Bobbi told Stan she would be back at her station to fill in her paperwork.

When she opened up the medical record, her hands trembled in earnest now. They were clammy and her breathing ragged.

She heard steps and called out, "I'm leaving soon, Stan."

When she looked up, though, Gen stood in front of the counter, looking down at her.

"Um...hi, Dr. Lambert."

"Stan called me about the ruckus, so I called the administrator, Jim McDonald, to fill him in about the arrest. I thought I would come see how you are doing."

Bobbi stood up, immediately regretting it. Her head swam with dots before her eyes, then she crumpled into the chair.

She came to shortly. Stan had been called, and he partially lifted her into the exam room and laid her on the table. Dr. Lambert stood to the side of the bed.

Bobbi tried to sit up, but Dr. Lambert held her down with a hand. "Not yet, Doctor." She nodded to Stan and he left them after closing the exam room door.

Bobbi breathed deeply. "I'm sorry. I passed out, huh?"

"What are you not telling us about your problem with violence?"

"Huh?" Bobbi began to feel trapped. She could feel her face flush with embarrassment. "Why would you say that?"

"A few weeks ago, at the dinner at Dr. Campbell's, you checked out of the conversation when Erin started to talk about violence in relationships. Then last week, she told me you looked like you would faint when you two were at Kenny's Tavern. Stan said that it was Mr. Myers and another man who got into an altercation at Kenny's that night. Erin told me that you did a grounding routine to help with your anxiety attack."

"Oh," Bobbi answered sheepishly. "Why were you talking about me with Mother Erin?"

"She brought it up after our last prenuptial session. In confidence between us as professionals, but I feel an obligation to bring it up now, because it seems to fit your current state of anxiety."

Bobbi sat up. "I'm okay now. At least I fended the bastard off and no one got hurt even further." She looked at the wall, then at Gen and pursed her lips. Several seconds ticked by, then she spoke, "I got out of an abusive relationship a year ago with another family medicine resident in Oregon. We'd known each other for a few months, had dated some. I really fell for her, but after she moved in, her personality took a drastic change. She became very controlling. Our fighting intensified pretty quickly. Finally, she put me in the ER when she shoved me into wall, and that's when I acted." Bobbi hesitated to reveal the next piece of information. "She's about Erin's size."

"Petite, like Erin?"

Bobbi nodded her head, not able to meet Gen's eyes.

"What can I do?" Gen softly asked.

"Nothing, thank you, Dr. Lambert. I've...been in therapy, took self-defense classes, and had been doing quite well, but I began to have these anxiety attacks again since moving here. Actually, since I met Erin."

"She reminds you of your ex."

"Not consciously, no, and then only in her petite frame. Otherwise she couldn't be more different." Bobbi continued, "When we first met, I came up with stupid reasons to really dislike her. I pulled my weight, got huffy with her. But she didn't go away, and I kept running into her."

"Will it be a problem working with her with mental health patients or any of your patients who are admitted to hospice?"

Bobbi took a big breath and ran her hands through her short hair. "I don't think so, Dr. Lambert. I confess that when we first ran into each other, she rubbed me the wrong way. But, now, looking back, we each were just doing our jobs. I let her get under my skin with very little provocation."

"Okay. What about the assault tonight? I can see

the contusions on your neck."

"A few days ago, Erin and I were at Kenny's Tavern, when Mr. Myers argued with another man. The argument escalated into violence, shoving. Milly, the owner, got punched in the jaw. Two other guys hustled them out of the tavern. I recognized Wes tonight as the same guy, but I thought I could handle him."

"Why didn't you get Stan right away?" Gen's frown didn't escape Bobbi's notice. She reckoned then that she'd failed to adhere to clinic protocols for patient disturbances.

"I'm sorry, Dr. Lambert." Bobbi felt herself blush a little at her weakness. "I guess I may be trying to make up for the times I let Stephanie have the upper hand. I still feel guilty about how I let a smaller woman control me physically." Bobbi's recent traumatic episodes always included this guilt. She felt like a weakling whenever she remembered Stephanie's attacks. Her mind would not shut off the image of her standing passively, shielding herself with her arms, but not defending herself from a smaller woman.

Dealing with the guilt had been a major part of her therapy after Stephanie left. But, would she have felt better punching Stephanie in return? Always, she came back to that question. Her counselor helped her reframe her thinking. It wasn't a matter of striking back, but of taking action to stop Stephanie's abuse, by legal means, and by removing Stephanie from her life. She couldn't control Stephanie, but she could control her response to Stephanie. Still, the lingering doubts haunted her, even though she'd gained some power over them. Nevertheless, since being around Erin, they had returned. Bobbi knew she had been ignoring them, hoping they would fade away. Unfortunately, the fight at Kenny's Tavern and today's assault were too close, triggering her anxiety.

Gen sat in one of the chairs. She looked tenderly on her. "What can we do to help, Bobbi? Do you need to see a counselor again? Take some time off to reduce stress?"

Appalled by these suggestions, Bobbi answered quickly, "No. No, that's not necessary. My counselor and I put together a program for me to follow when I have episodes. I used it at the tavern the other day, and it worked well. You...Well, you caught me before I could get myself in hand today."

"Have you ever passed out before?"

"No." Bobbi took a deep breath. "No," she said more quietly. "Too much adrenaline for my neuro system to handle, I guess."

Gen looked pensively at Bobbi. "I recommend you leave the on-call to me the rest of the evening, until Dr. Bright comes on duty at ten. Go home, get some rest, some exercise, whatever you need to do. I want to see you in my office tomorrow morning at seven to check how you're feeling. I don't want any more episodes while you're treating patients, and I imagine you don't either."

"You're right," Bobbi answered, feeling deflated and humiliated that Dr. Lambert told her to go home.

"I am not punishing you, Doctor. Please don't take it that way." Gen stood. "You look like a child who's had their favorite toy taken away."

Bobbi smiled weakly. "Sorry."

Chapter Twenty

The week flew by for Bobbi after the episode with Wes Myers and his wife on Sunday. No other major problems presented themselves, and Wednesday, her afternoon off, came. She'd arranged to take Erin out for dinner. She'd felt so bad about falling asleep after dinner at her house last Friday, she'd invited her out to make up for her faux pas. Echoes of her mother saying, "That was rude, Roberta Francene," would always haunt her actions in social situations, even at age thirty.

Needing some exercise in her overworked life, Bobbi went to the gym right from the clinic, did some cardio workouts, then swam for thirty minutes. She showered at the gym, picked up groceries for her sinfully empty kitchen, and drove home to do some much-needed housework. Her condo still had little furniture or accessories, but now the fridge at least looked as if someone lived there. While she still chastised herself for the low level of her homemaking, Bobbi couldn't scare up the energy required for furniture shopping. She felt lucky to have got the groceries, and now she would do some cleaning to round out her day off like a good domestic person should.

Bobbi dutifully cleaned the bathroom and kitchen, and vacuumed, then, feeling accomplished, caught up on her reading, sitting at her desk, going through several online journal articles that had been on her to-read list. After reading two of the articles, her phone beeped an alarm that she'd set for six-fifteen. She wondered how the time had got away from her and whether these articles would ever get read. She quickly changed into dark twill trousers, a gray button down, and darker gray cardigan.

Her drive to Erin's took less time because the roads were now clear of ice and snow. The clear road also made driving more relaxed. She hoped this dinner went well. She conceded that she liked Erin the more she knew her. She was a bright, perky person, not Bobbi's usual type, which leaned toward snarky and sarcastic, like Amanda. But somehow, perky met her current needs. Erin's priesthood made her curious, as well. Not many lesbians she knew could stomach the male dominance of the church, although for her, it was only hearsay. She'd never belonged to any church, so hadn't any experience with it.

And although those parts of Erin enticed her, Erin's tenderness toward her also warmed her heart. Yeah, who knew Bobbi Webster's heart could be warmed again after the fiasco of Stephanie? Erin, while triggering Bobbi's Stephanie-meter, turned out to be the opposite of her. Erin, while not innocent or naïve, put out vibes of contentment with her life. Bobbi sensed a calmness amid the chaos of parish life, and of demands from the needy congregants surrounding her. She doubted Erin took guff from anyone yet gave them a listening ear and let them down with kindness. Bobbi liked that combination. Was it called tough love, or something?

Then, there were Erin's assets to consider. Adorable, pixie-like face. Nice figure. Great smile with laughing, brown eyes. At five-foot-eight, Bobbi sometimes felt like a lummox next to small women, but Erin never made her feel that way. With Stephanie, Bobbi was reduced to nothingness. With Erin, Bobbi felt...cherished wasn't quite right. Validated. That's the word. Like she meant something in the world.

At first, Erin had treated her like the arrogant doctor she had been, and Bobbi felt bad about that. Erin was gentle and caring in Kenny's Tavern when Bobbi had her episode. She understood what was happening. Her pastoral counseling expertise guiding her, probably. Then when Bobbi'd fallen asleep after dinner, Erin had not been angry or vengeful, as Stephanie certainly would have been. She let Bobbi sleep, knowing it had been a long, draining week.

Did Bobbi need this kind of caring in her life? Boy, didn't everyone? Ever since Stephanie, she'd been a loner, dating the occasional nurse or other work colleague, but never letting things get close or go on too long. Even now, Amanda had been giving hints that she'd like to go out again. But Bobbi had lost interest. Maybe she'd lost interest in casual dating altogether? At any rate, Erin drew her unlike any Amanda could.

Erin answered her door, looking quite appealing and sweet, a red turtleneck bringing out her dark hair and eyes. She motioned for Bobbi to enter.

"I was surprised you could make it tonight. I thought you may be tied up with a Wednesday night church service."

Erin opened her coat closet and pulled out a red wool coat. Bobbi helped her put it on. "Not during Lent. We have a service early on Friday evenings, but no Wednesday service until after Easter. Then no Wednesday service during the summer."

"I see." Bobbi opened the door and let Erin lock

it. They got into Bobbi's SUV and headed to dinner at an Italian restaurant in San Sebastian that Erin had suggested.

"I want to apologize for going to sleep after dinner the other night. I wish you had woken me. I'm pretty embarrassed."

"Phooey." Erin gave her a dismissive hand wave. "You were exhausted. You could have just passed on the night, you know."

"That seemed rude."

"I would've understood."

There it is, Erin's thoughtfulness, Bobbi thought, and she expressed her notion. "Thanks for being so understanding. Not everyone gets doctors' behavior." They smiled at each other.

They drove into the restaurant parking area, hopped out of the SUV, and entered the small, dark space. A host led them to reserved seats overlooking a lighted pond area. While the grasses around the pond were still brown with winter, birds had begun to arrive in the area, and they watched ducks and Canada geese in the water and small finches feeding at a circular feeder hanging off a shepherd's crook.

Bobbi looked at her menu. "What's good here?"

"Anything, really. But I love their lasagna. It's what I usually have."

"How about their shells? I'm thinking shells and sauce."

"You won't be disappointed, I'm sure."

Bobbi smiled. "You know what you like, don't you? You are a person of definite opinions."

Erin slanted her head to the side. "Gee. I guess you're right. I know what I want, most of the time, anyway."

"That's a good thing, right?"

"In my family, if you didn't express yourself, you lost out. My three sisters and I could fight over the most insignificant thing. Once, we got into it over who got to talk to our grandparents first on the phone. We argued so loudly that Mom made us go to our rooms, and no one got to talk on the phone to them. I felt especially bad about that, because, not long after, our granddad died, and we hadn't been able to talk to him one last time."

"Big consequences." Bobbi watched Erin's face express her whole story. She's very charming and attractive. "Not to change the subject, but I also want to apologize for my behavior toward you."

"Oh?" Erin's face gave nothing away. *Her pastoral counseling face*, Bobbi thought.

"I've been pretty hard on you a couple of times. You remember, I'm sure. Mr. Mendes. Mrs. Stephens. Me—abrupt, condescending, edging toward rude."

"Oh…That." Erin smiled wickedly.

"You remember." Bobbi could feel her face heat up. "I need to tell you something." She cleared her throat.

The server arrived and they put in their order. Bobbi poured a glass of red wine for each of them. She raised her glass and said, "Cheers." Erin touched glasses with her.

"You were saying?" Erin looked intently at Bobbi. She could feel gentleness in Erin's gaze.

"Right." Bobbi took a sip of wine. "My reactions to you were not fair. I was in a bad relationship before I moved here. A girlfriend, Stephanie." Bobbi took a deeper draught of wine. "I, uh…Anyway, she was physically and emotionally abusive."

Erin looked at her intently for a moment, then said in a low tone, "I'm sorry." Erin touched Bobbi's hand quickly and then pulled back.

Bobbi didn't detect pity. It was more like supportiveness coming from Erin. "Yeah. Thank you. But you are about Stephanie's size. I mean, you're both petite, and...Well."

"Oh, God. That's got to be hard." Erin drank from her glass. "Do I trigger some PTSD? Have I done anything wrong?"

"No, no," Bobbi said immediately. "It's just...It's that, when I first met you, and I didn't know you, you reminded me of her, that's all. Totally unconsciously. You haven't acted in any way like her, please know that."

"But the night at Kenny's you were triggered?"

"Yes. It had nothing to do with you being there. The violence itself did it. And, please know, Erin, the more I know you, the less I think of Stephanie." Bobbi hoped Erin could hear her sincerity.

"More importantly, how are you doing with the triggers?"

"I had an episode at the clinic Sunday, while I was on call. The same guy who was in the fight at Kenny's has been abusing his wife. When I challenged him, he assaulted me—"

"Oh my God! What happened?"

"It didn't get out of hand, and I wasn't hurt or anything. He's been arrested on that charge, and Roxie helped me get his wife to the Babcock County shelter." Bobbi looked down at the table.

The server arrived with their entrees. Bobbi thanked him but didn't take up her knife and fork. "Do you want to say grace?"

Erin looked taken off guard. "Sure." She bowed her head, crossed herself, and gave thanks.

Bobbi bowed her head. When she looked up, Erin peered questioningly at her. Bobbi said, "That's it, there's not really more to the story. Why don't we eat?"

While they ate, the conversation flowed into easier territory. They discussed work and chuckled about their families. Bobbi remembered stories from medical school: One of trying to transfer an obese patient from chair to bed and being trapped under her body when they fell onto the bed. They both laughed.

Erin told a tale that happened during her training at the cathedral, of spilling wine down the bodice of a wealthy parishioner. Bobbi's eyes went wide.

Over coffee, Bobbi looked at Erin and said, "I have enjoyed our time together. I wondered, would you like to go out again? I mean...I like you. Would you be interested in dating?" Bobbi breathed deeply to contain her surprising nerves.

Erin gazed at Bobbi for a second. "I'm taken off guard a little, but yeah. I like you too, Doctor." She flashed her a bright grin, then leaned forward on the table. "I need to tell you about my situation."

Bobbi's nerves began to jangle a little more. What could this be?

Erin went on, "My parish has a few conservative, mostly older, parishioners. While the majority of my parish holds pretty liberal views, these two parishioners have power as members of my vestry—or board. They also had a big hand in hiring me. So, they convinced the parish to add a celibacy clause to my contract."

"What? I don't understand."

"My bishop doesn't care one way or another if her gay priests date or not, but my parish is a little behind the times. They wanted assurances that I would be celibate. They take a stance of loving the gay but hating gay behavior. Love the sinner, hate the sin."

"Son of a bitch," Bobbi spit out, then cringed. "Sorry for swearing. I'm just astonished. How can they dictate to you like that?"

"Well, it is what it is. I agreed to their requirement when I took the job last year. I didn't think I'd meet anyone to date out here. I've been in a couple of relationships over the years, but nothing serious. So, it was a no-brainer."

"But, that doesn't mean you can't date, does it?" Bobbi's frown got deeper.

"No. It doesn't. But I didn't want to lead you on that anything but celibate dating was possible for me. In other words, no sex, Doc."

Bobbi gulped and nodded. "Okay." She blinked her confusion. "This must be what my gay friends talk about when they talk about the church's stance towards gays being bullshit."

Erin quirked her lips in a rueful grin. "Yeah." She shifted in her chair and became more serious. "But, I never had any real trouble until now. The Diocese I came from couldn't care less about gays; they're very supportive and open. I don't flaunt my sexuality with my current little parish, but I don't hide who I am either. That's just not me."

"No, I can see it's not. You seem to be very easy in your skin."

Erin nodded. "My family taught me to be who I was. That I was loved by God, created by God just as I was, and that God charged me with being the best me I could be." Erin looked pensive, then continued, "There's a story from Judaism. A man named Eliezer worried he wasn't enough like Moses. A wise rabbi told him his job was not to be the best Moses, but to be the best Eliezer. My job is to be the best Erin, just as your job is to be the best Bobbi."

Bobbi drank her coffee, nodding quietly. This woman was very put together. How could Bobbi not be drawn to her? "So, about dating. Dating, but not get into sexual stuff. That's hard, Mother Erin." Bobbi smiled wickedly. "Do you think we could try it? I'm game."

Erin laughed. "I'm not sure I trust you. You have a devilish look on your face."

Bobbi chuckled. "Well, it couldn't hurt to try, and if things get out of hand, we can deal with it then. What do you say? How about going to the movies with me on Friday night after your service? I assume you can't do Saturdays because of your job the next day."

"Okay." Erin took Bobbi's hand to shake it formally. "It's a deal. Date with Bobbi Webster on Friday it is."

On the way home, Bobbi felt a little uneasy about their dating "deal," not sure where this was going. Or whether she could hold off her own sexual needs, either. The whole discussion had a surreal, teenage angst thing going on. But, she was willing to see where things might go. She took herself by surprise even mentioning the dating, but was glad she asked, and even gladder Erin had agreed. What did it mean, though?

At the door, Bobbi stopped and thanked Erin for a very good evening. She drew her into her arms and kissed her sweetly, not putting too much heat into it. Their first kiss. It lingered, as Erin melted into Bobbi's body and returned the kiss. Bobbi's lips longed for

Erin's soft ones. They kissed and kissed. Bobbi felt herself warming from the inside out. The Elf had some kissing moves. Bobbi finally broke the kiss and cuddled Erin into her arms.

"That was quite a kiss, Mother Erin." Bobbi looked down at Erin's beautiful smile. "Good night."

Erin stepped out of Bobbi's arms. "Good night. Thanks for a very pleasant night."

Chapter Twenty-one

Erin spent Friday morning at home, having some well-deserved Sabbath time. She swam at the gym to start the day, then came home to read a new novel. She met her friend Julia for lunch at Murphy's Diner in town.

Julia was waiting for her at a table. She rose and hugged Erin, they sat, and she asked with a smile, "What's new?"

Erin sighed, and answered. "Not much. Lent's been planned, and I'm working on Easter now. And by the way, I'm dating one of the doctors from the rural clinic. The one I told you about. The Take Charge one. So, I guess that's new."

"Oh?" Julia said non-committally, putting down her coffee cup and gazing at Erin.

Erin thought, *it's a bitch trying to get a rise from another pastor.* Everyone's trained to give off neutral vibes and not share how they really feel. "You know about my situation. I think I need to talk to the bishop."

Julia cocked her head. "Don't rush things, Erin. You're not there yet, are you? How many dates have you had?"

"A couple. She fell asleep on my couch the first date, so that date was not very date-like. Then we had dinner on Wednesday. We had a very good talk. She apologized for being so bossy and rude. Said I reminded her physically of her last girlfriend, who unfortunately, was emotionally and physically abusive."

"Wow. That's an extra load of anxiety to put on a relationship."

"I know. But now that she's gotten past that, she said she likes me and wants to see more of me. I like her too, since she's not so bossy. She's a caring physician. Very dedicated to her work. But, she's only here on a two-year fellowship. She started in January."

"You're afraid you'll get in too deep and then she'll leave?"

"Sure, there's that. But also, the deal with my parish and no sexual activity. I love the quirky group at my church. Still, it irks me that only a handful of parishioners have hijacked the other more liberal ones to dictate my behavior." Erin huffed out her exasperation. Their coffee and sandwiches arrived, and she stirred milk into her cup.

Julia chewed her sandwich and swallowed. She put her sandwich on the plate and lifted a piece of bread. "Darn. I told them no mayonnaise. Oh well." She scraped the mayo off with her knife, then replaced the top slice of bread. She took a sip of her coffee and said, "Do you have allies in your parish?"

"Yes. Several. Most of them winter in Arizona until the first of April." Erin fiddled with her utensils for a moment, then asked, "What would you do if you were me?"

Julia finished chewing. "If I were you, I'd wait until April. You may be able to date under the radar—"

"In this town? Where you even know the name of your neighbor's dog? My dating Bobbi has already been noted. One older woman brought it up to me on Sunday. She saw Bobbi and me leaving my house for dinner on Wednesday when she drove by the church.

She knows Bobbi. She's a patient of hers, or so she said. She wanted to make sure I was okay." Erin chuckled, putting air quotes around okay. "As if Bobbi would be making a house call. I called bullshit on her. Told her I was dating Bobbi. It's the gossip she was after. So, by now the whole parish knows."

"Okay, then." Julia drew out her words. "So much for flying under the radar. In that case, maybe a trip to the bishop is in your near future."

They finished their sandwiches and coffee. The server stopped by to ask if he could get them anything more. Julia grabbed the check from him.

"Hey." Erin tried to snatch it from her, but Julia pulled it out of her way.

"It's my turn to buy," Julia said.

Erin sighed. "Fine. But shouldn't the person being counseled pay, not the counselor?"

"Ha, ha," Julia smiled and said. "Wasn't much counseling. I think you know what you need to do. Take care of yourself and let the homophobes stew. They'll get over it."

"Maybe not." Erin stood. "Thanks for lunch and for the sounding board."

❧❧❧❧

The Friday Stations of the Cross service lasted twenty minutes, followed by a soup supper. Erin finished her duties around eight and went next door to change from her clericals into jeans and a pullover sweater.

She realized she felt comfortable with Bobbi. She was easy to talk to, now that they had come to understand one another better. While Bobbi wasn't into church, she had expressed genuine interest in her job as a priest and had participated in discussion with several theological questions at the Beer and Bible group. Bobbi's questions, while biblically illiterate, were far from naïve. Erin had been amused about Bobbi's reaction of disbelief, when others at the table talked of praying daily. Bobbi had never prayed, didn't know how, or so she said. Erin, herself couldn't remember a time when she didn't pray, even as a small youngster.

Bobbi had obviously committed herself wholly to medicine. She took many nights of on call, and went into the hospital when she needn't go, because she wanted to check personally on a patient's condition. She had been sincerely grieved to lose a baby on Ash Wednesday. Bobbi, a serious person in many ways, was, however, hard to get to know. She wanted to know what made Bobbi Webster tick.

Then the sex thing? Who knew where their relationship would go? Maybe Bobbi would decide Erin was too much trouble and go back to dating people like the nurse she saw her with at the brewery. Erin wouldn't blame her if she did. Priests carried a lot of baggage into a relationship.

Bobbi pulled into the driveway around eight-thirty. Erin met her with a big smile and led her into the living area.

"Hi. You're looking more rested than a few days ago." Erin took Bobbi's coat and they sat on the couch.

"No on-call this week. I switched out with one of the other fellows whose wife is due any minute. She went into labor earlier today, so I'm taking the rest of the weekend for him."

"You mean you're on call for forty-eight hours?" Erin said with alarm.

Bobbi ducked her head, a habit Erin noticed whenever Bobbi was embarrassed or self-conscious. "Yeah. No big deal. I've done it many times. What movie do you want to see?" Bobbi had her phone out, scrolling through the times and movie titles with Erin looking on.

They decided on a movie that started at nine-fifteen, so drove to the theater complex in a mall fifteen miles out near the highway. Erin bought the tickets, slyly looking up at Bobbi's face to register her lack of surprise. That was a good sign. The good doctor didn't assume she was the initiator in the relationship.

The movie, a science fiction-fantasy about a dystopian society, had earned an Oscar last year, and was just now coming to the local cinema.

They left the theater chatting about it.

"Do you like dystopian fiction?" Bobbi asked.

"Yeah. These wild fantasies are not so fantastic or unreal, given how the world is going right now. They give me hope that, even if the world goes sideways, into World War Three or something, that some survivors will challenge the status quo and work for a better society." Erin got in Bobbi's SUV.

"You're an optimist, aren't you?" Bobbi smiled at Erin as she started the car. "Do you want to go for a drink?"

"Let's go to my house. I have some beer and wine, if that suits you."

"Thanks. I looked at my finances the other day. I have quite a bit of debt from medical school, so decided I needed to stay home more and eat less take-out."

"I have some debt too, from my masters and divinity school both. And my job pays only half time, so some weeks I just scrape by. Mom and Dad help me too." Erin gauged the appropriateness of the next statement. "My school debt is about sixty thousand. What about you?"

Bobbi sighed. "One hundred and forty thousand."

Erin's heart dropped. "My God."

"It's only money," Bobbi said, shrugging.

"But how can you ever hope to get out of debt? Family practice in rural areas can't be that lucrative."

"Actually, family practice docs fall at the bottom among physician salaries, notoriously. Add rural practice, it's the lowest salary of any physician group."

"Wow. And you aren't worried?"

Bobbi shook her head. "I don't worry about money. I have an old car that suits me fine. I don't care much about living space—you've seen my sparse condo. I don't like jewelry and I don't need many new clothes. I live pretty simply. Well, except for my tech habit."

Erin took this in. "You know that's a spiritual discipline—simplicity of life."

"Spiritual, huh? For me, it's just how I grew up. Not much to spend money on in eastern Oregon. We lived on a ranch about forty miles from the nearest big town. We made our own entertainment, rode horses, played cards in the winter, hiked the mountains in the summer. But we worked hard. My parents weren't into making a show; they instilled in us a good attitude toward money."

"They didn't help you financially with medical school?" Erin wondered how Bobbi had survived.

"They didn't have the means. I had a couple of scholarships for undergraduate at the state school. I had rural scholarships for medical school and residency. Still, the debt added up. I worked weekends, as an aide at the local hospital during high school and college," Bobbi said matter of factly. "Did you work during school?"

"No. Mom and Dad insisted I focus on school. They took out parent loans and I took out student loans. Northwestern had scholarships for clergy kids, so that helped."

They drove into Erin's driveway. After getting in the door, she took Bobbi's coat and directed her to the couch.

"Beer or wine?" Erin called from the kitchen.

"Beer," Bobbi answered.

Erin walked in with two beers and handed one to Bobbi, then took her seat a few inches from Bobbi. She said, "I have a lot of respect for you, Doctor."

Bobbi grinned. "Why is that? Because I'm poor and not likely to get rich being a physician?"

"Well, yeah."

"Believe me, I met those guys in med school. The ones who ended up in high-end specialties; the oncologists, urologists. Don't even ask about the surgeons or those guys and gals who would take over their daddy's practice with little outlay required. I didn't hang out with them. I hung out with others like me, the primary care types, family practice, internal medicine, and pediatrics, and some of the obstetrics types too. I always wanted to work with people from cradle to grave, with minor and major problems. Where doctors see people over time, have relationships with families. And don't think it's all touchy-feely. I'm big on using my scientific mind. Diagnosis is like a mystery I can solve. Only I get paid to do it. And I get to help people at the same time." Bobbi drank deeply of her beer. "Also, FYI, the pay isn't exactly poverty level. I'll be making six figures this year and next in my fellowship."

"Gee, puts my measly salary to shame, doesn't it?" Erin reflected on their conversation. Deciding to move into other topics, she asked Bobbi about her family. "I remember you said you had two brothers, and your mom's a teacher, your dad a rancher, and they're all in Oregon?"

"Yep," Bobbi answered.

"Are you close to them?"

"Mom and I had the usual mother-daughter issues. I didn't wear dresses; she wanted me to put on makeup. That kind of conflict. But my folks are down to earth, practical types. I am too. I liked the way we were raised. If we did our chores, everything went smoothly. If we talked back or got crazy as teens, it didn't fly. We knew what was expected of us and we did it. Simple, our life, really." Bobbi sipped more of her beer. "How about you? Are you close to your folks?"

"I'd say somewhat. My sisters and I like each other, but my life is so different. They've got their husbands, and now are starting families, so we don't have as much to talk about, not much in common with a lesbian priest." Erin chuckled. "I'm close to my mom, but less so with my dad, even though we share a profession. He advised me during the ordination process, but he didn't butt in, didn't tell me how to do my job. I appreciated that. Mom and I joke around a lot. She's a nurse, you know, the nurturing kind, so that occasionally gets in the way. But overall, I'm happy with my family. We genuinely like each other, which I know sounds corny, but it's true. Not as much dysfunction as some families. No alcoholics or drug addicts. One sister was diagnosed with post-partum depression last year, but no real mental problems with us. We're kind of dull and boring, really."

"I think my youngest brother, the new-age hippie in Portland, might be doing his share of weed, but that's about it for us. It's legal in Oregon, but still, I don't like it. I had a bout with drugs in my teens. Not hard stuff, just weed. I tried some other stuff too and decided I didn't like it. I guess I'm just a beer gal." Bobbi finished her beer and plunked it down on the coffee table for emphasis, smiling.

Bobbi's phone rang. She dug it out of her pocket. "Sorry," she said, as she rose from the couch and went into the kitchen to answer. When she came back into the living area, Bobbi had a disappointed look on her face. "I'm afraid I have to go. One of my patients was admitted to BCH."

Erin came to her. "I'm sorry." She waited a minute, then said, "Listen, you're on call all weekend. How about I bring some dinner by your house tomorrow? Or wherever you are."

Bobbi looked surprised. "Holy shit. Oops, sorry. You don't have to do that. Don't you have things to do Saturdays?"

"I'm fine. I have to cook anyway. I might as well make it for two." Erin smiled and shrugged.

Bobbi grinned. "That'd be fantastic. Sometimes I'm scarfing down cardboard pizza from the break room, so real food will be a treat. Thanks a lot, Erin." Bobbi leaned in to kiss her.

Erin found her lips and kissed Bobbi back, bringing her tongue to taste Bobbi's lips and gently push between them. Bobbi responded in kind and drew Erin closer in a hug. She brushed her hand down Erin's back.

Erin began to feel the warmth of Bobbi's body all along her front. Bobbi felt both soft and muscular. She circled Bobbi's neck and played with her short curls. Both of their breathing deepened. Erin's lower core warmed with the telltale sensations of attraction. Her clitoris throbbed. She pushed Bobbi away slightly and ended the kiss. "Wow," she said softly.

"I need to get to the hospital," Bobbi muttered into Erin's hair. "Thanks for the beer. And for the movie." Bobbi pulled away, put on her coat, and neared the front door. She looked at Erin intently, drew her in for another kiss, then said, "Good night."

Erin shut the door, sighing like a love-struck kid. "Oh boy, Dr. Webster. We've got a long path ahead of us."

After tonight, she realized she wanted to address the short-term nature of Bobbi's time in Colorado. Even though she was not one to shelter herself from relationships, she knew she needed not to hurt Bobbi. Bobbi wanted to attain her goal of going back to practice in rural Oregon in less than two years. Erin wanted to be careful with both her and Bobbi's hearts.

She turned the outside light off and went into the kitchen to check what she could cook for Bobbi and her for dinner tomorrow night.

Chapter Twenty-two

Bobbi heard her phone vibrate on the countertop while she wrapped up her patient charting. She drew her hand over her eyes. She'd been at the clinic seeing Dr. Garcia-Brown's rescheduled patients all day Saturday, and just finished with the last of the Saturday walk-ins. Her stomach growled from missing lunch. She picked up the phone and answered, noting it was Erin's number.

"Hey, Doc. This is Erin's Catering Service. Where are you? Where do you want your dinner delivered?"

"Hi," Bobbi answered and laughed. "I'm still at the clinic. I've been so busy today, I forgot I'm getting a genuine meal tonight."

"I'll be there in twenty minutes."

True to her word, Erin walked into the clinic, carrying a small basket with a cloth covering it. Bobbi smelled wonderful odors wafting up and she tried to peek in. "Smells great. What d'ya have for me?"

"Roast chicken, biscuits, and a salad, with brownies for dessert."

"Yum," Bobbi said, rubbing her hands together.

Erin unpacked the basket while Bobbi grabbed paper plates and plastic forks from the break room cabinet. Bobbi helped Erin put food on the plates for each of them. Erin gave them each a biscuit and tossed the salad into two, small, brightly colored, plastic bowls she had brought.

"I'm starved," Bobbi said. She grabbed utensils and raked food into her mouth, her eyes closing in ecstasy.

Erin ate across from her at the break room table and grinned at Bobbi's expression. "You're easy, Doc."

"What do you mean by that?" Bobbi joked, frowning.

Erin laughed. "Been busy today?"

Bobbi sighed. Between bites, she said, "Been crazy. Dr. Garcia-Brown's patients were rescheduled from yesterday. I also had the usual Saturday walk-ins. By the way, his wife had a baby girl around two this afternoon, and everyone's fine. But, I've barely had time to breathe."

Erin shook her head. "Glad you're able to take a break—"

Bobbi's phone buzzed. She sighed and answered, walking into the hallway for privacy. Two minutes later, she reentered the break room. "I've got to get the exam room ready. A kid probably needing stitches coming in." Bobbi quirked her head in apology and left Erin.

A few minutes later, Erin popped into the exam room Bobbi had been preparing. "I left the rest of the brownies in the fridge."

Bobbi looked up from her work and moved to the door. She took Erin into her arms, whispering, "I appreciate you coming over with dinner. Thanks." She kissed her, hugging her tightly to her body. When Erin pulled away, Bobbi felt the loss of warmth and softness. Erin made Bobbi do a happy dance inside.

Stan led the boy and his parents down the hallway. Bobbi waved to Erin and brought them into the treatment room. "What have we got here, young man?"

❧ ❧ ❧ ❧

On Sunday morning, Erin walked into church ready for the late service, seeing about forty people filling the pews. She stood in back, waiting for the pianist to take up the first hymn, when she thought she noticed a familiar head of short, curly, dark blond hair. Bobbi sat in one of the back pews by herself, reading the bulletin, a hymnal open beside her on the pew.

Astounded, Erin finally realized she needed to proceed down the aisle when the first strains of the hymn played.

After the service, Bobbi met her in line with the other parishioners, and shook her hand.

"Mother Erin, good to see you." Bobbi had a smug smile.

"And I'm astonished to see you." The line of parishioners behind Erin looked intently at them. "I'll see you at coffee hour."

Later, in the small parish hall, Bobbi walked up to Erin, both of them holding Styrofoam cups of hot coffee. Bobbi held a cookie in her other hand.

"I'm so surprised that you're here," Erin said.

Bobbi merely smiled enigmatically in return.

"You're not going to tell me why you're here?"

"No reason. I had a good sleep last night for a change. I wanted to see what your Sunday looked like. What you might say in a sermon. I liked it, by the way. The sermon." Bobbi still smirked.

Erin looked at Bobbi askance. "I don't know that I trust you. You're not a church person, and I always distrust the motives of those who don't go to church."

"Why would you do that? I'd think you'd want new folks coming." Bobbi ate her cookie and took a sip of the coffee. "Are you free for lunch? I can't promise I won't get called in."

Erin gazed at Bobbi. "I have some things to take care of after coffee hour. Can you give me forty-five minutes?"

Bobbi finished off the cookie in one bite and downed the last of the coffee. "Sure. Can I wait upstairs for you?"

"My office is open. Just go down this hall and to your left. It's the last door on the right. Can't miss it."

"See you later." Bobbi winked.

Chapter Twenty-three

Bobbi walked around the overstuffed bookshelves in Erin's office.

Seminary reading looked as bad as medical school. She picked up a very large tome on theology, which seemed to be equivalent in size to Bobbi's internal medicine textbook. She flipped through the table of contents. God. Creation. Sin. Salvation. Holy Spirit. Church. Sacraments. The list went on. What was Eschatology?

Bobbi sighed, replaced the book, and walked slowly around Erin's office, looking at icons on the credenza. She smelled a sweet spiciness in the room. The desk was very neatly arranged, but she laughed at the Jesus bobblehead and some finger puppets of guys with beards lying across the front, along with a collection of several stuffed sheep.

"Like my kingdom?" Erin quipped, as she entered the office while taking off her vestments. She hung up her robe.

"It's full of books. Looks like my apartment when I was in med school. And what's that smell?" Bobbi asked, watching Erin sit at her desk and rev up her laptop.

"Frankincense. I get it at the local marijuana shop." Erin grinned. "If you can wait a few minutes, I have to send some emails and update our web site with my sermon."

"Can I do anything to help?"

"Just be patient, is all." Erin typed away.

Bobbi sat in one of the old chairs and reread the service bulletin, much of which was in a foreign language to her. Introit. Gloria. Sursum Corda. Sanctus and Benedictus. Even though her Latin was confined to medical terminology, Bobbi could make out some of the words. But why did they still use Latin and Greek? It left her confused.

After a half hour, Erin sighed. "Okay. I think that'll do it." She rose from her desk. "Ready? Let's go next door to my place. I'll change clothes." She turned to Bobbi. "Actually, do you mind if we don't go out for lunch? I'm kinda beat."

Bobbi looked at Erin's drooping face. "Dumb me. Of course, you're tired."

Erin shrugged. "I usually take my pastoral nap on Sunday afternoon."

"Geez. I'm sorry. I should've realized you'd be taxed after Sunday morning." Bobbi pondered a second. "I can cook brunch. How would that be? You can relax. Do you have eggs?"

Erin's eyes brightened. "Really? You'd cook for me? Yes. Yes. Yes." Erin hugged Bobbi. "I think I love you." Erin stepped back out of Bobbi's arms, her eyes wide with shock.

Bobbi smiled, amused at Erin's statement. She chuckled softly.

"I...Wow, you know what I mean."

Bobbi was enamored of Erin's endearing blush. "I got you. You're happy I'll cook us some omelets."

"Whew. Thanks for understanding."

They got their coats on and walked next door. Erin went into her room to change, after showing

Bobbi the layout of her kitchen and everything she'd need for making brunch. Bobbi found an apron on a hook next to the fridge and collected all her ingredients to make spinach and cheese omelets.

Erin came back dressed in jeans and a top. Bobbi looked down at her feet and raised a brow. "Bunny slippers?"

Erin playfully smacked her arm. "Don't make fun of a priest's Sunday afternoon comfort. What do you wear when you get home?"

Bobbi made a show of thinking hard. "Let's see… normal jeans, normal flannel shirt, normal sneakers. You know, normal stuff."

"Smartass." Erin neared Bobbi and rubbed her hand over her back. "Get back to work, chef."

They both laughed. Bobbi liked the easy banter between them.

In a short while, Bobbi plated her finished omelets and added pieces of toast, while Erin poured the coffee she'd made. They sat across from each other at Erin's dining table.

Erin said grace. "Thanks. This looks amazing, Bobbi."

"I forgot I knew how to make these things. I do so little cooking for myself. It's no fun cooking for one and eating alone."

"Know what you mean, but I try. My mom instilled that habit of cooking in me."

"My mom did the opposite. I worked outside with Dad and my brother Matt after school, so we came in tired and hungry. Dinner was always on the table. Even though Mom had to be as tired as we were, coming from a long school day, wrangling third graders."

"Was there a division of labor by sex on the

ranch?"

"Not so much. Dad used me like the boys. And Mom made all of us do housework. We had to keep our rooms clean, the bed made, clothes picked up. When we hit thirteen, we each did our own laundry after we got a laundry basket for Christmas."

Erin looked surprised. "Impressive."

Bobbi shook her head, remembering the laundry failures. "I didn't say we did laundry well. All of us had our share of accidently dyed shirts and shrunken wool socks and sweaters."

Erin gazed into Bobbi's face tenderly. "I love to hear you laugh." She took Bobbi's hand.

Bobbi rose from her chair and took both of the plates to the sink. She came back and took Erin's hand to lift her from her chair, then drew her into her arms. "I've been wanting to hold you since I saw you this morning in church."

Erin snuggled and hummed. "This may be better than a pastoral nap."

Bobbi felt her soft, small body and felt protective. She hugged her more tightly, then bent to kiss her.

They kissed, standing next to the dining table, for some minutes. Bobbi began to heat up, her tongue found Erin's, and the kisses deepened. "Oh, God," Bobbi intoned. She felt she was about to enter the zone of no-return.

Erin led Bobbi to the living room sofa. They explored each other's bodies, caressing shoulders and entwining fingers in hair. Bobbi thought she might burst if something else didn't happen soon.

She drew back and they peered at each other. Bobbi breathed deeply. "Crap," she said.

"What?" Erin asked.

"I'm pretty heated up. How about you?" Bobbi stroked Erin's soft, smooth cheek, her heart about to pound out of her chest.

Erin seemed to contemplate her next statement. "Will you come to bed with me? I really want to make love with you."

"What? Wait, we can't do that." Bobbi stood and became agitated. "This isn't how it's supposed to go, Erin. You're supposed to be celibate. I'm not going to be the one to make you lose your job." She turned to find her coat draped on a chair. "I need to go."

"Don't go." Erin leaped up. "Don't, please. I'm sorry."

Bobbi kissed Erin briefly and took her into her arms. "What the hell are we getting into?"

Erin shook her head against Bobbi's chest. "I shouldn't have put you on the spot. I'm just so attracted to you. To your mind. Your body. Your gentle soul. I don't know what to do. Loving you is the right thing, I know it." Erin stepped back. "Please stay. Let's talk this through. I can't have you leave like this."

Bobbi's head reeled.

"Please, Bobbi. Don't make this harder by skipping out on me. Let's talk. Please."

Bobbi, still spinning with emotion and confusion, heard Erin's plea. Her fear rose. Erin had all the qualities she was drawn to. She was bright. Cute. Smart. Didn't take herself too seriously. Bobbi loved her independence. Aloud, she shocked herself by saying, "Am I falling for you?"

Erin led them back to the sofa. "Sit and talk to me. Tell me how you feel."

Bobbi smiled wanly. "I think I need a drink to get through this."

Erin shook her head. "Me too. I'll get us each a beer."

Erin came back with the beers. "Now, enough stalling. Spill it, Doctor."

Bobbi sipped her beer and inhaled deeply. "I like you a lot. I like the time we've spent together. I like you more than a casual thing, but I'm afraid. I'm leaving to go back to Oregon next year. You have your church here. I don't want to hurt you." Bobbi quirked her lips in a lopsided grin. "Hell, I don't want to get hurt either."

"I agree to both of those feelings."

They drank their beer in silence. Finally, Bobbi weighed her thoughts and asked, "Do you think we could date without...you know?"

"I don't see how, if I were truthful," Erin said, looking up into Bobbi's eyes. "I'm really turned on by you."

"Me, too." Bobbi kissed Erin. "I don't want you to get into trouble. But, hell, this isn't fair." Erin's situation was so artificial. So focused on appearances and rules.

"I know, sweetie, I know." Erin caressed Bobbi's cheek. She sighed.

Bobbi held Erin close, stroking her hair, thinking. She broke the silence. "What would happen if we...if you weren't celibate?"

Erin leaned back out of Bobbi's arms. "At the very least, I would need to go talk to the bishop, in person. The parish has a problem. Or, some of them. Well, more accurately, about two or three of them—"

"Two or three?" Bobbi was appalled. "How can they blackmail you like this?"

Erin hung her head. "I know. I know. It's just

the way it is. They're parish leaders. Big givers to the coffers. One is the matriarch of the parish, was even baptized here. She's—"

"Oh, Erin," Bobbi took her in her arms again, her heart breaking for her. "You don't have to live like this, do you?"

They sat quietly, Bobbi rubbing Erin's back gently. "Do you think we each need to think this over? I feel like my head's whirling. I don't know anything. Are you as confused as me?"

"No, not confused. Torn." Erin took Bobbi's hand in hers. "We have a lot against us, if what we feel is deeper than a fling."

"This is nothing like a fling." Bobbi gazed on Erin. She hadn't felt her heart so warmed by another woman. A sense of hope flooded around her fear.

Erin smiled warmly.

"What does this mean?" Bobbi asked.

"We can't figure everything out today. I think I need to see the bishop before anything else happens between us." Erin kissed Bobbi gently.

Bobbi returned the kiss with passion. She took Erin's face in her hands. "I need to be truthful with you. I'm not a religious person. This morning, in your service, I felt I had entered another universe. A place I'm not sure I'm comfortable in." Bobbi pursed her lips. "I don't know about the church and God thing, Erin. I'm sorry I have this problem. Is that a major stumbling block for you?"

"Nope." Erin smiled serenely. "I'm not worried about you. To quote Elizabeth I, 'I don't have windows into men's souls.'"

"What about lesbian's souls?" Bobbi grinned, wanting some comic relief from their intense discussion. Her smile fell away. "Are you sure? Isn't it important that people close to the priest be able to support them?"

"I don't see what the problem would be. You're very loving, generous, and giving, Bobbi. You do support me. You're as worried as me about our celibacy issue."

"True. But I can't...I don't understand your calling, why you do the church thing. I don't understand prayer or worship or having a building that's used only one or two days a week for a God I can't be certain exists. I don't fit into your religious world." Bobbi stopped to gauge Erin's reaction to her real questions.

Erin scrunched her face, thinking. "I'd be glad to answer all your questions. You ask good ones, but not ones I haven't dealt with before, from parishioners and non-parishioners alike. In fact, I know some long-term church attenders who don't understand prayer and some who don't pray in their daily life. All of our vestry wrestles annually about the lack of our church building being occupied or rented. How to get more groups and people to use our space. How to share our space graciously, which is easier said than done. And, whether you're a Christian or not, at one time or another, many people question God's existence. I did when I was a teen. Occasionally, even now, I'll have a day that challenges my faith down to my bones. I wonder where God is, how to reach Her, how to pray."

"What *do* you pray about?" Bobbi asked plaintively.

"Everything," Erin answered immediately. "For sick and dying people. I pray for my family every day. I pray for the world, especially places of conflict and injustice, death and destruction. I pray for our nation, which is especially hard since the last election. I pray for those in need or trouble, the homeless, those in prison. I pray for our earth and the human greed that destroys it. I pray for everything and everyone. I pray for Walter, my biggest critic at Holy Spirit church. And for my biggest supporters, too."

"I don't hear you praying for yourself." Bobbi raised her brows.

"Hoo, boy, I pray for myself more than anyone else! When I can't come up with a good sermon. When I want to kick someone's butt. I pray all the time for my temper, my ability to mouth off before thinking. I never pray for patience, though."

"No?"

Erin chuckled. "When I pray for patience, I invariably get a problem that makes me wait for a solution. And wait." Erin paused for a beat. "Have you ever prayed with a patient?"

The question took Bobbi aback. "Wow." She thought for a moment. "I have. I just remembered. A family asked me to pray for their daughter with them. A teen who had meningitis. We were just starting treatment for her, I was handing her over to the specialists, but they knew me as their physician in my residency in Oregon. I felt so bad for them, because they could lose their daughter. So, I prayed with them. I don't even remember what I said or how I said it. I didn't feel uncomfortable doing it. I just did it. Words came out of my mouth. And we all cried. I remember so well, the crying." Bobbi wiped a hand over her mouth. She blinked and inhaled deeply.

Erin quietly watched her.

Sitting on the couch, holding each other, they talked quietly about Erin's predicament. They came to no decisions, other than to continue dating.

Erin led Bobbi to the door at six p.m. Their kiss was lingering, soft, gentle, and comforting.

"I needed that good-bye," Bobbi said, nuzzling Erin's neck.

Chapter Twenty-four

Erin was terrified. She and Bobbi were taking the beautifully sunny March afternoon to go out to Yancy's Triple D Ranch to ride horses. She'd ridden once or twice as a child, bouncing around on jolting ponies without much control. While she had not fallen, the experience did not make for a comfortable ride nor a love of horseback riding.

Bobbi picked her up in her SUV and they arrived at the ranch, where Yancy, in jeans, boots, and a tan canvas jacket, met them in the drive. Erin gave her a tight smile.

"Good to see y'all. Ready to ride?" Yancy grinned at Erin.

Erin grimaced. "I'm really scared. Nothing's going to happen to me, is it? Will they bite? Do they buck?"

Yancy looked with concern on Erin's white face. "Let's take it easy. First, we get to know the horse. I picked Honey, who's a very gentle horse. She does lessons with all ages of people. She's never bitten anyone. She'd only buck if startled out in the open, so trotting around the paddock will be very safe. I will be there with you. Bobbi will ride Golden Girl while you're learning your seat. Don't worry. Rule number one: if you relax, the horse will relax. They can sense your anxiety."

"That doesn't ease my tension much, Yancy.

Now I'm worried about the horse *and* myself."

Yancy and Bobbi laughed.

Bobbi said, "You're making this a big deal."

Erin sputtered. "You bet. I'm a city girl, not ranch hands like you guys."

Bobbi looked at Yancy. "Maybe we could do some relaxation exercises."

Yancy shrugged. "Okay."

Bobbi held Erin's shoulders. "Give yourself a moment. Breathe deeply."

Erin inhaled.

"Count to ten. Breathe out."

Erin exhaled.

"Repeat ten times." Bobbi continued to keep her hands gently on Erin's shoulders as they rose and fell.

Erin closed her eyes and completed the exercise. She felt the tension leave her shoulders and her face lose its tension. Of course, this felt like prayer to her. She chuckled to herself that Bobbi had just helped her pray. "That was wonderful. Thanks."

"Feel like you're ready?" Yancy asked.

Erin nodded. Yancy helped Erin meet Honey and taught her to use the currycomb and brush, then left Erin to finish grooming. The horse's huge bulk still intimidated her, but she felt her intense fear ebb away.

After grooming, Yancy led Erin to Honey's side. "We're going to clean out her hooves." Yancy leaned into Honey's side and picked up her rear hoof. She picked out debris all around the soft frog, brushed the site, then set her hoof on the barn floor. "Your turn now." Yancy handed a surprised Erin the pick and put the brush near her.

Erin amazed herself by finishing the other three hooves. Honey stood very still, obviously a pro at being groomed.

Yancy helped her bridle Honey, then gave her the saddle and assisted with placing it correctly on Honey's back, instructing her quietly all along. Yancy's patience impressed Erin and she gratefully accepted her quiet reassurance.

Erin smiled at the tacked-up horse. "I did it." She brushed her nails across her chest.

Yancy laughed. Bobbi had tacked up her horse and led him to the mounting block out in the paddock. Chill air met them as they led Honey out. Bobbi mounted and waited with her horse a few feet away from the mounting area.

Yancy instructed Erin how she would mount Honey and settle into the saddle before squeezing her sides to get her to walk. Erin inhaled and exhaled, and while still uncertain about this whole expedition, she climbed the steps of the small wooden platform, feeling less anxious. She looked down at the saddle and the horse's head, standing still before her. "It's a long way to the ground."

Yancy patted Erin's leg. "Not that far. Now swing your right leg over gently and slide into the saddle. You can grab her mane if you want. Here are the reins."

Erin wiggled her butt into the saddle, blew out another big breath, then patted the horse's neck. "Good girl, Honey." She pressed her lower legs gently into Honey's sides and slowly and calmly began to walk around the edge of the paddock.

"Remember about using both the reins and your legs to turn her."

Bobbi, on Golden Girl, preceded them in a slow walk around the paddock, also bolstering Erin's confidence.

For the next hour, Erin learned to steer the horse at a walk, to trot and not bounce around, and trot and turn at the same time. Erin smiled and laughed as they rode the paddock.

At the end of the hour, Bobbi took Golden Girl for a quick ride down the ranch road, while Erin and Yancy took off Honey's tack and brushed her down. Yancy let Erin feed Honey a small bucket of oats in her stable before letting her out into the pasture with the other horses.

Bobbi arrived back just as Erin and Yancy exited the barn, walking toward the ranch house. Erin waved jauntily to her and smiled widely.

As Erin and Yancy entered the house and each got a drink of water, Erin said excitedly, "I'm so proud of myself."

"You should be. You did great. You're a regular cowgirl now."

She cleaned up the horse smell on her hands. Bobbi walked into the house and cleaned up, then they all met in the great room, sitting on the couch.

"There's a chill in the air in here. I'm going to start the fireplace," Yancy said.

After the gas fireplace began to give off warmth, they all relaxed on the sofa in front of it.

Gen soon opened the front door and came in with a chill breeze. "The wind," she said breathily, brushing her hair back from her forehead. Yancy left the couch and met her with a brief kiss.

"I've got the supper in the oven. I followed the instructions to the letter."

Gen chuckled at Yancy. They hugged for a moment. "Hi, everyone. How did your riding go?"

"Great," Bobbi and Erin both said at the same

time.

"Lots of fun," Erin added.

"Let me get changed. Yancy, please get our guests something to drink. I'll be right down." Gen walked up the open stairway.

"Beer, wine? Something stronger? Something non-alcoholic?"

Yancy got beers for all three and they settled before the fire, warming themselves and sipping their drinks. When Gen came back down, they were talking about Erin's parish.

"Wow." Yancy looked at Gen. "Did you know about Erin's homophobic parish?"

"I wouldn't call them that," Erin put in.

Erin told Gen about the arrangement she had with her parish, while holding hands with Bobbi. Bobbi squeezed Erin's hand, and Erin smiled at her tenderly.

"It's more than the Roman Catholic church would do," Gen answered, referring to the church's stance against women and gay priests. "But still, they aren't treating your love with equal respect."

"No lie," Yancy answered in a disgusted tone. "What will you do?"

Erin looked at Bobbi. "I've got a meeting with the bishop next week."

Just then, a knock came on the door. Yancy brought Roxie and Kate into the great room. Everyone greeted each other with friendly hugs.

Roxie brought two bottles of wine into the kitchen area and opened one. She brought glasses back for her and Gen. "I brought the Chilean red we talked about."

"Ooh, goody." Gen grabbed her wine glass and swirled the dark liquid with relish.

"We were just talking about Erin's upcoming meeting with her bishop," Bobbi said.

"Oh, baby cakes, is that coming up next week?" Roxie looked with concern at Erin.

Erin nodded. "No big deal. Bishop Margaret and I know the score. She'll be supportive, I think. Although I don't know how it all will play out."

Bobbi squeezed Erin's shoulders.

They ate dinner together, enjoying banter about homophobes they each had encountered in their lives over the years. They laughed and drank and laughed some more.

After dinner, they brought out the instruments they'd transported, Bobbi's banjo and Erin's violin. "Time for some music," Bobbi announced.

They tuned up to each other while the others gathered close.

Bobbi and Erin played quiet folk tunes from Bobbi's sheet music.

Gen and Kate sang along, while Roxie played makeshift shakers made of beans in a closed plastic container. Yancy laid back on the sofa, enjoying the little concert.

The music swirled around the three couples in jaunty rhythms. Bobbi and Erin traded leads. Bobbi picked tunes that Erin would take up with the violin while Bobbi played background chords. Then they would switch leads again.

Pausing between pieces, they played six selections, watching each other for rhythm and tempo changes. They played easily together, to Erin's delight.

"That does it for me," Bobbi said after thirty minutes. "My hands aren't up to playing any more tonight. I haven't played in some months and my callouses are getting callouses."

Yancy stood. "More beer?"

"No thanks. I have an early day tomorrow."

"That was fantastic," Gen gushed.

"Wow, you guys played well together. Are you sure you haven't done this before?" Roxie asked.

"No. It was fun though," Erin said, grinning at Bobbi.

Kate added, "Y'all are good. I'd like to hear more some time."

"We'll have to do this again soon," Erin said, looking at Bobbi.

Bobbi nodded enthusiastically. "Sure, I'd love it. Maybe I'll practice a little more before the next concert."

They all laughed.

Chapter Twenty-five

"Come in, Mother Erin." Bishop Margaret Stanhope's aide led Erin into the bishop's swank office overlooking a busy street in Denver a few blocks from Colfax. "The bishop is still in her meeting but will be here shortly. Can I get you something? Coffee? Soda?"

"Diet pop, please. Thanks, Brett." Erin exhaled. Brett brought her a Diet Pepsi and a glass of ice. She sipped her drink and prayed silently, breathing deeply. It wasn't that she was nervous as much as uncertain about how the meeting would help her.

She looked over the books on the bishop's shelf, the usual theology books and references. The bishop's icon collection crowded the entire wall opposite the large windows looking down on the street. Erin walked around, checking the different saints and styles of icons on the wall, enrapt by the bishop's treasures.

"Sorry, Erin. Meeting ran late." The bishop, a medium-height woman in her late fifties, with silver and brown short hair, rushed in with a breezy greeting and hugged her. "How you doing?" she asked as she and Erin took chairs directly across from each other.

"I think you can guess why I'm here." Erin went right into the discussion, hoping it was the right tactic with her busy bishop.

Bishop Stanhope grinned. "Let's start with a short prayer, huh?" The bishop reached out and grabbed

Erin's hand. "Gracious and loving God, we thank you for the faithful witness of all our gay, lesbian, trans, and bi priests in this diocese, but especially for the ministry of your servant Erin. May you continue the good work you have begun in her. Amen."

Margaret sat back and said straightforwardly, "Now, how can we get this parish to treat you with respect? How can we get them to recognize you as a person in your own right, whose love counts just as much as your parishioners' do?"

Erin, taken aback by the bishop's quick assessment of her problem, said, "Thank you, Bishop. That's my problem exactly. How? Those three parishioners are the leaders of the parish. Have been for decades." Erin conjured up in her mind the images of steely faced Walter.

"But who are the new leaders?"

"The new leaders?"

"The ones who are coming up the leadership ranks, who know you and like you just the way you are. Those are the ones you need in your corner. They will help put the others in their place." The bishop raised her hand. "Don't look at me like that. Your parish system contains progressive genes. I've known Holy Spirit parish for many years. They've led the diocese in refugee ministry since the 1990s. They've done many ministries with children of addicts in the past and are working now with other youth. You've got good underpinnings at Holy Spirit."

This news surprised Erin. "I didn't know."

"Oh, yes." Margaret smiled wisely. "They need only to remember who they are to come around, my friend."

They talked of tactics, of meetings Erin could

convene, with the new leaders in control. The bishop gave her ideas for going forward with a plan, and by the end of the half-hour meeting, Erin felt buoyed and energized. She had a plan, with the bishop's blessing.

When Erin arrived home, she immediately called her parish leader, Charlotte Stephens, to meet her for coffee the next morning.

⊲∿⊲∿⊳∿⊳∿

"Hi, cutie," Bobbi entered Erin's house the next evening, tossed her coat on the sofa, and kissed and hugged her.

"Hey, yourself." Erin giggled. "You look like a drowned puppy."

"I forgot my umbrella this morning. It was bright and sunny. Who thought I would need one this evening?"

"You're on call at eight?" Erin brought a pot of hot tea to the living room with two cups. "Sugar and milk, right?"

Bobbi sat and stirred her tea. "I assume I'm here because you have news."

"I do." Erin smiled enigmatically. "I met with the bishop. I've begun my campaign against the homophobes in my parish."

"Wow. That's fast work. I knew you were a Mighty Mouse." Bobbi grinned wickedly.

"Shush, now. The bishop advised me to get the good guys from Holy Spirit solidly in my corner, so I'm having a meeting tomorrow night with the leaders of my parish, some of whom have been in Arizona for the winter. They're all back home now and I have enough support to remove the stipulation on my contract."

"You do? That's great." Bobbi took Erin's hand and stroked her knuckles.

Erin could barely keep her energy in. "Yeah. I want you to come to the meeting."

Bobbi gulped the hot tea and coughed.

Erin patted her back. "You all right?"

Bobbi rasped out, "I'm fine. Whew. Better." She finally caught her breath. "Geez, Erin. Do you think that's wise? What do you want to accomplish by me being there?"

"I thought it would be easier if there were a name and face of the person I'm dating. It's harder to reject a real person than an idea."

"Oh." Bobbi looked skeptical.

Erin didn't expect this reaction from her. "You don't have to if you don't want to come. I'd understand. It's a lot to ask. You'll be outed to my whole parish."

"That doesn't bother me. I think by now lots of folks know who I am. Some little kid pointed me out to her mother at the clinic the other day and asked if I was the gay doctor." Bobbi chuckled.

"Oh, God, no." Erin covered her mouth with her hands. She grinned but said, "I'm so sorry, sweetie." She took Bobbi into her arms. "We're surrounded by stupid, straight people."

Bobbi drew back from a hug and kissed Erin tenderly. "I'll do whatever you think is best, Mother Erin."

"Okay, tomorrow night at six. Be here or be... queer." They both laughed, but Erin couldn't tell if Bobbi laughed from amusement or from nerves. She realized it was a lot to ask of the church-phobic doctor.

Chapter Twenty-six

Welcome, everybody," Erin said to the assembled group of seven sitting on the couch and dining room chairs gathered in the living room at the vicarage.

Charlotte, the same woman she'd spent time with in the hospital when she'd had pneumonia several weeks ago, sat the closest to her, as the parish's leader. On Charlotte's right were the two negative parishioners, Helen and Walter, whose stipulations the rest of the vestry had agreed to for Erin's contract. Allies of Erin's, Mike and Jennifer, sat across from them. The group rounded out with two people Erin considered neutral, Clarice and Tom. She wished she knew them better; nevertheless, her interactions with them in the year since she'd been hired had been positive. She just wasn't sure where they stood on the issue of her sexuality.

Bobbi sat with a stoic face on Erin's left, looking definitely outside her comfort zone. Erin squeezed her hand.

"I've called this meeting because I want to be up front with you about my personal life. I'd like to introduce my girlfriend, Dr. Roberta Webster." Erin watched carefully as everyone reacted.

Helen and Walter gasped.

Mike smiled at Erin, then at Bobbi, and said, "Welcome to our meeting, Dr. Webster."

Clarice smiled, but Tom's smile was tight and didn't reach his eyes.

Jennifer, however, rose from her chair, clasped Bobbi's hand, and said warmly, "Great to meet you, Dr. Webster."

Charlotte took over the meeting. "We're here tonight to discuss the special clause in Mother Erin's contract that we signed one year ago. I want us to decide tonight whether to retain it or strike it and sign another contract." Charlotte sat primly and looked each person in the eye. "Everyone will have a turn to express their stance. I, for one, am against the current contract we negotiated about Mother Erin remaining celibate. I don't believe we should treat any class of person with a different set of rules. I abide by my baptismal covenant to respect the dignity of every human being and I don't believe it is respectful to treat Mother Erin's love as less than anyone else's."

Walter shook his head. "Her lifestyle is an abomination to God and I'll show you right in the bible where it says that. We hired this young woman, thinking her behavior would remain chaste. That she would not practice her deviant lifestyle while a priest in our midst. I don't think we need to change one damn thing. I abide by Jesus's stance of loving the sinner but hating the sin and she should remain celibate. She owes us that, since we were open enough to hire her in the first place." He puffed out his cheeks, which had turned red, and crossed his arms on his chest. Next to him, Helen's face remained a mask of distaste.

Jennifer spoke up, "But, how can you be a Christian and say those things? Jesus never said anything at all about homosexuals. Mostly he preached for compassion, for not accumulating wealth, and for forgiveness. Love God, love your neighbor. That's the message he taught. How can we treat Mother Erin with less respect?"

"I agree with Jennifer," Clarice said. Walter looked daggers at her. She ignored him. "I've been studying on this issue. Mother Erin is our first gay priest, but she's not likely to be our last. I believe God made her just the way she is and God loves her, and we should, too." Clarice returned Walter's pointed stare.

"Why, Clarice, how can you say that?" Helen said, her mouth looking like she'd sucked a lemon. "You know the bible says the homosexual lifestyle is an abomination before God. It's not natural. God did not make people who love the same sex."

"I'll tell you how I can say what I said, Helen. My own son came to out Stewart and me about three weeks ago. To tell us he was gay. He waited until college to act on his feelings and he's dating now. I've never seen him happier, and Stewart and I are both happy for him. That's how I can say what I said. Because I love my son no less than when he kept his secret. The poor guy had known all through high school he was gay and was afraid to tell us." Clarice looked at each person pointedly. "How can I treat Mother Erin with disrespect when I love my own son, no matter what?"

"I knew that boy was weird." Walter pointed his finger at Clarice.

Erin gasped, eyeing Walter in a new, less flattering light. Tonight, he was showing his true colors as a worse bigot than she'd thought.

"Walter, I don't care what you think. You're stuck back in the '50s when all priests were men. It's a new day. Get with the program." Clarice's face got red. She frowned at him. "Psychiatrists today say that being gay is not a mental illness. It's not a lifestyle. It's not something people choose." She looked around the ring of people. "Who in God's name would choose to be ostracized? To be an outcast to a whole group of bigots like you, Walter? Kip's life was miserable until he could be himself. I'm just sorry it took him so long to tell us. Now Mother Erin just wants to love another person. I don't think we should stand in her way. Jesus's commandment at the Last Supper was to love others as he had loved us."

"I'll tell you right now. If y'all change her contract, I'll take my pledge and leave this church in a heartbeat." Walter stood, his face scrunched with hate.

"Please remain calm and seated, Walter," Charlotte said.

He lowered himself to the couch, but his pouting face made his point.

"Blackmail is not pretty," Mike said. "No one should get their way because they threaten to take away their pledge. I don't believe that's how churches are supposed to work. As the leaders of Holy Spirit parish, we should be listening to one another, not coming to snap judgements and pontificating our position as gospel truth."

"No one person rules our vestry." Charlotte glared at Walter.

The room got quiet. Walter's cheeks still spouted red spots. Helen fidgeted with a hanky in her lap.

Witnessing the conflict swirling around her, Erin breathed deeply, then spoke evenly and calmly. "I know this is a difficult issue for some of you. Please know that I will abide by whatever contract terms you decide upon. If you decide tonight not to change the contract, I will accept it. But, truthfully, I ask you to consider my situation as a human being who wants to love and be loved just like anyone else."

Helen puffed out her chest. "I do not believe in gay priests, to begin with. But two different gay priests applied for our position. There was nothing we could do. I've been heartsick from the beginning, I can tell you." She sniffed into an embroidered hanky, then sat very straight, even regally.

As Helen reminded Erin of Maggie Smith as the Dowager of Downton Abbey, she struggled to contain a grin.

Helen continued in a huffy tone, with measured speech, "I've been a communicant of Holy Spirit church since the day I was born. I was baptized here. My parents were staunch members and generous supporters for forty years. My father was senior warden several times. My mother chaired the altar guild. I've chaired every committee at one time or another. You know I give more than most." She looked smugly at Erin. "I don't think I can continue to support you, Mother Erin, should you go against our policy. As I say, I have never believed in gay priests to begin with."

Tom spoke for the first time in the meeting. "What do you mean, you don't believe in gay priests? They're not unicorns, Helen! Mother Erin's one of the best priests we've ever had. I've heard nothing but good feedback from other parishioners. Her sermons have lots of meat in 'em. I hear her pastoral visits really help people, although I can't speak from my own experience 'cause I've not been in the hospital, knock on wood. She knows her stuff better than the last joker who was here, who read his sermons like they was a boring story. And they were. If you're that unhappy, Helen, why're ya still here?" Tom politely looked at

Helen.

"Well," Helen huffed. She turned her head away from Tom.

Tom added, looking at the group, "Not only is Mother Erin a great priest, she's got us doing the things we used to do. Working with the children in the low-income housing across the street. Giving help to refugees and immigrants. Giving baskets to poor families at Christmas and Easter. I'm happy with her, and don't care if she's gay, or straight, or what."

"The poor should be working instead of sponging off churches. That's another mark against her, as far as I'm concerned." Walter pointed his finger at Tom.

Tom shook his head. "I go with treating her like any other priest. I didn't like the special clause in the first place. Any other priest would've just done their thing, whether married or not. I don't think it's right to treat Mother Erin any different." Tom looked around and sat back in the walnut dining chair. "That's all I have to say."

"I agree," Clarice and Jennifer both spoke at once, then laughed lightly at the gaff.

Mike added, "You can count me in as well. I voted 'no' on any special contract clause for that reason. Granted, single priests should show an example in their lives, but gay priests have only received the ability to marry in the last couple of years. I think as long as Mother Erin's discreet, she should date like any other single priest. And Dr. Webster isn't a parishioner, so Mother Erin isn't doing anything wrong."

All but Helen and Walter were nodding their agreement with Mike.

No one said anything more for some moments.

Finally, Charlotte said, "Do any of you have any

more comments about changing the contract?" She waited. "We're going to take some moments of silence, to pray about this decision."

The room fell silent; they could only hear Walter's heavy smokers' wheeze.

After three minutes, Charlotte broke the silence. "Are we ready?" She looked for confirmation to each person. "Then, as senior warden, I call the question. Should we change Mother Erin's contract to exclude behavioral stipulations of celibacy?" Charlotte paused. "Those in favor, say aye."

Erin held her breath.

"Aye," all but Walter and Helen said.

"Those opposed, nay."

Walter and Helen, together, said, "Nay."

"Are there any abstentions?"

Silence.

"It passes. We will officially, as of today, remove the celibacy stipulation on Mother Erin's contract. I will visit the attorney tomorrow and see to it." Charlotte smiled and winked at Erin. "We love you, lady priest." She patted Erin's hand.

Erin's shoulders relaxed in relief. She hadn't realized the depth of the parish's caring for her.

"Now, is there any other business?" Charlotte asked, looking around. Walter and Helen looked as if they had swallowed poison. "No? I declare this meeting adjourned."

Everyone rose from their chairs. Walter, stormy faced, walked directly up to Charlotte. "You'll receive my written resignation tomorrow." He huffed out the door.

Helen, with pursed lips, grabbed her coat and slinked out after him.

Clarice stepped to Erin. "You didn't know about Kip's coming out, did you?"

"I didn't. That was a brave thing you did tonight, Clarice. Thank you." Erin hugged her.

Clarice, with tears swimming in her eyes, replied, "I had no choice. I love you both." She picked up her coat and put it on. Tom waved, said good-bye, and walked into the spring night behind Clarice.

Jennifer, Mike, and Charlotte remained. They gathered around Erin and Bobbi.

"I can't thank you all enough for your support. I'm sorry about Walter's resignation," Erin said.

"He'll be back," Mike said.

"How can you be sure?" Jennifer asked.

"Where else will he go? He loves all the rituals of the church. He's been at Holy Spirit church since his family moved to Colorado in the 1960s. He won't leave entirely. I predict he'll be back for Easter."

Erin was skeptical. "That soon? I don't know; it's only two weeks away."

Bobbi hugged Erin from the side. "I don't know exactly what happened tonight, but I felt you all support us in our relationship. Thank you."

"It's great to see you with my underwear on, Dr. Webster." Charlotte nudged her with her elbow, laughing.

Bobbi's eyes got wide, then she smiled. "Oh. Right. I seem to see when you're wearing a patient gown, Mrs. Stephens."

Everyone snickered.

Charlotte sighed. "I think that went well. I agree with Mike that Walter won't stay gone for long. And, now, dear lady priest, you do what you need to be a whole person. Knock it out of the ball park."

Jennifer and Mike looked at Erin with warmth. Erin felt her face redden.

Jennifer looked at Charlotte and said, "I need to get home to the kids, but thanks for calling this meeting. We did the right thing. If anyone in our parish doesn't believe that, they can choose to go somewhere where their brand of Christianity, if you can call it that, is preached."

Erin scrunched her face, nodding. "I hate to say it quite like that, Jennifer, but you're right. We're branded as progressive Christians and now the parish is beginning to act like it. I appreciate this movement certainly, for myself. But more importantly, I appreciate that this town has a place for Christians who accept that all people are God's children, and all people have worth and dignity."

"Hear, hear," Charlotte said with gusto.

She, Jennifer, and Mike said their goodnights and left.

When the door closed, Erin took Bobbi in her arms.

Bobbi blew out a large breath. "Wow."

"Yeah, wow."

Chapter Twenty-seven

I thought we should talk," Erin said into the phone to Bobbi, who stayed at the clinic for Wednesday night walk-ins, a new service at Ryan Delaney Rural Clinic. "Are you free tomorrow night?"

"Just a minute." Erin heard muffled voices, then Bobbi came back. "Tomorrow night? Yes. I should be clear by seven."

"Thursdays are my days at the mental health practice in town. Why don't I make dinner at your place and you can eat as soon as you get home?"

"You don't have to cook for me, Erin," Bobbi said.

"I like to cook for you. Someone has to take care of you." Erin laughed.

"Ha, ha."

Erin could hear the smile in her voice. "Tomorrow, then. Bye, sweetie."

❧❧❧❧

On Thursday, Bobbi finished up her last patient, a young child with strep throat. She brought her tablet out to the nurses' station and entered her notes.

"Dr. Webster?" One of the nurses handed Bobbi the phone intercom.

"Yes," Bobbi said into the phone.

"Dr. Webster, you have a visitor here. What do

you want me to do with her? Her name is," papers shuffled, "Dr. Stephanie—"

Bobbi broke in, "I'll be right out." Her heart rate skyrocketed. What the hell is she doing here? Bobbi turned to Doris, the nurse at the station. "Doris, will you please dial the police?"

Doris raised wide eyes. "Sure," she said, staring at Bobbi.

"Right now."

Doris punched in the numbers. She handed the phone to Bobbi. "Hi, this is Dr. Webster at Ryan Delaney Clinic. We need an officer to remove a visitor from the premises...Good. Thanks." She handed the phone back to Doris.

"Something I can do, Doctor?" Doris said quietly.

"An ex who was abusive is in the patient waiting area. I want her removed. I have a no-contact order on her in Oregon. Let's keep this calm and quiet, okay?" Bobbi groaned inwardly, feeling put out both by Stephanie's presence and Bobbi's need to breach her own privacy with Doris and perhaps others in the clinic. She didn't want her dirty laundry to be this week's gossip at the Ryan Delaney Clinic.

Doris nodded, her face looking on Bobbi with concern. "I'll go out and see that she's removed." Doris strode confidently down the hall to the waiting room.

Bobbi exhaled slowly. She knew she could do this. Just stay calm.

She finished the medical chart, powered down her tablet, and put it in the locked drawer at her cubby behind the nurses' station, where each of the three fellows had been assigned their own personal space. Then she sat and tried to stay focused, thinking about what may be going on in the waiting room.

Why was Stephanie here? How had she found her? Bobbi racked her brain. Oregon Health Sciences Family Medicine alumni newsletter? Maybe the administers of Ryan Delaney Clinic had posted the news of the incoming rural fellows on the internet. Stephanie, always one for finding what she wanted and going for it. Damn.

Doris stuck her head around the corner into the fellows' small hallway. "Here you are. All taken care of."

Bobbi stood. "What happened?"

"One of the deputies, Rick, came in. I met him, pointed her out to him, and told him of your restraining order. He walked right up to her and led her out of the building. They were outside. I could see her motioning with her hands at him, and she didn't seem happy."

"Right." Bobbi blew out a big breath.

"You okay?" Doris put her hand on Bobbi's forearm.

"I'm fine, Doris. Thank you for helping out. This stays between us, okay?"

"My lips are sealed." Doris made the lip-zipping motion. "By the way, I saw she was driving a red sports car of some kind. Sorry, I'm not up on car models, but it's hard to miss."

"Got it. Thanks, Doris. You're a gem."

Doris turned slowly, taking one last look at Bobbi, then walked away.

Bobbi got her breath under control. Her hands shook and were clammy. She wiped perspiration from her forehead. *She could be waiting for me anywhere. What if she follows me home? Or to Erin's?* Bobbi rubbed her head where she felt a headache coming on. She closed her eyes, still sitting at her desk in her cubby.

How long until I can leave? She wanted to run home and shower before Erin came over. God, if Stephanie shows up while Erin's there…

Finally, Bobbi put on her coat, deciding that Stephanie couldn't possibly know where she lived, could she? She walked through the staff entrance into the cool early evening air. The sun was about to set at six-thirty, since Daylight Saving Time started last week. She could make it home in plenty of time before Erin arrived.

When Bobbi got home, she picked up a few things in the small, sparse living area. She hopped into the shower very quickly and was still towel-drying her hair when someone knocked on the door. Erin's early by five minutes.

She pulled on jeans and a sweatshirt, wrapping the towel around her neck to wipe at her damp hair, then walked through the condo and pulled open the door, ready to hug Erin.

"Hi," Stephanie said. She stood dressed in a blue ski jacket on her small frame, her bleached blond curls teasing her cheeks.

Bobbi's heart ramped into high gear, as she grabbed the door close to her body and blocked the way into her condo. "You need to leave. Now," Bobbi rasped out vehemently.

"That's no way to treat an old…what were we, Bob? Lovers? Girlfriends?" Stephanie smiled slightly.

"The police will arrest you if you don't leave."

"Bob, what is wrong with you? I come in peace. I know we didn't end so well. You were so out of sorts. But it's a new day. We've both moved on. Let me in, it's getting chilly out here."

Bobbi stood her ground. "I told you. Leave now

or I'm calling the cops. I have a restraining order on you. You're violating that order." Bobbi swallowed hard, holding herself together and trying mightily not to panic.

When Stephanie reached out her hand as if to caress Bobbi's cheek, she jerked her head back, putting her off balance, and in a wink, Stephanie shoved the door open and stepped into the apartment. "An order only lasts for the months laid out by the judge. And it's not binding in a new state." Stephanie smiled arrogantly.

Bobbi stepped back. "I'm expecting someone any second. If you don't leave, they will call the police."

"Why are you so antagonistic, darling?" Stephanie wandered nonchalantly past Bobbi to look around the room. "Still not Suzy Homemaker, I see." She picked up a picture of Bobbi's family and looked at it. "How are the folks in Oregon?"

"Put that down."

Stephanie looked up from the photo and dropped it onto the couch.

"What do you want, Steph?"

"Can't I visit my ex? I'm in town for a couple of days and wanted to drop by."

"Right. You're just in the middle of eastern Colorado by sheer luck. Not buying it. I repeat, you need to leave. You and I are over." Bobbi opened the door fully, her heart pounding in her ears.

"I'm not ready to leave yet." Stephanie took a seat on the couch.

Bobbi inhaled.

"Knock, knock." Erin peeked around the open doorway. "Hello?" She came into the room and immediately stopped when she saw Stephanie.

"Aren't you going to introduce me to your new girlfriend?" Stephanie smirked.

Bobbi clenched her fists. "Erin, this is Stephanie."

Erin looked at Bobbi then at Stephanie. "Hello."

"Aren't you the cutest thing? I see Bobbi likes us petite types." She lay back into the couch. "Are there refreshments?"

"Erin came over to cook dinner. You need to leave. Now." Bobbi fisted and unfisted her hands.

"You're quite rude, you know. I can watch you eat."

Bobbi stepped slowly closer to the couch. "You need to leave. I won't say it again. I'll just call the cops."

"Do they have cops here? I met some bumbling idiots at the clinic today. That was also rude, Bob. What in the world has gotten into you? You used to be so compliant. You knew what I wanted, and you did it, or you knew the consequences." Stephanie stood up and into Bobbi's personal space.

Erin, wild-eyed, looked at them each in turn. "Folks, this is getting ridiculous."

Stephanie looked at Erin again. She grinned. "I agree. Let's all sit down and visit."

"Erin, please call 911." Bobbi didn't take her eyes off Stephanie. Her breathing became loud and raspy, her hands clammy. She recognized an anxiety attack about to start. She inhaled deeply and began to count to ten.

Erin pulled out her phone and punched the numbers.

Stephanie leapt at Erin, grabbed her phone, and flung it toward the wall, where it cracked open and fell to the floor in pieces.

"Now, wait a minute," Erin yelled, her face

scrunched in anger.

Bobbi moved out of her way as Erin lunged for Stephanie, gripped her by her jacket front, and shoved and pulled her toward the still-open door. Stephanie, taken off guard, struggled, but was no match for Erin's rage. Erin shoved Stephanie out the door and closed the door before Bobbi could react.

Stephanie screamed outside the door, kicking and pounding it, while Erin pushed the locks closed. Bobbi grabbed her phone and called 911.

"That creep broke my phone. I want to press charges," Erin huffed, her face bright red.

Bobbi breathed to calm herself, then talked to the police, looking at Erin. She closed her phone. "Are you okay?" She took Erin in her arms. "That was amazing."

Erin let out a small sob. "Whew. That was intense. Is she still out there?" Erin looked through the window next to the door.

Bobbi saw Stephanie at her SUV, running her key along the side panel. "That son of a bitch."

Sirens closed in and the sheriff's car pulled up. Stephanie ran to her sports car and tried to close the driver's door, but the deputy kept her from it, then pulled her out of the car.

Bobbi walked out onto the front porch. The other deputy came to her and asked what the problem was. They remembered Stephanie from earlier in the day at the clinic.

Stephanie, being cuffed, yelled, "The little one assaulted me."

"She broke my phone," Erin told the deputy.

Bobbi put in, "I asked her to leave several times, but she wouldn't go. When I asked Erin to phone 911, she grabbed Erin's phone and threw it—"

"So I decided it was time for her to go. I grabbed her and shoved her out the door. I did not harm her." Erin sniffled and wiped her arm across her face.

Bobbi moved closer and hugged her with her left arm, while the deputy wrote down the details. "Do you want to charge her for damage to property?"

"Yes."

By this time, the other deputy had Stephanie cuffed and led her to the squad car, while she still screamed obscenities and struggled against him. Bobbi and Erin stood on the porch until the car drove away.

Deputy Rick said to Bobbi, "You need to get a restraining order in Colorado. The one in Oregon has expired, we found out earlier today. And, it doesn't apply across states."

Bobbi looked at Erin, then said to the officer, "Thanks. I'll do that as soon as possible. I need to make an appointment with the judge, right?"

"Yes," he said. "Well, we're done here, I think. You may need to make a formal statement at the courthouse later this week about today's trouble. If you need anything more, just call." He handed Bobbi his card and left.

Erin and Bobbi walked back into the condo.

Erin said, "You go relax. I have the stuff to cook with, while you rest." Erin kissed Bobbi lightly and shoved her gently toward the bedroom, then turned to her kitchen duties.

Bobbi went into her bedroom to finish what Stephanie had interrupted. Her whole body trembled. Sitting on the bed, she practiced her grounding routine until she felt calm enough to help Erin with the cooking.

Later, while they ate, Erin asked about Stephanie and Bobbi's relationship.

"I'm very ashamed." Bobbi pushed her food around her plate.

"Why ever for?" Erin stopped eating and looked on Bobbi with concern.

"When Steph and I lived together those three months, she shoved me around like I was a child. I was overwhelmed and really frightened of her. She could come at me with such ferocity."

"Like she did with me tonight, grabbing and breaking my phone?"

Bobbi nodded, tears brimming in her eyes. "I never could confront her like you did tonight. I tried, but I didn't have the courage, or something. She always threatened to up the ante. She would throw my things in the trash. One day I came home to all my dresser drawers emptied at the front of the apartment building. Humiliating." Bobbi wiped her eyes with her napkin. "Sorry, I'm blubbering about this." Bobbi gave Erin a wan smile.

"Come here, sweetie." Erin took Bobbi's hand and led her to the small couch. "I don't need to tell you what this is all about. You know the score with abusive relationships, right? How the perpetrator makes the victim feel it's her fault, makes the violence about some picayune thing she's done? You know that you suffer from trauma, and that your thinking still has to catch up with your body's automatic reactions to her."

Bobbi nodded, sighing. "Yeah." She looked intensely at Erin. "I can't seem to get away from the feelings of being a total coward. She's only five feet high, but she had me under her thumb the entire three months. I couldn't sneeze without her consent. Why couldn't I've stood up to her?" Bobbi blew out a big breath, shaking her head.

"I take it that's a rhetorical question?" Erin asked.

Bobbi nodded, and said, "I know, I know. I hated myself with her."

Erin engulfed Bobbi with her small arms. Bobbi let herself feel Erin's loving hands stroking her back tenderly. It felt so good, so comforting.

Bobbi laughed.

"What?" Erin pulled back and asked.

"I thought maybe I would ask you to my bedroom tonight. Celebrate a little after the parish meeting." Bobbi chuckled and looked down at Erin's hands holding hers. She smiled ruefully. "I'm not feeling very amorous. Sorry." Bobbi hugged Erin tightly.

"Oh, sweetie. I didn't come over tonight expecting anything but a warm cuddle and some food." Erin kissed her.

Bobbi felt safe in Erin's arms, protected by her tenderness, in a way no other woman had made her feel. She deepened the kiss. Erin moaned. Bobbi and Erin's tongues played, making Bobbi's whole body warm up.

Erin pulled back and raised her brows. "Not amorous, huh?" They both laughed.

"I can't help it. You turn me on something fierce."

"Are you rethinking your previous statement?" Erin's eyes twinkled with mischief.

Bobbi grinned widely, then sobered. "I want our first time to be special, Erin. I want us to be together with love, not just—excuse the phrase—a lust-filled fuck-fest."

At those words, Erin giggled. "I see." Erin snuggled into Bobbi's arms. "I'm with you." She pulled back. "Are you all right? Have you gotten Stephanie's visit out of your system for tonight? You know, I will go to the court with you to ask for a restraining order. I've been there a few times with one parishioner for the same issue."

"Geez, sorry to hear that," Bobbi said. "You don't have to come with me. You have enough on your plate with the fall-out from Tuesday's meeting. I'll ask for a couple of hours off on Friday to go."

"Do you have an attorney?"

"No. I didn't have one in Oregon. Maybe it would help."

Erin stood up and found a professional card in her purse. "Here, a parishioner of mine. Good guy." She scribbled a name and handed it to Bobbi. "He's on the web."

Bobbi kissed Erin. "Thanks, munchkin." It felt good to infuse a little humor into the aftermath of Stephanie's presence.

Erin gaped at her. "Hey. No name calling." They kissed again then cleaned up after dinner. Bobbi grasped Erin closely as they said their good night.

Chapter Twenty-eight

Easter day approached, but first, Erin had to get through several services during Holy Week, the entire week prior to Easter that commemorated Jesus's last week on earth. She and Julia traded off churches for two services. Julia led the Thursday service and Erin led Good Friday. Attendance was spotty, as the weather continued to be cooler than normal for mid-April. A few scattered tulips and hyacinths around the churchyard had the gall to come up with snow still clinging to their green leaves, but nothing had bloomed yet.

That week, Bobbi worked every daytime shift and four nights. Spring break for the local schools did not affect her but did several of her colleagues. She and Gen both took extra nights on call for staff who had children, while Erin busied herself with church. Consequently, Erin and Bobbi saw little of each other the whole week.

On Easter Sunday, Erin and Julia hosted a joint Lutheran-Episcopal service at Julia's church, which seated several hundred people. They expected perhaps two hundred.

Bobbi wrapped up her Saturday night on-call by admitting a woman to the hospital with gall bladder disease. She now was being prepped for surgery, so there was nothing more for Bobbi to do. On a whim, she decided to go to Erin's ten a.m. service to see what

Easter was all about. Finding parking difficult, she finally spotted an opening a couple of blocks away in a residential area. She entered the church, still dressed in khakis and a cotton pullover sweater over a blue button-down shirt.

The deputy had escorted Stephanie out of town, she heard on Friday. So, feeling like she'd dodged yet another Stephanie moment, she relaxed in her pew, blinking to keep her eyes open. Charlotte Stephens waved at her from a pew across the aisle toward the front. Mike, Jennifer, and Clarice all sat together with several others who looked to be their families, toward the middle of the church. Even Helen sat primly toward the front, next to a man with very little white hair ringing his crown like a halo. Bobbi reckoned that Helen's faith perhaps took precedence over her dislike of Erin's "lifestyle." People who used that word about gay, lesbian, bi, and trans people always made Bobbi laugh. As if getting groceries and watching TV was a lifestyle any different from a hetero one.

Suddenly organ music swelled and incense floated by, leading in a procession of robed choir members and ministers. Erin and Julia took up the rear. When they reached the front of the church, the hymn ended and chanting began. Bobbi let herself be carried away in the calming rhythms.

Immediately after the chanting ended, Bobbi was astounded to see Walter sneak into one of the pews toward the back, with an older woman, probably his wife. Both were dressed in their best clothes. The woman's gray hair had been coiffed and lay inertly on her head. Looks like Mike had been right about Walter. While Walter, in principle, disagreed with gay clergy, he didn't let that interfere with his attendance on Easter. Bobbi smiled to herself to see his stern face some pews behind her.

As the service continued, Bobbi then felt the elation of the congregation rise, with special music from horns, a rousing anthem by the choir, and even singing from a children's group, who made Bobbi smile through her tiredness. Music took up most of the program for the morning, Erin's sermon was thankfully short, but the communion took much longer than Bobbi's first experience, due to the long line of people queuing in the aisles. Bobbi joined them when her pew was called forward. She watched what people did at the altar rail and copied them when a robed minister, neither Erin nor Julia, gave her bread and another gave her wine. Surprising to her, the wine was real.

After the service, Erin looked busy talking with parishioners. Kids ran around the churchyard, some in little suits with ties, others in jeans and sweaters. She noted she wasn't the only person not dressed up. Bobbi waited inconspicuously at the end of the nave, off to the side of the queue of folks through the door. Erin and Julia greeted some with hugs, others with handshakes.

Finally, the queue dwindled and Erin and Julia strode past her down the aisle toward the front of the church.

"Hello, Mother Erin," Bobbi whispered loudly as she passed without noticing her.

Erin turned. "Oh." She stepped into the pew and hugged Bobbi fiercely. "I am so glad to see you."

"Me, too. It's been a long week for both of us." Bobbi drew back. "You look exhausted."

"Ditto, Doc." Erin grinned and stroked her cheek gently. "Let me get out of this getup and we can walk down to the vicarage."

Later, as they gathered on the couch with snacks, snuggling into each other, Erin said, "We have to watch *Mary Poppins.*"

Bobbi leaned back, her mouth agape. "*Mary Poppins?* You're kidding."

"No way. I've had a huge crush on Julie Andrews since I first saw this movie on TV when I was a kid. It's how I knew I was gay. It's my post-Easter gift every year for getting through hell week." Erin sat erectly, looking proud.

Bobbi sniggered. "I guess I'll survive Dick van Dyke dancing with cartoon penguins."

Erin turned on the movie from her online film stash, and the first strains of the overture played against an image of Julie Andrews drifting down on an opened umbrella. She grabbed a pillow and stuffed it between her and Bobbi. "You don't have to watch it if you don't want to," she said in a huff, while grinning.

Bobbi smirked, snagged the pillow, and threw it on the floor, then snuggled against Erin. When Erin began to sing along with "Just a Spoonful of Sugar," Bobbi knew it was useless to protest, so she shook her head and let Erin have her movie, falling in love a little more as Erin's adorable, thin soprano belted out each successive song.

Bobbi ate some grapes, and tried to focus on the movie's light banter, but felt her eyes lowering precipitously. Finally, she gave in to her exhaustion.

Erin shook her. "Hey. Time for dinner, Dr. Narcolepsy."

Bobbi roused herself. The day had waned. "What time...?"

"Four. The lamb should be done in a little while."

Bobbi shrugged off the afghan lying across her legs. "Wow, sorry. I seem to fall asleep around here."

"Am I that boring?" Erin stood over the couch with her legs spread and her arms akimbo.

Bobbi, struck by her cute pose, took hold of her waist and pulled her down to the couch. Erin shrieked, as Bobbi tickled her sides.

"Stop." Erin giggled and screamed.

They tussled playfully and fell onto the carpet. Bobbi sat up, straddling Erin, and gently pinned her arms above her head. She panted, leaning in for a kiss. Erin wriggled under her, broke one arm free, and began to tickle Bobbi in return. Laughing and screaming, they wrestled to be on top. *She's stronger than she looks*, Bobbi thought.

Finally, both breathing hard and cackling, Bobbi rolled off Erin and lay down beside her on the floor. She took her in her arms and kissed her deeply. Erin reciprocated by pushing her warm tongue between Bobbi's lips. Bobbi moaned. She ran her hand down Erin's front, finding warmth along her shirt and cardigan. Bobbi's heart raced with the sensations of softness, warmth, and growing desire, and with the tenderness Erin produced in her.

Bobbi looked down at Erin's face, holding her in her left arm and using her right hand to trace her pert nose and smooth skin along her cheeks and jaw. "You are amazing. Every time I'm with you, I find something more that draws me to you. Your bravery. Your integrity as a priest." She touched Erin's eyes gently. "You make me want you so much."

Erin stroked Bobbi's hair. "I love your curls right there." She tugged at the curls on Bobbi's nape.

Bobbi felt the warmth on her cheeks. Bobbi kissed

her deeply, gently, then more insistently, pushing open her mouth and exploring with her tongue. Erin hummed. Bobbi felt her core heating up. Her clitoris throbbed and she felt the hot wetness between her legs.

They kissed for some time. Then Bobbi parted Erin's cardigan and tugged her shirt out of her yoga pants, stroking her abdomen in small circles. Then higher, caressing her breasts over the smooth fiber of her bra. Erin sat up and took off her sweater and shirt. Bobbi reached behind her and unhooked the bra. Erin looked into Bobbi's eyes as the bra slid down her arms and her breasts, with small pink nipples, emerged.

Bobbi nearly cried out with happiness when she palmed one breast, testing its heft. "So soft. Beautiful." Bobbi leaned in and kissed it, then nipped it lightly. Erin bent her torso up to Bobbi's mouth. Bobbi warmed even more, felt herself wanting a slow journey all over Erin's body. Her heart beat with deep wanting. Not lust, but something much truer and more loving, and sensitive to Erin's needs and wishes.

"I'll give you twenty years to stop that." Erin leaned her head back, her face a mask of desire.

Bobbi shifted Erin down to the carpet. Erin put both hands on Bobbi's chest. "Wait."

Bobbi struggled up out of her fog. "What?"

Erin whispered, "Let's go somewhere more comfortable."

Bobbi sat up. "Is this what you want? Don't push it. I can wait if we need to." Bobbi hoped like hell Erin didn't say no.

"Yes. Oh God, yes." Erin pecked Bobbi on the mouth, stood up, and pulled Bobbi up. She led her into the bedroom.

Bobbi stood in the doorway of Erin's bedroom

and smiled at the mix of Chicago Cubs paraphernalia and Jesus and Moses puppets, in the turquoise room. All was neat and tidy, and the room smelled of Erin's citrusy shampoo.

Erin tossed the bedspread off to the floor and drew back the cover and sheets.

Bobbi grabbed her waist and took her in her arms. As they kissed, Bobbi's breathing ramped up in excitement.

Erin unbuttoned Bobbi's shirt. "You're wearing too much between me and thee."

Bobbi, in turn, pulled at the elastic of Erin's lycra pants, gently and slowly lowering them, savoring the moment. She was about to make love to this beautiful woman. Her heart played a rhythm of love and compassion, as she tried to convey those feelings with the gentle movement of her hands on Erin's clothes.

Finally, they both rested onto the bed, fully nude. Taking a moment, Bobbi let her eyes caress, along with her hand, the beauty she saw before her. "Wow. You're amazing." She kissed Erin's cheek, her neck, down to her breasts, taking them in with lips and teeth and tongue. Sucking, oh so lightly, on her nipples, producing purrs of pleasure in Erin's chest. Bobbi smiled at the sound.

Erin pressed Bobbi into her breast, while sifting her fingers through the short strands of her hair. Bobbi kissed Erin's torso, her abdomen. She teased her navel with short licks, making Erin emit low chuckles.

Erin brought Bobbi up to her lips and kissed her passionately. "We really are together. I can't think of a better way to spend Easter Day celebrating life."

Bobbi leaned on her right elbow and stroked Erin's cheek. "Is this a resurrection for you? It feels like one for me." Bobbi hesitated, while continuing to caress Erin's breasts softly. "You feel so right in my arms. When I'm not with you, I feel lost somehow. I can't explain it."

Erin's eyes widened. "Now I know that it must be Easter. You've just given me light and love. I hope you can tell."

Bobbi's heart swelled. She hugged Erin close while stroking her sides and hips. She gripped Erin's backside and caressed the small mounds of flesh.

They fell together in a rain of kisses and strokes and murmurs of pleasure, tenderness, and gentleness. Bobbi thought she would stay in this bliss forever. Then they both breathed hard and fast, and the lovemaking took on a more urgent pace.

Bobbi found Erin's inner thighs, kissed them languidly until she reached Erin's very wet labia. She circled her vaginal opening, creating heat within her own core. Her whole body throbbed. Erin's yoni turned red as Bobbi stroked along its length.

"Yes, right there."

Bobbi took her time with unhurried, feather-light touches all along the inner labia, as Erin became saturated. She wanted to convey all she felt by loving Erin's body.

Erin panted. "Don't tease me."

Circling the clitoris, then stroking harder, Bobbi watched Erin buck with energy. A pink flush rose on Erin's body and her muscles tightened. Bobbi's own arousal heightened and screamed for release. Her heart beat in her ears. Erin looked so beautiful in the throes of orgasm, writhing, her mouth open to the world, drinking in bliss.

When Erin calmed, Bobbi snuggled into her arms. Erin stroked Bobbi's small breasts and wended her way south with kisses. Anticipation sent Bobbi into spasms of delight. She was so ready when Erin's mouth, warm and wet, found her clitoris. Bobbi fell back onto the bed with the tingles of excitement focused between her legs. Her orgasm came quickly. She stiffened. "Yes, Erin. Erin."

They lay together in the late afternoon, watching the sun cross the floor in stripes from the window blind. They caressed and kissed on the no-hurry plan. Bobbi felt sated, happier than she had in months, with Erin in her arms. Small Erin. Beautiful Erin.

"I can't believe you're in my arms." Bobbi kissed her. "You bowl me over."

"Your gentleness. Wow." Erin held Bobbi's face in both hands. "I thought I would die of anticipation," she joked.

"I'm glad you didn't."

Erin snuggled into Bobbi's neck, then gave her a questioning look. "Do we need to talk about where this is going? You and me."

Bobbi dreaded these kinds of questions. She had some lingering uneasiness about her short-term stay at Valley View. She'd be off, hopefully to Oregon, in another twenty months. She pondered Erin, marveling at her in her arms. Her silky skin, her petite arms and legs. Her lovely breasts, abdomen, the pink in her cheeks. "I don't know about you and me in the long run." She felt Erin stiffen in her arms. "We've established that this is no fling. You and I have clicked somewhere more important in our lives. A place that makes me happy and content to be around you. To make love to you. We've just begun our relationship on another level. I think we have to go into the future and see where this relationship leads us. I know I want to be with you."

"And I with you. I think I'm falling for you, Doctor Bossy Pants."

Bobbi squeezed Erin closer to her. "God."

"Are you okay? I didn't mean to scare you." Erin sat up.

"No, no. I didn't mean it like...I'm good with that. I love that you may be falling for me. I really like you lots, too, if you haven't picked that up by now, Elf."

"Oh." Erin leaped up from the bed. "Lamb." She grabbed a long T-shirt from the bathroom.

Bobbi, startled by Erin's abrupt departure, immediately got up and pulled on her clothes while Erin clanged pots in the kitchen.

"Whew. The lamb is just fine." Erin shut the oven door. "But it *is* done." She turned around.

Bobbi exhaled in relief. "I thought the house was on fire the way you sped out of the bedroom."

Erin flipped a dishtowel at her. "You made me forget the dinner."

The towel hit Bobbi on the arm and she gripped it, then tugged it away from Erin and ran at her with it. Erin squealed and ran into the living area, crouching behind a chair. Laughter rent the air as Bobbi chased her around the room. When she caught her, they hugged and giggled like children.

Bobbi kissed her. "I got you, Elf."

The doorbell rang.

With wide eyes, Erin whispered, "Oh my God." She called out, "Just a minute." Then she sprinted into the bedroom.

Bobbi played it cool, sitting on the couch with the Sunday paper, when Erin came out, looking dressed, if not exactly put together. She had on the yoga pants and a black T-shirt with a cross in the upper corner. But her hair stuck up in the back; her makeup had smeared.

Bobbi stifled a chuckle.

When Erin answered the door, Charlotte Stephens stood, still in her fancy Easter dress and matching hat, holding a covered pie plate. "Happy Easter, lady priest." She raised the plate.

"Come in. Come in. Happy Easter to you, Charlotte!" Erin's voice sounded unnaturally high.

Charlotte took two steps into the room and glanced at Bobbi with meaning. Bobbi nodded. "Mrs. Stephens. How are you?" She stood.

"Not as good as the two of you look," she quipped. She winked at Bobbi.

Erin's face turned dark red.

"I won't stay. I baked my usual coconut pie for Easter. I made an extra one that I thought you might like. My family went out for Easter brunch in Denver and we just got back, so sorry if you've already eaten. I smell something wonderful."

Erin inhaled. Bobbi saw her struggle for composure. "No, we were just about to get dinner on the table, so the pie will go great. Thanks so much, Charlotte." Erin took the pie, set it on the small foyer table, and hugged Charlotte.

"Do you eat pie, Doctor? You look pretty skinny to me."

"Oh, yes. In fact, I love cream pies. Thank you, Mrs. Stephens."

"I think you can call me Charlotte, now that you're intimately acquainted with our lady priest." Charlotte smiled wickedly. "You might want to comb your hair, dear." Charlotte sniggered while brushing her hand through the back of Erin's messy hair.

Like teens who'd been caught making out, Erin and Bobbi could only stand awkwardly and stifle their giggles.

"Okay." Charlotte broke the spell. "I'm off. Good to see you both. And have a fine evening." She strode to the door, Erin opened it, and she marched out.

Bobbi and Erin looked at each other and broke out into gales of laughter, holding their sides, bent over.

Chapter Twenty-nine

Erin called Bobbi the next day around noon, hoping not to interrupt patient care. She answered on the first ring.

"What are you eating, Doctor?"

"Nothing."

"I miss you. You left before I woke this morning. I didn't get my morning kiss."

Erin heard rustling. Bobbi whispered, "I'm going to my cubby where there's some privacy." She came back. "I didn't know we had a morning kiss. Is that a thing?"

"Certainly. Haven't you heard of the famous South Side Morning Buss? All Chicagoans know it like they know the L routes."

"I see. Buss, like in kiss, not public conveyance, right? I must be an ignorant Oregonian. I'm sorry if I exceeded the boundaries of polite Chicago society," Bobbi teased.

Erin laughed. "How's your day and why aren't you eating?"

"My day is slow. No one does bad things to their bodies on Easter, except maybe eat the ears off chocolate bunnies, which is not exactly a medical crisis." She paused. Erin detected something else going on. "I'm not eating because..."

"Yes."

"I don't want to tell you this."

Erin quietly said, "I'm listening."

Bobbi huffed. "When I got home to change for work this morning, a small gift was waiting for me."

"What do you mean?"

"My front door had been beaten. Marks and dents all over it."

Erin's pulse raced. "Bobbi. Who do you think it was? Did you call the sheriff?"

"No. I had to rush to get to the clinic. I'll call them this evening."

"Is it Stephanie?" Erin named her nemesis.

"Don't jump to conclusions, honey. I don't know who it is. I'm sure the sheriff's staff will see if the neighbors saw or heard anything."

"You sound tired, sweetie." Erin weighed her next statement. "Listen, you know I've taken vacation this week. Can I come over and fix dinner? I don't want you to be alone right now...Well, and I want to be there. I want to be near you."

"Geez, you don't have to do that. It's your time off. Do something for yourself. You don't want to be involved in my weird junk this week."

Erin heard the vulnerability under the bravado.

"Not only that, I thought you were going to Chicago to be with family and friends?"

"I am, but not until Thursday. I'm staying in Chicago this weekend, since I'm not serving at church on low Sunday."

"Low Sunday?"

"You know, the Sunday after Easter when no one comes to church."

"Oh. Got it. Sometimes I need a dictionary with all the church terms you use." Bobbi's voice lifted a little from the tired rasp.

Erin let out a low chuckle. "Okay, so I'm coming over tonight. I'm packing an overnight bag. I'm cooking you some dinner. So...there."

"Okay, lady priest. Actually, I'll be very happy to see you. But remember what I said. Doctor's orders. Get some relaxation time."

"Yes, ma'am," Erin said, laughing. "See you later."

⊱⊰⊱⊰⊱

Erin shivered when she saw the door to Bobbi's condo from her car. It looked as if it had been rammed with something large and sharp. Dents and scrapes covered the gray metal. One hole, about four inches in diameter, marred the right side, next to the knob, as if someone had tried to gain entrance.

Bobbi pulled up just then and Erin exited her car with a grocery bag. "Do you have any spices at all?" She held up the bag to indicate the food that needed some ingredients.

Bobbi hugged her closely. "Hi to you, too. And yes, smart aleck, I have spices. I have herbs. I have sugar and flour and milk and beer and..."

Erin stuck her tongue out.

"What's that for?"

"For being cheeky." Erin took Bobbi's hand to walk to the door.

Bobbi took the grocery bag. "What's for dinner, Elf?"

"We're not back to the elf-calling are we? And it's lamb stew using yesterday's leftovers. But I need some bouillon. Do you have that?"

"Yes." Bobbi opened the door. "I need to get you

a key."

"Oh?" Erin raised her brows.

Bobbi shrugged. "Let's get this party going." She stepped into the room, put down the bag, then grabbed Erin around the waist and kissed her deeply.

Erin felt her pulse rise as she relaxed her body into Bobbi's arms. "You're such a good kisser. I'm so lucky to have a girlfriend like you." Erin brushed her hand over Bobbi's jaw. "Not bad to look at. Smart. Compassionate. But a bit of a smart aleck."

"Moi?" Bobbi feigned shock. She reached to shut the door.

Erin stood next to her, gazing at the damage, and shook her head. "I'm a little worried for you." One arm slipped around Bobbi's waist. "You're calling the sheriff, right?" Erin looked up into Bobbi's eyes, which had lost some of their spark.

"Let me take a quick shower and then I'll call." Bobbi slumped her shoulders.

Amidst the anxiety floating in the room, Erin busied herself by cutting vegetables and lamb into cubes. As she threw everything into the stew pot, Bobbi strode into the kitchen, rubbing a towel on her head, her complexion gray.

Erin looked on her with tenderness, cupping her jaw. "Did you ever eat today?"

Bobbi shook her head. Then she raised her hands, "Don't get high and mighty on me."

"Why don't you go lie down? Dinner will be ready in about an hour."

"I called the sheriff's office. They'll be here any time now." Bobbi blew out her cheeks.

Erin nodded. "Go on, sit down." She pushed her lightly in the middle of her back.

In ten minutes, a knock came. Erin came out of the kitchen, wiping her hands on a towel. Bobbi sighed and opened the door. Deputy Rick Santana stood with another deputy, Rosa Martin.

Bobbi let them look at the damage to the door. "I don't care about the damn door, but the fact that someone tried to gain entry into my home while I was gone has me really bugged." She raked her hand through her head.

Erin stood next to Bobbi. They all sat in the living area and Rick wrote Bobbi's statement of the details in his small notebook.

"I reported to you last Friday that Dr. Stewart was escorted out of town. We've not spotted her little car since. We wouldn't have let it go by, that's for sure." He flipped through pages in his small notebook. "I see we came out to the clinic two weeks ago, and you pressed assault charges against a Wesley Myers. He just got out of county lockup."

Her heart in her throat, Erin watched Bobbi closely for her reaction.

"I figured as much," Bobbi said. She shifted on the sofa.

"We'll see what the neighbors say. Maybe someone caught him in the act. Although we didn't get any reports from this area of town last night." He closed his notebook and stuffed it in his shirt pocket. "Thanks, Dr. Webster." He tipped his hat to Erin. "Reverend." The deputies left in the squad car, trolling slowly down the street.

"Come on, let's get you something to eat before you fall on your ass." Erin grabbed Bobbi's hand and led her to the table.

Erin dug into her bowl of stew and bit into a

biscuit she'd made with a mix. Bobbi'd hardly touched her food.

Staring down at the table, Bobbi suddenly looked up to Erin. Her blue eyes danced with energy. "I think Wes Myers has a drug problem," she blurted out.

Erin set her fork on the plate, her eyes wide. "What?"

"Wes. He's skittish; I noticed it that Sunday night at the clinic. Did you see how skinny he is? At the tavern. And wan, even bordering on jaundiced, like he might have liver disease."

"Wow."

"I'm going to tell the deputy." She jogged into the living area, and got her phone off the foyer table.

Erin caught snatches of the conversation as she went into the kitchen to put Bobbi's plate into the oven to keep warm. When she got back to the dining table, Bobbi put her arms around her waist and swung her around. "Deputy Rick liked that theory. They're getting a search warrant from the judge to check out his house and car. Maybe we'll get him some help."

"I'm so impressed that you figured this out."

"Well, let's not count the chickens. No eggs have hatched yet."

Erin smiled to see her much more relaxed. "We'll see." Her shoulders dropped from the release of tension and she snuggled into Bobbi's arms. "You need to eat now."

"I'm as hungry as a bear," Bobbi said. "Bring it on, Elf."

Erin playfully nudged Bobbi's arm. "Will you stop with the elf thing? You may give me a complex. And you know what happens then?"

"What, cutie?" Bobbi kissed her neck.

"Stop it." Erin batted at Bobbi's head lightly. She crossed her arms on her chest and produced a tough-guy accent. "If ya mess wid us Sout Siders we'll have ta sic da Irish Mafia on ya. Ya know, Bugsy Moran and his bunch?"

Bobbi picked her up and kissed her deeply. "I'll take on the Irish any time, Elf."

Erin hollered. Bobbi replaced her feet on the floor. They hugged tenderly. "You're staying, right?" Bobbi whispered.

"Oh, yes." Erin purred into Bobbi's ear.

Thirty

When Bobbi arrived at the clinic on Tuesday morning, Yancy was just sprinting up to the staff door. Then, Gen's office door stayed closed most of the morning, even after Yancy left an hour later. Careful of Dr. Lambert's privacy, Bobbi didn't mention Gen's closed door during the morning with her nurse Doris, as, together, they moved patients into exam rooms and through assessments and treatments. At noon, Bobbi stood at the counter, entering information into her tablet. Gen walked up to the counter, her carefully coiffed hair in place, with her usual energy, and talked with Sheila, her nurse. When she left out the staff door, Bobbi knew something had happened. She'd never seen Gen take time off without scheduled vacation, and she'd not been ill since Bobbi started at the clinic in January.

❧❧❧❧

"I'm so sorry," Erin said.

Yancy hung her head, but Erin could see her eyes were teary. "Gen's making tea. Would you like some?" Yancy pointed toward the kitchen end of the great room.

They all sat quietly for a while at the dining table, sipping their tea.

Gen began the conversation. "I'm a little shocked

at my reaction, more than anything else." She wiped tears from her cheeks. "I'm really shaken up by this news." She looked intensely at Yancy, then at Erin.

Erin waited to let them talk about their feelings.

Yancy stroked Gen's back, both of them looking sorrowful. Erin could not feel exactly what they felt, but she knew this kind of loss—a special kind of grief focused on the loss of a dream—many times was as difficult as a physical death.

Gen continued through her sniffles, "I thought we might have some problems conceiving through artificial insemination, but I hadn't anticipated that I wouldn't be able to conceive at all. I'm so disappointed." She wept into Yancy's shoulder.

After Gen's crying had subsided, Erin asked, "Yancy, how are you doing?"

Yancy looked at her with red eyes. "I don't know. I'm still in shock, I think. You know I'm turning forty-two this summer. My biological clock slowed its ticking dramatically this year, if you know what I mean, so I'm not a good candidate, either."

Gen smiled wanly and swept an errant tress off Yancy's cheek.

"Yes, I see. Gen's and your issues are different but lead to a similar outcome. I'm so sorry. You were ready to be moms, weren't you?"

Both Gen and Yancy nodded.

"I know I was, and Yancy had come around, once I convinced her she'd be a great parent. She's so patient with kids." Gen looked tenderly at Yancy, who smiled and kissed her cheek.

Erin watched their display of affection, thinking what a supportive couple they were for each other, even in their vast difference in styles and personality.

"I'd suggest you two take some time to grieve before considering other options. I know you want to move on, but your sorrow is real and should be treated with care."

"Yes, I agree," Gen said. "This one," she nudged Yancy, "may have a harder time with waiting than me."

"Oh, in what way?" Erin directed her question to Yancy.

Yancy sighed deeply. "I'm the one who likes to run from feelings. I don't like when I feel out of control. And I like to get things settled. Get the problems fixed. In fact, before I met Gen, I was in bad shape because of my inability to grieve losses I'd had in my twenties and then again in my thirties. I lost close people. My brother. My dad. My significant other. I entered therapy just as I met Gen. I don't think we'd be together if I hadn't gotten my shit together. I'm not good with long processes, like grieving."

"How were you going to handle nine months of me incubating a baby, darling?"

Yancy's mouth gaped. "Hey." She nudged Gen back. "I would've coped...mostly."

Erin smiled at their banter, seeing it as a good sign they were working through their news. "What can I do?"

"You can pray with us," Gen said.

Erin nodded. She gathered their hands in hers, bent over them, and prayed for their healing from their shock and grief.

While driving home, Erin prayed for Gen and Yancy silently. Their plight had touched her. Listening to their grief had awakened some thoughts about her own biological clock, tick-ticking away. Gen and Yancy, crying about unborn children, made her wonder about her own stash of DNA material resting quietly and each month coming out of hiding, pushing one small ovum into the world, only to be met with silence. Yes, she wanted children too. She'd not, up until this moment, felt her chance to be somebody's mom getting smaller by the moment. At thirty-four, she had time, but not endless amounts of it. A shocking thought. For the first time, she wondered whether Bobbi wanted children.

Wow. And that thought startled her. Don't rush this, she told herself. Bobbi and she just had entered a new phase of their relationship. She felt so good around her. Bobbi met her needs for brightness, tenderness, integrity, and in a very lovely package. Their banter kept her grinning, made their time together fun, but did not exclude deeper conversation. Bobbi also had been stepping deeper into her own spirituality, attending the Beer and Bible group, and showing up to see what church was all about a couple times. She suspected Bobbi would label herself an agnostic. One who questions God's presence. Erin could deal with Bobbi's nascent spiritual journey.

Chapter Thirty-one

The clinic's quietness calmed Bobbi after a night of on call. No one had yet arrived to start the day and she had the staff lounge to herself. She pushed the filter full of coffee into the machine and turned it on, smelling the wonderful promise of caffeine in the air as it poured into the carafe. Waiting for the machine to finish, she grabbed clean cups from the break room dishwasher, stacked them in their places on the cupboard shelf, and left one out next to the coffee maker for her own use.

Rubbing her tired eyes, she hoped the caffeine would energize her sleep-deprived brain. Late spring, and the farmers and ranchers had begun working outside more. During the early evening, she had doctored more than one minor agricultural accident: a deeply embedded splinter, an ankle sprain, a laceration caused by barbed wire. Then during the night, two children arrived from the same family with suspected strep throat. The cultures would be back today, but she had started preventive antibiotics.

Finally, at three or thereabouts, a pregnant woman called. Bobbi called the obstetrician, only to find out that she was on vacation. The woman had not entered full-on labor yet, so Bobbi remained on alert for another call from BCH. She had no patients this morning, thankfully, so decided to get some rest on the couch in the lounge, until sunlight pouring through the window into her eyes woke her at six this morning.

Feeling peckish, Bobbi inserted money in the snack machine, picking the least sugary thing she could find. Just as she unwrapped the package of trail mix, behind her, Gen said, "I see your nutritional intake is as balanced as usual."

Bobbi whipped around, clutching her chest. "Crap. I didn't hear you come in, Dr. Lambert."

Gen smiled. "Sorry. I'm a little early. You may have noticed I snuck out of the clinic early yesterday, so I've got tons of paperwork sitting on my desk and my first patient at nine."

Bobbi handed her the cup she held. "You may want this, then."

"Thanks." Gen cupped her hands around the white porcelain. "Smells great. What are you doing here at the crack of the day?"

"Ms. Stephens in labor at BCH, with Dr. Lawton-Mills on vacation this week, so I stepped in last night to admit her. No problems when I left at four-thirty. Dilating well and on schedule. BP staying low. Baby's heart rate steady and strong." Bobbi reached into her mind. "I think it's her third child...Yeah. Things should move along well."

Gen flinched, turned pale, and mumbled, "Thanks for the coffee." She left the break room.

Feeling flummoxed at Gen's quick departure, Bobbi put the pieces together. As soon as she'd mentioned the Stephens woman's labor, Gen reacted. Yesterday's closed door, Yancy's arrival, and Gen's early departure. She'd heard from their obstetrician, probably. Bobbi shook her head. While she didn't know exactly what was up with Gen and Yancy, it had to be something about their attempt to become pregnant.

Artificial Insemination, or AI, could be dodgy at best, so if Gen had any medical issues, she and Yancy would not be able to conceive naturally. Bobbi pursed her lips and sighed. She felt sorry for them. How would she feel? Did she even want kids? She liked her nieces fine enough, but never thought she'd have the time in her career to become pregnant, let alone be a mother. Maybe, if she found the right person who would be the other parent, it could work out. Did Erin want children? Bobbi stopped in her tracks. Wow, where did that thought come from?

The phone buzzed, interrupting Bobbi's mental processes. It was the hospital. After answering and getting the latest on Ms. Stephens, she poured the coffee out in the sink, grabbed her backpack, and left the clinic for BCH.

❧❧❧❧

When she finally arrived at her condo at midday, Bobbi wearily stripped off her scrubs and hit the shower. Nothing felt as good as the hot water sluicing away stiffness and tiredness. She laid her head back against the tiles. The front doorbell rang.

Who in the hell? Bobbi yelled out she would be there shortly, while she raced to pull her clothes on over her still wet skin.

She looked out the peephole. It was Wes Myers in camo pants and a black T-shirt. She took a deep breath. Should she call the sheriff? She grabbed her phone off the foyer table, her hand trembling slightly while she put it in her pants pocket. Swallowing air into her lungs, she braced herself and opened the metal door.

She stared at Wes.

He smirked, two front teeth missing. "Well, ain't you going to invite me in, Doc?"

"What do you want?" Bobbi glared at him from the middle of the open doorway, bracing her core and placing her feet wide to block his entrance.

"Nothing. Just a friendly visit. Since you been at me, I've been in jail twice. That wasn't very nice. I didn't like that." His beady eyes bored into her.

His pupils were dilated, his color a light grey, and he sweated in the cool spring air. She was sure he was high on something.

Bobbi closed the door behind her and stepped onto the porch, wishing she'd taken the time to put on shoes. She knew the guy in the duplex next door was probably out for the day, but Wes wouldn't assault her in broad daylight, would he?

She watched him closely. His face was waxy, his hands shaking. Definitely on something.

In a flash, he reached into his pocket, whipped out a pocketknife, and stuck it into her belly. "That's for messing with me, you dyke bitch." He grimaced, then laughed, as he pulled the knife out and ran for his truck.

She looked up at him fleeing, as she slid down onto the porch. The pain in her stomach shocked her, but not as much as the blood oozing out onto the concrete porch.

Wes fled in a rusty red pickup truck, the tires screeching.

Bobbi told herself to remain calm. She pressed her hand onto the wound spreading sticky, warm blood across her t-shirt. Steadying wobbly legs beneath her, she stood and stumbled inside. She groped her phone from her pants while she dropped onto the chair and dialed 911.

Her head swam but cleared a little after placing it between her legs, despite the discomfort of bending at the waist. She answered the emergency operator in a raspy voice, between breaths. "Stabbing...At 745 Fairview Drive. The new condos."

"Who's been stabbed?" The calm voice asked.

Bobbi raised her head and decided lying down would help her. She put her feet up on the sofa arm. Shock. Must not go into shock. "Me...Bobbi Webster."

The operator kept her on the phone until Bobbi heard the sirens approaching her subdivision. Had she left the door unlocked?

The doorbell rang, then two EMTs flung the door open and strode immediately to her on the couch. "Bobbi Webster?" a short woman asked.

"Yes." Bobbi breathed deeply but winced with the pain.

The woman kept her talking while pushing her hand away to press gauze on her stomach. Bobbi groaned in pain. The other EMT wrapped a blood pressure cuff on her arm.

"When did this happen?"

Bobbi could feel her brain going fuzzy. She gulped and answered in a weak voice, "Just now. Five minutes tops...I'm a doctor."

The short woman who was at her side wrestled the long sleeves of her t-shirt up her arm and started an IV. "Yes. I know. I've worked with you a couple of times, bringing in a patient to BCH. I'm Beth Stephens. You delivered my nephew earlier today. And my grandmother is Charlotte, whom I think you know." Beth smiled kindly, taping the IV line to her arm.

Bobbi, trying to focus, dipped her head, the best she could do as a nod. Charlotte. She liked Charlotte.

The EMTs transferred her from the couch, then strapped her onto the gurney and slid it out the door. The older one, a man, was on his radio to the ER.

Bobbi recognized a neighbor who stood next to her front walk. The gray haired woman, her face a mask of concern, asked, "Can I call anyone for you, Dr. Webster?"

The woman's face whizzed by her. Bobbi steeled herself for the bumpy drop onto the ambulance floor. "Please call Mother Erin…Holy Spirit Church." Bobbi closed her eyes with the effort it took to speak. Why did she say that? Erin was busy. And Bobbi didn't like the idea of Erin seeing her so incapacitated.

The ambulance door banged shut; the young woman—was her name Stephens?—sat next to her and kept tabs on the IV and her blood pressure.

"Pressure one hundred over sixty and steady. Hang in there, Doctor. You called so quickly I think you won't have lost much blood."

Bobbi could manage only a slight nod. She lay back, wincing from the pain shooting through her abdomen. "Anything internal nicked?"

Beth shook her head. "Hard to tell. They'll take care of you in the ER; don't worry. It certainly wasn't an artery, or you wouldn't be talking to me."

If it had been an artery, she certainly would *not* be talking. She laughed to herself to think of it.

"Something funny?" Beth asked.

Bobbi wanted to reply, but darkness took over. The next thing Bobbi knew, the door of the ambulance flew open, and hands guided the gurney onto the pavement, then whooshed through automatic doors into the brightly lit ER.

In a haze, she recognized the voice of Jaime Garcia-Brown. Her eyes fluttered open. He had his stethoscope on her chest, while the EMTs shouted out numbers for pulse, temperature, blood pressure, and IV fluids. Hands held her on both sides and slipped her onto the exam table of one of the ER rooms. Someone cut off her t-shirt and attached EKG leads.

"Hemorrhaging. Two or three centimeter laceration of indeterminate depth. Let's stem this bleeding." Jaime shouted orders to several people around her bed.

Bobbi was determined to stay awake, not to go under, but it was becoming harder and harder. The pain kept her both awake and wanting to escape from it.

"Get me a unit of B positive." It was Amanda.

"Amanda," Bobbi whispered.

"Hey, Bobbi. Don't talk. We've got you." Amanda laid a hand on her arm. "You're doing well. Blood pressure still stable. We're managing the bleeding first, so you can go for a CT scan."

Jaime poked his head in her vision. "Good afternoon, Bobbi. Looks like you had an encounter with the wrong guy."

She gulped as the pain washed over her. "Wes," she rasped.

"Your BP looks good. You bled out some, so we're giving you one pint of blood. I want to see what the damage looks like inside." Jaime nodded to the staff surrounding Bobbi. "Okay for CT. Let's go."

One of the nurses and an ER tech guided the gurney through the doors to the Imaging Department. Bobbi could hold on no longer and gave in again to the darkening of her vision.

An imaging tech woke her to get her into the CT machine. It whirred around her for minutes, then she was glided out and slid onto the gurney again, to return to the ER.

The ceiling lights swept by her vision like a carnival ride. She held onto consciousness and measured her breathing through the pain.

Amanda met her in the curtained space. "Mother Erin is here for you. Do you want to see her?"

"Let's get me fixed up first. What's the verdict on the internal damage?"

"Let me get Dr. Garcia-Brown."

Several minutes passed before Jaime came into her line of vision. "Good news. The radiologist says no important structures were severed. No puncture of the intestine, spleen, or gall bladder, or even the stomach. Some damage of soft tissue and the rectus and transverse abs, but nothing needing surgery. Missed the abdominal aorta, thankfully. Seems the knife went in at a shallow angle from the left, so didn't penetrate below three or so centimeters into the ab wall. You'll heal just fine with no movement for a few days, then you can do some therapy. I'll put in some sutures and you'll be good to go. How's the pain?"

"Could do with something, Jaime."

She heard him call for morphine drip and for lidocaine.

Amanda appeared at the bed to inject her IV, smiling down at her. "Good news, Bobbi. Just a few stitches."

The morphine soon had Bobbi struggling with the fuzziness in her brain.

Jaime pushed the suture cart into the space. "I

didn't ask whether you wanted somebody more skilled, you know, since this is above your bathing suit area. Do you want me to call Hunsaker, the plastics guy?"

Bobbi grinned and laughed softly, immediately regretting it. She moved her hand in dismissal.

While Bobbi swam in the pool of near-consciousness, Jaime and Amanda prepped her belly and stitched up her wound. She woke when the surgery light above her bed suddenly flashed brightly in her face.

Amanda stood over her, bandaging her belly. "All done." She smiled. "You're going up to the med-surg floor for observation."

"No way. That's not indicated." Bobbi tried to raise her head from the bed, but it got only a few inches before she collapsed back on the treatment table.

"Sorry, doctor's orders. You've had a transfusion, and we need to monitor your BP and blood counts. You know that." Amanda stilled, then continued checking Bobbi's vitals.

Jaime returned to her bedside. "How you doing?"

"I'd be better if you'd let me go home."

"Not going to happen. You know the drill. Observation for at least twelve hours. If you're a good little doctor, you can go home tomorrow morning. Any questions?"

Jaime looked pleased with himself, but Bobbi wanted nothing more than to knock the grin off his face. She pouted and shook her head.

"Hello?" Erin peeked around the curtain. "Is this where I can find a certain doctor who has become a patient?"

Bobbi smiled faintly. "The Elf. So glad to see you."

Erin went to the bed, looking intently into Bobbi's eyes. "Hey, there." She kissed Bobbi's forehead, while stroking back her hair. "How are you?"

Jaime said, "Need to see to another patient. You okay?"

Bobbi quickly eyed him and said, "Go. I'm good. Thanks, Jaime."

He waved a salute and slid around the curtain.

Amanda said, "Jeannie from med-surg is on the way to take you up. Glad you're okay, Bobbi." Bobbi smiled at her, as Amanda squeezed her shoulder and gave Erin a quick wink.

"Thanks," Erin said to Amanda. To Bobbi she said, "So. Tell me what happened."

Jeannie from med-surg came into view around the curtain just then. "Ready for a trip?"

"I suppose. Doesn't sound like I can avoid it. But I'm really all right."

"Sure, Dr. Webster. But you—"

"Know the drill. I get it." Bobbi winced. It hurt like the devil, she felt weak, and her head seemed stuffed with cotton. She blinked.

Erin took one arm, Jeannie the other, and they helped her stand and shift her feet to lie on the rolling bed. They tucked her under a sheet. Jeannie pushed it out the doors toward the elevator, Erin in tow.

After Bobbi had been rolled into Room 202, and Jeannie had checked all her lines, and given her the bedside call button, she left her and Erin alone.

Erin sat. She grasped Bobbi's left hand and stroked her skin.

"Don't look so worried," Bobbi said in her raspy voice.

"Was it Wes?"

"Yeah."

Erin threw her head back and groaned. "Oh, God. He could have killed you, darling." She gripped Bobbi's hand more tightly while her eyes spilled over with tears. Erin grabbed tissues from Bobbi's bedside table, sniffled into one, and said, "I'm sorry. You don't need me here blubbering all over you." She looked intently at Bobbi's face. "You need some sleep, sweetie. It's been a long day. You look exhausted."

Bobbi's eyes drooped, as if to agree with her. "I'm okay."

"Why don't you get some rest? I'll be back for dinner."

"Sure. You don't have to come back tonight." Bobbi yawned.

Erin leaned over and kissed her sweetly on the lips.

Bobbi hummed. "See you later."

Chapter Thirty-two

Yes, I'm sure." Deputy Rick sat in Bobbi's living area in the only chair, following up from yesterday's interview in the hospital. "It was Wes. He wanted revenge for me having him arrested and stashing his wife in a shelter and away from him." Bobbi shifted uncomfortably on the couch. She wore her rattiest sweatpants and an old, long-sleeved OHSU t-shirt.

"Any witnesses?"

Bobbi sighed. "No. One neighbor came by while the EMTs were loading me. I think her name is Dobbs. I've met her before, but don't know her well. She lives two doors down. Retired teacher."

"Hmm." Rick stuck his lower lip out. "Let me go talk to this neighbor. Hopefully she saw something. We also can try for some DNA from the blood. In most stabbings, the suspect ends up cutting themselves as well. I hope you still have the clothes you were wearing?"

"Oh." Bobbi stood up gingerly. "Let me get them. The hospital sent them home with me this morning in a bag." Stepping carefully and slowly, Bobbi held a large white plastic bag and handed it to the deputy. She clutched her stomach while she sat back on the couch with a small groan.

"Anything else you remember?"

Bobbi blinked, remembering Wes's glazed look.

"Yes. His pupils were dilated and he sweated even though it was mild yesterday afternoon. I suspect he was high on something. It reinforces our conversation the other day." She more than suspected. Perhaps this issue would explain his behavior, although it would never give him an excuse for it. But drug abuse could be treated.

"Like weed?"

"No. I didn't smell weed. I imagine he's using something more potent. Coke. Meth. I'm not a drug abuse expert, but his low weight and the other signs are there." Bobbi wiped her hand wearily across her forehead. "Oh, and his truck was old. Red. Sorry, don't know the make or model. Had a lot of rust."

"We can check his plates. I'll bring you a picture to identify." Deputy Rick nodded, writing more in his small pocket notebook. "Do you mind if I take these clothes? And I'll do some legwork with the neighbors. Call if you remember anything else I should know." Rick put on his cowboy hat. "And get well, Doctor." He turned. "Don't get up, I'll find my way out."

After the deputy shut the door, Bobbi slowly made her way over to lock it. She laid back down on the couch. Her mind replayed the image of the knife puncturing her belly, over and over, like a video loop, as soon as she shut her eyes. Her heart beat out of her chest. His beady black eyes, bad breath, and toothless grin haunted her every time she closed her eyes. She wondered how long this video would loop through her mind as, finally, her tiredness won out and she slept deeply.

≈≈≈≈≈

Erin finished her to-do list for her days off. It had been difficult to keep her mind on her work, as the attack on Bobbi made her crazy with fear for her. Seeing her looking so pale in the ER was horrific. She cringed about the whole episode with Wes, from the fight in the tavern, to the episode at the clinic, and then at Bobbi's own house. Sighing deeply, she grabbed her phone and called in an order at Ranchero, the best Mexican restaurant with take out. Glad that it was still light out at six p.m., she locked up the church and drove toward town.

When she arrived at Bobbi's, she used her new key and entered quietly. On the couch in the dark interior, she caught Bobbi's outline on the small sofa, covered by a quilt. Erin gently pushed the door shut and locked it, then tiptoed into the kitchen with the food, where she placed it to warm in the oven. She crept back into the living area and peered down at a sleeping Bobbi.

Her hair, matted with sweat, and her pale face prompted Erin to caress her cheek with tenderness. Bobbi brought out her maternal instincts. She could have been much worse off; Erin shivered with the thought.

She blew breath from her puffed-out cheeks. What was she doing with this woman? Did Bobbi need her, really, or was it Erin's wishful thinking? Bobbi functioned at a high professional level, making decisions affecting others daily, protecting their health and wellness, even saving lives. Erin's heart swelled with the compassion and patient-focus of Bobbi's work, even though Erin did not always agree with her methods.

Did Erin's more-spiritual approach clash with Bobbi's, or had it been Bobbi's more scientific mind?

Not the message as much as the way the message was delivered? Both worked for others' wellbeing, but toward differing goals. Erin strove toward spiritual depth and wellness. Bobbi strove toward bodily wellness. Bobbi may characterize her aim as whole-person wellness: mental, physical, and emotional wellness, which Erin appreciated more the more time she spent with Bobbi and understood better what made her tick.

Take Wes, for example. Bobbi's motivations to save him from himself all hinged on his drug abuse, which she identified as the nucleus of his explosive, physically violent behavior. Bobbi's ordered mind found a source of Wes's difficulty, so could now identify methods of treating it. To Erin, Bobbi operated much as she did. When an underlying source of spiritual angst could be pinpointed, a path to a parishioner's or client's spiritual health became clearer. The difference between her and Bobbi's professional approaches lay in the lenses with which they searched the heart and soul, or, in Bobbi's case, the body and mind. The bottom line: both Erin and Bobbi tried hard to assist people in their journey toward wholeness.

Quietly, Erin pulled a book from her messenger bag, turned on a floor lamp, and sat to read in the chair next to the sofa, looking up occasionally to check her sweet Bobbi.

Bobbi stirred thirty minutes later.

"Hi, sweetie. Did you get some rest, I hope?"

Bobbi yawned, inhaled deeply, and smiled at Erin. "Hey there."

Bobbi's tired eyes called to Erin's motherly instincts again. Her arms longed to hug Bobbi to her, but she willed them to her sides, wanting not to impose herself upon Bobbi. Dragging the chair closer to the couch, she said, "How are you doing?"

Bobbi's eyes avoided hers, and she said quickly, "Really well. I smell something good."

Erin recognized Bobbi's independent streak in her avoiding telling her how she really felt. "Do you think you could eat some Mexican? I have the fixings for two fajitas. One chicken, one beef."

Bobbi did not try to get up, which was a red flag to Erin. She couldn't imagine the pain she was in, but her body said it for her, stiffly lying under the blanket.

"Chicken sounds good."

A kiss on the cheek before going to the kitchen left Erin nearly crying. She pushed down the tears threatening to fall. "Tell me you didn't sleep on the couch all day. You should be in your bed," Erin called from the kitchen.

No answer came. Erin frowned. Bobbi wasn't taking care of herself. Darn medical types. Her mom was the same way. She took care of everyone else when they were sick, but when she had the flu or a bad cold, she still went in to work. Even her dad's admonitions about spreading things to other people didn't disturb her mom. Bobbi stoically pushed on, just like her mom.

As Erin brought in the fajitas on plates, she decided to take the doctor by the horns. "I'm in charge now, Dr. Webster. Just call me Nurse O'Rourke. You will do as I say. You're going to eat as much of this as you can, no whining. Then I'm getting you to the bed, where you should be, after a nice, hot wash up."

Bobbi's eyes got wide. "What? You're not in charge of me, Elf." She winced, laughing lightly.

"Think again, Doc. The Elf has spoken. Now, I've got your fajita fixed. You will eat it." Erin stood over the couch, put the plate on the chair seat, and assisted Bobbi from a lying to a sitting position. Erin, taking on her tough love stance by standing akimbo, watched over Bobbi as she ate.

Bobbi glanced up to her. "Aren't you going to eat?"

"I'll eat after you've eaten and I've got you into bed."

"Your meal will get cold."

"It's warming in the oven."

Bobbi sighed loudly and then tucked into her food, eating most of it, while Erin watched.

Finally, Erin asked with a tinge of concern in her voice, "Do you know what's happening with Wes?"

"I heard from the deputy around three this afternoon. They did a sweep of his house and found lots of drug paraphernalia. He was cooking meth in his basement. Dumbass. He could've blown up his wife and him both. They talked to his wife at her new place of work. She hasn't seen him for three weeks, which was comforting to hear. But they've yet to pick him up. Rick said they've got some leads and hope to nab him in the next twenty-four hours."

"That's good news. I'm staying here. At least until he's arrested and behind bars."

"What?" Bobbi looked up from her plate with distress on her face.

Erin figured she'd receive this response to her temporarily moving in. "No argument, remember. Nurse O'Rourke in charge. My mom and dad decided to make the trip from Chicago to see me this weekend, instead of me going there. You shouldn't be here by yourself. So, I'm staying this next week."

"Not just until they nab Wes?" Bobbi's face now

looked confused.

"Well, I misspoke. I'm staying until Wes has been put away *and* you're healed and can take care of yourself. Although that proposition is pretty dicey, given your lack of self-care." Erin grinned cheekily. "So there."

Bobbi finished her plate. "I'm not going to argue. If you want to waste your precious vacation shacked up as my personal slave, who am I to say no?" Bobbi yawned.

"Now, wash-up time, then bed." Erin took the plate into the kitchen, came back, and helped Bobbi to the bathroom.

Chapter Thirty-three

The next morning, Bobbi's phone rang after breakfast. Her mom.

"How are you doing today?"

Bobbi huffed. "I'm doing better every day, Mom. My wound is healing. Erin stayed over last night in full-mother mode, flitting around me as if I'm incapacitated. I'm letting her think I'm unable to function so she feels useful."

"I heard that," Erin shouted from the bathroom, where she had just showered.

"I'm glad she's there, child of mine. Dad and I've been worried about you. More than when Stephanie put you in the ER. This guy and his knife could have been the end of you. I've not been able to think about anything else, so, since I'm off for spring break starting Friday, and I'm flying down for a couple of days. I'm not asking, I'm telling." Her mom's voice got commanding.

Bobbi knew she couldn't stop this steamroller called Mom from its beeline straight for her. "I'd love to see you, Mom," she said, trying for upbeat and welcoming in her own voice.

When Bobbi got off the phone, Erin came from the bathroom, dressed in clean clothes, looking fresh and bright. Bobbi expected her to take flight any second, like a sprite with wings. Bobbi smiled and said, "My mom will be down Friday for a few days. We're having a convergence of parental units this weekend, it seems."

"Oh." Erin stopped toweling her wet hair and said, her big brown eyes widening, "Where will we put them all?"

"I thought they all could stay at the vicarage," Bobbi said, wondering if her mom would really agree to lodge a county away.

"Hmm. And supposedly I would stay here with you?" Erin looked skeptical.

"Well, yeah. Do you have a better idea?" Bobbi felt she was about to be overruled, unfortunately. She ached to have Erin here, but her plan seemed about to crumble.

"I think your mom should stay with you. She's been in Oregon stewing over you, so she needs to be around you. You need to let her bustle around and take care of you."

"My mom, bustle around and take care of me?" Bobbi said, wide-eyed. "You're projecting your mom onto mine, or your own mothering methods onto my mom's very different ones. My mom's more the 'up and at 'em' type. It'll be boot camp here, not a coddle-your-kid weekend."

"Oh." Erin stuck out her lower lip. "Poor baby." She wrapped Bobbi in her arms. "I would coddle you. My mom would nurse you. My dad would pray for you. We're all big saps when it comes to sick-room tending."

"I think I knew this," Bobbi said, smirking. "My family comes from the stiff-upper-lip society. How do you think I made it through med school? I'm one tough cookie."

Erin patted Bobbi's chest. "Well, this cookie had

a bite taken out of her a few days ago. I want to see the cookie repaired and back to normal before someone decides to dip her in milk."

Bobbi hooted, then clutched her midsection and grunted. "Damn."

"See what I mean? You need some coddling."

"Fine, you can duke it out with my mom, who is known as the terror of third grade students in Ketchum, Oregon."

᠅᠅᠅᠅

On Friday afternoon, Bobbi got a text that Fran Webster had arrived at the Denver International Airport and wended her way to Valley View in a rental car.

Erin finished up laundry, brushing aside Bobbi's attempts to help fold sheets and towels. "Go sit down. You're as jumpy as a cat."

Bobbi nodded. "Okay, okay."

"Are you nervous?" Erin asked, as she put the folded sheets in the closet. "It's just your mom."

"Ha. No adult ever says, 'it's just my mom.' Don't you know that? Also, I still haven't heard about Wes yet, either."

The doorbell rang. Bobbi hadn't heard anyone drive up. She jumped with nerves. Peeking through the door, she saw her mom holding a small carry-on bag. Her hair whipped around in the wind.

Bobbi opened the door. "Hi."

Fran Webster plopped the case onto the floor and took Bobbi in a light hug. "Don't want to hurt you. Let me see you." She pushed Bobbi apart from her and raked her gaze along Bobbi's abdomen, then back up to her face. "I think you'll live, Roberta Francene."

"Mom, this is Erin O'Rourke."

Fran sized up Erin while shaking her hand. "Where's the rest of you?" She laughed lightly.

Erin laughed with her. "Good to meet you, Ms. Webster."

Just then, Bobbi's phone rang. From her peripheral vision, she caught Erin taking her mom into the bedroom to unpack. "Yes, Dr. Webster here."

It was Deputy Rick. "Good news, Doctor. We found Wes Myers at his buddy's house in Johnson County. He's safely in the county jail, being arraigned on a $100,000 bond this afternoon on charges of aggravated assault and drug possession and manufacture. We also charged him with a hate crime, since Colorado protects persons by virtue of sexual orientation and you said he called you an offensive name. We interviewed your neighbor, Ms. Dobbs. She *did* see him attack you with the knife and said she came over as soon as she could. She identified Wes's truck, but didn't hear your conversation with him."

"That's very good news, Deputy. What do I need to do? Do I need an attorney?" Bobbi asked.

"It never hurts to consult someone. You have recourse to a civil suit as well as the state courts. I have your statement about the attack, we are running the DNA, but I don't think we will need it, given Ms. Dobbs' witness statement. The prosecutor will be in touch with you very shortly."

"And who's the prosecutor for his case?"

"State's Attorney Lynn Sanderson. She's pretty young, very aggressive."

"I see." Bobbi ran her hand through her hair. She definitely didn't need all the hassle Wes Myers stirred

up but having a good prosecutor may help. She needed
not so much to be avenged for the attack, as to see that
Wes never attacked anyone else. "I have a question,
Deputy. What if I dropped the assault charges and left
you to deal only with the drug charges? I want to see he
gets some help, not just jail time."

Rick paused. "That'd be in the prosecutor's
hands, how she charges him. Right now, he's being
charged with assault with a deadly weapon, unlawful
manufacture of meth, and criminal possession of a
controlled substance. You can talk with Lynn about
the sentence bargaining process, if you want. You'll
hear from Lynn soon."

"Thanks." Bobbi sighed. They talked a while more
about the arrest and Bobbi's part in Wes's charges. She
closed the call and sat down on the sofa with a sigh.

Erin's hand snaked around her shoulder and
rubbed her neck briskly.

"I'll give you ten years to stop that," Bobbi said
under a groan of pleasure, as the anxiety of the week
lessened for a moment under Erin's warm hands.

"Let's have something to eat," Erin said, kissed
Bobbi on her head, and went into the small kitchen.

Bobbi felt exhausted. So much happening in such
a short time. She tiredly pulled herself from the sofa
and met her mom coming out of the bedroom. "Did
you have a good trip, Mom?"

"It was fine. How are you holding up? Your dark
circles have dark circles, so you'll hit the bed early. I'll
take the sofa out here."

"Huh uh. That sofa will kill you." Bobbi could
see her mom had arrived like the cavalry, taking over.
"You can sleep with me in the bed."

"Where's Erin sleeping?" Fran looked over at

Erin, working at the stove.

Bobbi sighed, missing Erin even before she had left. "We decided she'll stay at the vicarage tonight. She's driving to pick up her folks at the Denver Amtrak station tomorrow around seven-thirty. So, an early start for her." Bobbi sat on the sofa with another groan, keeping her hand placed on her stitched stomach.

"Have you met them?"

"No."

"If you're okay here, I'll help Erin in the kitchen and pump her for information." Fran smiled wickedly and winked at Bobbi.

"Mom…" Bobbi whined. "Leave her alone."

Fran laughed.

Bobbi laid her head back and closed her eyes for a moment. The next thing she knew, Erin kissed her on the forehead. "Do you want something to eat, sweetheart?"

Bobbi blinked. "What time is it?"

"Time to eat. Early evening. I need to go home fairly soon."

"I don't want you to leave, you know."

"You've played the sick card for two days and I've played the good girlfriend; now I have to play the good daughter." Erin gently helped Bobbi up and over to the kitchen table. "We've got good food. Your mom even made some biscuits. How about that?" Erin pointed to a basket overflowing with steaming goodness.

Bobbi took in the fragrances: biscuits and vegetable soup. Warm and cuddly food. "Just what the doctor ordered."

Fran spoke as she brought another plate into the dining area, "And I also made a cobbler from some peaches I brought from Hendley's Orchard."

Bobbi shook her head. "And I told Erin you weren't the kind of mother to coddle me. Guess I'm eating those words, quite literally."

Fran gave them both a look of mock hurt. "What a thing to say—that your mother would not mother you. I never."

They all three grinned. "Well, I, for one, am glad to be coddled. But I'm also jumping out of my skin to get back to work on Monday."

"Monday?" Erin nearly shouted.

Bobbi dug into the food, ignoring Erin's negative response about work. "Oh, Mom, these are fantastic." The biscuit melted in Bobbi's mouth, causing her to moan. "And the soup tastes so yummy, with those fresh veggies." Bobbi eyed Erin, who had yet to take a mouthful of food. "Are you okay?"

Fran looked back and forth between the two women.

Shock still on her face, Erin said, "It's only been a week and you're going back to work? What doctor allows this?"

"Gen said I could decide for myself when I felt well enough to take clinic patients. I'm not allowed to be on call, she said, until the stitches are out, in case I'm alone and need assistance with a patient. I need to get back to work, Erin. I'm going crazy just sitting around doing nothing. I don't want the other fellows and attendings working overtime just to cover my patients any longer than necessary."

Bobbi's mom, eating her soup and biscuits, said between bites, "That sounds reasonable to me."

"Oh?" Erin said, her brows knotting. "I just worry that you're doing too much too soon. You have a tendency to ignore your tiredness. I don't want you to go in too soon."

"It'll be all right." Bobbi flashed her a smile, trying to look as confident as she could, even as her belly ached after sitting at the table for ten minutes. Erin's words washed over her in warmth and caring, and she looked on her tenderly. "I appreciate your care for me, you know."

Erin smiled, took Bobbi's hand, and stroked along her knuckles gently. "I do care, Dr. Take Charge."

"Watch it, Elf. I may be inclined to a tickle session."

"Don't you dare. You'll hurt yourself and I'll kick your butt." Erin spooned soup into her mouth, but Bobbi noticed the slight smile curling her lips.

"Okay, girls, there will be no tickling or butt-kicking on my watch," Fran chided, shaking her spoon at them. "Get back to eating, 'cause the doctor needs to get to bed, and the priest needs to get to her house. Chop-chop."

After they finished eating, and Erin and Bobbi had kissed goodnight, Fran shooed Bobbi into the bathroom to wash up and get ready for bed. Bobbi got into bed, and, shortly after, Fran entered and sat down on the edge of the bed.

"I like her," Fran said simply.

"I do too."

"She's good for you. She doesn't mess around, speaks her mind. My kind of woman. Well, good night, kid. Sleep as long as you need tomorrow. I'll take care of whatever comes up. But I'm making pancakes for breakfast, just so you know." Fran patted Bobbi's knee, rose from the bed, and shut the door quietly.

Bobbi smiled at her mother's retreating form. She understood her mother's reticence in speaking of emotions. None of her family was particularly good at sharing deep, inner thoughts. They got things done. The Websters were practical, earthbound, grounded ranchers, not rhetoricians.

But Erin. How glad Bobbi was to have Erin's skill with emotions, her support in putting herself out there. Bobbi relaxed into the bed, her pain pill kicking in after the soreness caused by sitting up at the table. Her eyes fluttered closed, the smile still ghosting her mouth, as she thought of what Erin's parents would be like. Short? Clever? She chuckled. Coddling?

Chapter Thirty-four

I don't know why we didn't think of taking the train before. It beat the heck out of flying out of O'Hare." Erin's dad, Scott, laid their two pieces of luggage inside the door at the vicarage. "Nice digs, honey. Nicer than my first vicarage. Remember, Meg?"

"How can I forget mice, bats, sagging floors, and breezy windows?" Meg, Erin's mother answered.

Erin shut the door behind them and led them into the downstairs bedroom of the Victorian house that served as her parish's vicarage. "The vicarage was built in 1894, so it's seen its share of priests over the years. You guys can take this guest room. I'm upstairs. I've got a little study up there too. The bathroom's just down this hall. When you're ready, I've got some brunch ready."

Erin had not seen her parents for a full calendar year, her longest absence from them, and they looked good to her, stepping out of the sleeping car at Denver's Amtrak station with their bags. Her dad looked tousled, yet still his energetic self, with his salt-and-pepper, thinning hair its usual neat and short style. Mom's jeans and hoodie outfit looked cute, making her seem forty-five, not sixty-five. She was Erin's height, but had lighter brown hair with some wisps of gray, swept back off her face in a curly cut. They embraced for a long time on the platform, until her mom had noticed that they were blocking the flow of people coming to and from the train car.

On the way home, they talked about Holy Spirit and the parish discussion that led to her amended contract. Scott and Meg were particularly worried about Bobbi, even though they'd never met her. Erin chose to keep quiet about Bobbi's previous troubles with her ex-girlfriend Stephanie.

While Scott and Meg unpacked and freshened up, Erin called Bobbi around eleven. "Hi, Doctor. Are you behaving yourself?"

"Hi. I'm good. How was your parents' trip?"

Bobbi sounded tired, so Erin wanted to make her call short. "Good. We thought we'd bring dinner over tonight for you and Fran. How's pot roast sound?"

"You don't have to do that. Mom can cook, you know."

"That's not the reason. My mom needs to cook to feel needed, so you'd be doing us all a favor, 'cause until she can cook, she's going to drive us crazy."

"Oh, well, to save everyone's mental health, we'll just have to concede to her needs." Bobbi yawned. "Sorry."

"Did you not sleep well?"

"Not the best. Damn drugs. I've never been great at pain pills. They put me to sleep quickly, but I wake a couple hours later." Bobbi yawned again.

"I'll let you go. We'll be over around five. We can have a glass of wine—well, some of us can have a glass of wine—before dinner."

"I missed you last night, Elf."

"I missed you too, Doctor Take Charge." Erin chuckled. "I hope you've been resting today."

"Yeah. Mom's been like a busy bee, cleaning my condo. And she just left to get some stuff for the kitchen. And more towels. Evidently, she says I'm lacking in guest accommodations. I forgot I only have a couple of towels for the bathroom, and the kitchen doesn't have much in the way of pots and pans. You may have noticed."

Erin shook her head. "Oh, I noticed. It's like entering a third world country in your condo…Oh, damn. Wait. That sounded like a privileged American talking, sorry. Anyway, glad she's getting you outfitted. I better let you go so you can go back to doing what you were doing, which I hope was reading or watching TV and resting."

"I'm watching baseball. It's like watching paint dry and puts me to sleep in minutes," Bobbi replied wryly.

"I like that. Go Cubbies. See you soon, sweetie."

❧ ❧ ❧ ❧

Fran opened the door to Erin and a lithe man and short woman in their sixties, waving them in with a "Welcome."

Bobbi called hello from her perch on the sofa, then slowly rose to greet them all.

"Hello, Bobbi. It's so nice to meet you. We've heard so much about you." Meg took her in a gentle hug. "You look just as Erin described you. I'm Meg and this is her father, Scott."

Scott shook Bobbi's hand with a warm smile.

"How are you feeling, sweetie?" Meg asked kindly. She looked at Bobbi directly with the same dark eyes as her daughter, and at the same small height and build. Looking at Meg, Bobbi thought she was seeing the older Erin standing in front of her.

"I'm doing better every day, Ms. O'Rourke."

"None of that. I'm Meg to you. And this must be your mother."

"May I introduce Fran Webster?"

Meg and Scott shook hands with Fran, and they all sat down around the sofa with extra chairs from the kitchen table.

Seating herself next to Bobbi on the sofa, Erin took Bobbi's hand in hers. "Did you get any rest today? I still see dark circles."

Meg said, "Oh, Bobbi. We're so sorry for your troubles. Are you sure us being here is okay? We don't want to tax your energy."

Fran spoke up, "We Websters are tough. It's good for Bobbi to move around, to help heal her wounds and get her energy level back to normal. We wouldn't think of not having you come. I'm so glad to meet Erin and you all, too. It's the first time I've been allowed to meet any of Bobbi's girlfriends' parents. A red-letter day, heh?"

"Oh, Mom," Bobbi said, turning hot with embarrassment.

"We're glad to make the connection with you, too," Scott answered. "I understand you're a teacher. I've always admired those who can teach. I would be the last person who could corral a classroom of children."

"Now, Scott. You know you've taken your share of confirmation class kids over many years. It's no different. In fact, it may be worse. Some of those kids were being pushed by their parents to become confirmed."

"Not me," Erin said with a grin.

"Oh, I remember well," Meg answered. "You skipped the whole thing. You were acting out, getting independent at age thirteen."

Bobbi smiled at the interplay between Erin and her mother. She raised her eyebrows when Erin caught her eye. "I'm glad to hear you weren't a goody two-shoes."

"And you were?" Fran asked, laughing.

Bobbi looked at her mother, surprised she would want to air their family secrets.

Fran glanced at the O'Rourkes, then at Bobbi, while Bobbi groaned. "My dear daughter, at age fifteen, decided she'd try a few drugs."

"Oh," Erin said, surprise in her voice. "What, exactly, did you experiment with, Doctor?"

Bobbi felt all eyes on her. She could kill her mother for bringing this up. "Mom," she said in her whiny tone. "I was very young, and, well...stupid. Besides, Chucky dared me and Jen—"

"And here's where I say, if Chucky dared you to fly the Columbia Gorge without a plane, would you do that?"

Erin and her parents hid smiles behind their hands, watching the two go at it.

Meg said, "This sounds way too familiar. Miss Erin pulled some stunts too, didn't you, my little darling?"

"Hey, who invited these parents anyway, Bobbi? I think it's time to get dinner on the table." Erin tugged Bobbi gently to stand from the sofa.

Laughing, Bobbi stood gingerly, holding her stomach. "Don't make me giggle like this, please."

Erin and Bobbi worked on setting the table and getting pot roast sliced and onto the table. "Don't you even think about carrying that heavy plate of meat," Erin chided Bobbi.

"Who, me?" Bobbi smirked. She loved when Erin fussed over her, but not too much. A woman could only take so much maternal fussing around her.

Erin grabbed the platter and called "Dinner" into the living area. The three parents came and sat. Erin asked, "Would you say grace tonight, Dad?"

Scott said a short prayer and they dug into their meal. Conversation swirled easily among the group. Bobbi described her rural fellowship. Erin told stories about her issues with her parish.

"See, that's why I never went back to church," Fran said adamantly. "People who profess Christianity can sometimes be the biggest bigots going, then claim it is their faith. I never heard of such hypocrisy."

"I don't know, Mom. I've been to Erin's church a few times. Only a small minority pushed the archaic celibacy clause. And even they backed down when confronted. Her biggest enemy came back to church after threatening to quit and take his pledge with him."

"I've seen it before," Scott added between bites of potato. "I'm proud of you, lassie." He winked at Erin.

"I am too," Meg added. "It happens with medical staff too. Those ignorant types who refused to see gay people during the AIDS crisis. They made my blood boil. One physician quit when my hospital made their policy clear about treating all people without prejudice. None of us were sad to see him out the door."

"Yes, and then there are the teachers who gossip about the students who seem a little too sissy for their cowboy philosophies. When this one came out to us, we just ate dinner and asked that she be careful and bring her girlfriends home so we knew who they were. Didn't we, Roberta Francene?"

Bobbi shook her head at her mother and

continued to eat.

When they had finished dinner, the O'Rourkes demurred to stay longer, citing Bobbi's need for rest.

Erin took Bobbi's hand and led her to the bedroom, as her parents said good-bye to Fran. "I miss you, sweetheart." She kissed Bobbi tenderly.

Bobbi moaned into the kiss. "Wow, do I ever miss you." She stroked Erin's cheek, and kissed her deeper.

"Hey, lassies, time to stop the sparking," Erin's dad yelled from the living area.

They both chuckled. Bobbi ducked her head, nuzzling into Erin's hair, and sighed.

Erin drew away slowly, pecked Bobbi's lips once again, and said, "I'll see you tomorrow afternoon, probably around dinner time. My dad's preaching tomorrow."

"Good. I wish I could stand sitting for the duration of your service to hear him."

"You're fine. I understand." Erin smoothed Bobbi's top over her chest. "Take care, Doctor."

❧ ❧ ❧ ❧

"I like Bobbi very much," Meg stated, while Erin drove home to the vicarage. "She's very intelligent, naturally, but also self-deprecating and sweet in a way I don't see in physicians I'm friends with. She takes her job very seriously, I can tell. You say she wants to start rural practice in her home town in Oregon?"

"Yes," Erin answered, pulling into the left lane to pass a slow pickup truck.

"And her goals would take her out of Colorado, I take it. Where does that leave your relationship?"

Erin glanced at her mother. She didn't want to

get into her and Bobbi's private affairs. "She *is* a great doctor. But, we haven't gotten that far, Mom. We barely started a more intimate relationship at Easter, so I don't know what the future holds, if anything."

"She looks at you with so much love, I can't believe that. You love her too, don't you." Meg's statement came out as a fact.

"I think I do."

Meg nodded her head in her wise fashion. "Your dad's asleep back there," she indicated the back seat. "I think the trip took it out of him." She looked tenderly at him.

Erin drove the rest of the way wondering whether Bobbi and she had garnered enough forward momentum together to keep what they had alive. She thought maybe they did, but they hadn't broached anything long-term yet. She thought they probably were monogamous, although that hadn't come up either. She knew she certainly wasn't seeing anyone else. Maybe Bobbi still dated Amanda. Amanda certainly made herself known the day Bobbi came into the ER. But now that Erin thought about her, Amanda hadn't pushed herself on Bobbi that day. She'd been kind to Erin, too, as if she knew they were seeing each other. So, perhaps Bobbi no longer dated Amanda. Erin wouldn't blame her if she were still dating her. Amanda had a lot going for her—smart, a good nurse, from what Erin had witnessed. And other, ahem, assets.

When they got to the vicarage, Erin's parents said their good nights. Erin got ready for Sunday by laying out her clericals. It felt good to be on vacation, with her dad taking over the service tomorrow. She'd originally had the congregation doing a stripped-down service, but when her dad offered to take over, she thought her parish would like it.

❧❧❧❧

Sunday flew by for them. The service went well. Parishioners liked her dad's sermon. Walter especially made positive comments after the service, while in line to greet Scott. Erin sighed when she heard him sucking up to Scott. What a jerk that guy could be. Her dad took it in stride, not taking the bait of being complimented on anything he did as a priest. He was her role model in his reaction to these kinds of parishioners who clearly wanted to butter up the priest.

After lunch, they all settled into naptime. Erin had a difficult time dropping off to sleep. Her stomach started to ache, thinking about her mom's questions about Bobbi's moving to Oregon after her fellowship ended. She and Bobbi needed to address these issues some time, but when would they be ready?

Then, Wes Myers' behavior. Frightening. She hoped, like Bobbi, that he would be sentenced to some kind of drug rehabilitation, although he would have to go to Denver, the nearest facility, from what Roxie had told her. She saw some folks with addiction in her practice with Roxie, and some who'd come from the Denver drug treatment programs. Rehab never really ended for the poor souls with addictions. Would Wes be able to sustain his program if he did get sentenced to rehab? Would it take care of his anger issues or were other deeper problems driving his dysfunctional behavior? For Bobbi's sake, Erin prayed it did. Erin had been praying for healing for both Wes and Bobbi.

Chapter Thirty-five

"D r. Webster?"

"Yes."

"Come in. I'm Lynn Sanderson. It's good to meet you. I'm sorry about the attack you sustained. Are you doing all right? I hope this meeting will not be too taxing for you."

Bobbi shook hands with a woman about her age wearing a dark skirt suit that fit her as if it had been tailored. Ms. Sanderson stood slightly shorter than her, her dark hair pulled back into a neat bun, giving her a professional air. Her legs were muscular, her hips and bust curvy. Not fat, but not slim either. *Probably works out*, Bobbi thought. Bobbi noted a large diamond on her left hand, with a gold band. "I'm doing much better, Ms. Sanderson. I went to work yesterday and lived to tell about it." Bobbi smiled.

Ms. Sanderson only nodded. "Let's get your statement and then you can go."

All business, this woman, just like Deputy Rick said, Bobbi thought. Bobbi went over her statement, then Ms. Sanderson's assistant produced it for signing in minutes, Bobbi signed it, and that was it.

"Before I go, can I ask about sentencing Mr. Myers to rehabilitation for his addiction?"

"Yes." Ms. Sanderson rifled through materials on her messy desk and handed Bobbi a pamphlet. "Please take a good look at these victims' rights. You have the right to be present during any court proceedings, including sentencing hearings." Ms. Sanderson gazed directly at Bobbi. "The case looks to be open and shut. The defendant's attorney will most likely advise him to plead guilty, given the weight of the evidence against him and his prior contact with you. We'll then move to the sentencing phase. A probation officer will prepare a document in support of the sentencing for the judge's use, detailing Mr. Myers' history of convictions and other pertinent background that would affect sentencing. During the sentencing hearing, I can either read your victim impact statement, or you can deliver it in person. You also have a right to no contact from the convicted person."

Bobbi took the pamphlet and eyed it briefly. "My main goal is to be assured Mr. Myers receives appropriate treatment."

"I understand. Because you're a physician, your statement might carry more weight than normal. But ultimately, the judge will decide herself. Our judge takes these types of cases very seriously. She doesn't normally use mandatory sentences for drug charges. She likes to take each case on its merits." Ms. Sanderson took Bobbi's signed affidavit and handed it to her assistant. "While we can only register our thoughts on sentencing, the judge will take it from there. I've worked with Judge Latimore on several cases since I became a prosecutor. I have a good record with her, and she listens to me. I'll take this under advisement and talk to Mr. Myers' attorney. But I can't promise anything." She stood from her desk chair and held out her hand to shake Bobbi's. "Thank you for coming by today, Doctor."

Bobbi shook hands. Evidently, the meeting had

ended. Bobbi felt slightly rushed. Ms. Sanderson was already busying herself with paperwork on her desk. "Thank you. When might I hear about all this?"

Ms. Sanderson looked up from the desk. "Mr. Myers will enter his plea today at three, so it depends on how crowded the judge's docket is. I'll be in touch."

⚜⚜⚜⚜

Erin entered Bobbi's condo on Wednesday evening. Bobbi stood at the stove, stirring something. "Hey, Doc, what's cookin'?"

Bobbi turned and kissed Erin gently on the lips. "You're a welcome sight. I missed you this week. I assume your folks got back to Chicago all right? Mom left yesterday morning for the airport. She made a bunch of food that she froze for me. She was a cooking fool yesterday. I'm warming mac and cheese in the oven. Thought we'd have frozen peas." Bobbi smiled.

"Good. See, she did coddle you. And you had me believing she was a hands-off mother."

"Yeah. She surprised me a little too. It felt nice having her rushing around doing things. Of course, she made me a little crazy, 'cause she wouldn't let me help."

"You went to work Monday, right? Did you stay all day, or were you careful?" Erin still harbored fears of Bobbi doing too much too soon.

Bobbi grinned. "You're a little mother yourself, Elf. And yes, I only stayed for four hours. I saw patients for two hours in the morning and two hours in the afternoon. And yes, I tired pretty quickly and felt sore when I got home. I took something for the pain, laid down, and Mom fed me. Are you satisfied?"

Erin stroked Bobbi's cheek. "I only worry because I care. You know that, don't you?"

Bobbi kissed Erin deeply, holding her close around the waist and pushing her body into her. Erin's heart rate spiked. She loved the feel of Bobbi's taller form, toned from working in the gym, but still definitely feminine.

Bobbi whispered, "And I care about you, too, Mother Erin."

They ate their mac and cheese, Erin commenting on Fran's yummy, cheesy concoction.

"Mom never has a lot of time to cook because of her job, so I think she enjoyed the down time here with me. She laughed and joked with me, which we haven't done for a few years. School can really wear her down, you know?"

"Like my mom. Nursing takes a toll." Erin finished her plate and grabbed Bobbi's to take to the sink. "By the way, you went to the attorney's today. What happened?"

"Piece of cake. I made my statement and had it notarized there. Then she sent me home with a victims' rights pamphlet. I'm to write a victim impact statement for the sentencing phase. The attorney called to tell me that Wes pled guilty today. Next Wednesday is the sentencing hearing, which gives the court enough time to prepare background information for the judge. And my impact statement can be given in person or via written communication. I'm writing it and having the prosecutor enter it into the proceedings. I don't really want to see Wes's beady eyes ever again."

"Wow. Things are moving fast." Erin stroked Bobbi's hand. Bobbi looked less anxious. "I'm glad to see you looking more relaxed. Are you ready to put this episode behind you?"

Bobbi sighed. "Boy, yeah. I've got an appointment in Denver on Friday. Yancy gave me a name of a good therapist."

"Oh, sweetie, that's great. I'm so proud of you, taking your life back. Getting help." Erin kissed her chastely. "Oh, and another thing. I've helped victims with impact statements before in my pastoral counseling role. I could help if you want. No pressure."

Bobbi took Erin's face in her hands and stroked her cheek gently. "You're a keeper, Elf. Thanks, yes. I thought I'd draft something tomorrow and then I'll have you look at it."

After dinner, Bobbi and Erin cuddled on the couch, reading. Then at nine, Erin took her leave. They kissed at the door, Erin's heart doing a happy dance at how everything seemed to be calming down in their lives: Wes had been convicted, Bobbi was recovering, and her parish had a more welcome stance toward her.

Chapter Thirty-six

Sentencing day came. Bobbi worked at the clinic, seeing patients in both the morning and afternoon sessions, but her mind wasn't on the job. She called one patient by the wrong name and got another's diagnosis incorrect, talking about what the last patient was being seen for. Both episodes embarrassed her. She prided herself on how well she connected with patients. Getting names and diagnoses mixed up didn't figure in good patient rapport in her world.

Erin texted around noon to say she was coming by with some take-out lunch.

Bobbi sighed in relief when she hugged Erin in the break room.

"I'm not particularly hungry," Bobbi confessed.

"I imagined you wouldn't be," Erin said tenderly. "Don't feel you have to eat. I also brought some fruit. You may want to keep some for later in the afternoon if you feel hungrier then."

Bobbi shuffled. "I wanted to let you know...I..."

Erin waited patiently for Bobbi to continue.

Bobbi led Erin out of the break room to her cubby so they could have some semblance of privacy. "I called Amanda. We went for coffee yesterday at noon. As we suspected, she knew we were seeing each other. But she responded well. She thanked me for having the good manners and thoughtfulness to tell her face to face that you and I were an item. I like her a lot and I hope we'll continue as friends."

"You did good, Doc." Erin nodded. "What time does court convene?"

"They should be over. It was to start at ten this morning, but I've heard nothing from the attorney." Bobbi ran her hand through her cropped hair, mussing it even more, she imagined. "I'm not nervous, really. I'm more hopeful that the judge will do the right thing. But I can't say I'm not on tenterhooks waiting for the news."

Erin pulled Bobbi down for a kiss, her hands circling Bobbi's neck. The kiss lingered and deepened.

"Ahem." Gen stood just outside the cubby. "Sorry to interrupt, folks."

Bobbi and Erin broke apart quickly.

"Doctor, you have a call on the clinic line."

"Oh." Bobbi looked at Erin meaningfully. "I've been expecting some news on the sentencing," she said to Gen.

Gen nodded, and as she turned to leave the cubby, she patted Bobbi on the shoulder without saying a word. Bobbi sighed with her heart open. Gen had been a great support these past few days.

Before Bobbi went to answer the call, she asked Erin, "What was that kiss for?"

Erin whispered, "A sign of coming attractions. We haven't made love in days. I've missed you terribly and presume that you can handle some passion tonight."

Bobbi waggled her eyebrows and smirked. "Be right back. Hold that thought."

"Yes, this is Dr. Webster."

"Doctor, this is Paul Frank, the assistant DA.

Ms. Sanderson asked that I call to inform you of the outcome of Mr. Myers' court date today."

"Yes?" Bobbi bit her lower lip.

"Judge Latimore took her time questioning Mr. Myers. She then went into chambers to study carefully all the sentencing support documents, including your witness impact statement. She just came out of chambers a few minutes ago."

Bobbi inhaled to steady her nerves. *Just get on with it*, she thought impatiently.

"As we expected, and she stated in her preliminary remarks, she gave your VI statement more credence than she normally might, given that you're a physician. She sentenced him to rehabilitation."

Bobbi exhaled the breath she didn't realize she'd been holding. "Oh, thank God. That's great news. She did specify a treatment facility?"

"No. Drug court staff will work with his parole officer to come up with a plan for him. In the meantime, he's to receive medical care for addiction. He looked in bad shape, so we surmised he might already be feeling the effects of detox. He's being treated by one of the prison doctors and will be at the county prison medical facility until he's transferred to rehab."

Bobbi nodded her head. "Yes, I see."

"Do you have any questions?"

"So, is this business finished? Do I need to do anything else?"

"You will be informed at the completion of his rehab and may need to give another victim statement then. We'll keep you informed should that be the case down the road."

"Thank you." Bobbi felt like gushing, but held back. *Be professional*, she admonished herself. "Thank you so much. I'm very pleased with this outcome."

"If that's all, then, have a good day, Doctor."

Bobbi nearly ran down the hall to let Erin know the good news.

Chapter Thirty-seven

That night, Erin and Bobbi gingerly made love, fully aware of Bobbi's continued healing, but also triumphant to have ended the bad business of violence surrounding them.

Sweetly, Bobbi came to Erin. Tenderly, Erin held her and coddled her into a slow, burning explosion of pleasure.

When Bobbi regained her composure, she said, "You make my heart sing, Elf. Can I return the favor?"

"Not tonight. There'll be other nights or days...or afternoons or mornings...or..." Erin stroked Bobbi's short, unruly hair. "Are you tired?"

"I'm...not tired, so much as relieved. Happy for Wes and his future health. And for his wife, who may have a chance to get her husband back whole." Bobbi turned to face Erin in the bed. "Don't get me wrong, I'm not so naïve to think one trip through rehab will solve all his problems."

"You know, only forty-three percent of addicts complete treatment and eighteen percent remain clean and sober after five years."

"Whew. Not the best results. I remember how many times some celebrities have been through rehab. It's scary. As a physician, I wonder if just leaving people alone with their own willpower wouldn't be just as effective. But I would never deny anyone medical support through the detox phase. I've never treated anyone, it's not my specialty, but addiction specialists use a whole cadre of drugs to aid in patient functioning while the illicit drugs come out of the neuro system."

Erin sighed. "I'm praying pretty hard for Wes and I'll keep it up as long as I'm here in Colorado."

"Praying, yeah. I have a surprise for you." Bobbi looked like a small child, as she continued. "I've been reading up on it. I found out that people who meditate regularly have lower blood pressure and heart rate, sleep better, and report better well-being. Reports of medical and nursing staff praying with pre-surgery patients show that surgeries have fewer complications, all else being equal. Less bleeding and better blood pressure control. But for me, the review of these scientific papers held more credence when they researched patients' use of personal prayer to help transform the meaning of their illness. Chronic disease, like cancer, especially."

"Praying thanksgivings daily improves one's gratefulness. My personal daily discipline includes nighttime journaling that focuses on my whole day, but specifically on giving thanks for the blessings of the day, even days when things went to hell in a handbasket."

Bobbi yawned. "So, we agree that prayer can have good effects. What I'm still uncertain about is how prayer works."

Erin chuckled. "I wish I knew the answer to that, too. Most times, I feel God's presence during my prayers. But occasionally, I feel like I'm talking to an empty universe."

Bobbi swallowed hard.

"Not often. But, sometimes, when the day has been long and difficult, I wonder where God is. It's part of my faith, to question and search. It's part of my priesthood, to help others to question and search too."

"You don't have all the answers, Mother Erin?" Bobbi quirked a smile.

"No way, Doctor. Just as you don't. You can't heal everyone, just like I can't spiritually help everyone. I believe staunchly in people's freedom to choose whether they can love a God who loves them whether they love Her or not."

"I've wondered where God is for Wes. And for me. Although, I've felt God's presence more and more since I've got to know you. I see patients in a different light, now. I see their struggles more readily than I did when I first started to practice in Colorado. Remember when you were seeing Charlotte Stephens and I bawled you out for having a communion kit in an isolation room?"

Erin said, "I don't think I'll forget it soon."

Bobbi laughed. "I apologize for that arrogant doctor. I know now that your pastoral presence with Mrs. Stephens may have been as important as my medical treatment. Not that prayer would heal her miraculously, but that your prayer and presence and the—what do you call it?—sacraments gave her something solid to cling to in her discomfort and anxiety."

Erin's eyes turned liquid in the dim light of Bobbi's bedroom. She sniffled. "Thank you, darling."

"I still don't know what this means for my religiosity. You know, whether I can do church. I still feel like I'm on another planet in that place, hearing a foreign language I've never heard. Seeing rituals I haven't a clue about. I *do* like the singing."

Something in Erin leaped for joy at Bobbi's confession about singing in church. She knew parishioners who'd come into the church because some part of the liturgy drew them in. God put desires in people's hearts: Bobbi's desire to sing was big.

"Maybe you could bring your banjo and play with the singers some time?"

"Ha, Elf. I just said I'm not sure about all this and you're inviting me to be part of it? Hold your horses."

"But don't you realize singing is God calling you to church?"

"What? Wait a damn minute." Bobbi sat up in bed.

Erin sat next to her, placing her hands on Bobbi's chest. "Don't get bent out of shape, darling."

"And that's the second time you've called me darling. I thought I was sweetie? What's going on?"

Bobbi looked at Erin's nude body and then at her own. She snickered. "What are we doing?"

Erin laughed raucously at the absurdity of being nude in bed having this major theological discussion. They settled down, both yawning.

"I think it's time for sleep, Mother Erin. Even if you can't answer my theological questions while naked," Bobbi quipped.

Bobbi cuddled Erin until Erin heard her breathing rhythmically. Erin carefully disengaged Bobbi's arms from her waist. She sighed in happy contentment.

Epilogue

January, Eighteen Months Later
"Why did we have to move in the dead of winter? It's freezing out here."

Bobbi took a box Erin had been wrestling and set it down in the living room of their new house. They'd worked out a rent-to-own deal with the widowed, older man who owned it. He lived in Bend now, just recently having left Ketchum due to his failing health.

"I thought you were Chicago-tough? Where's your winter coat, Elf?"

"I didn't want to get it dirty, Dr. Take Charge."

Bobbi looked around at the mess of boxes and furniture in the living room and felt overwhelmed. "What should we do first?"

Erin wrapped her arms around Bobbi's neck. "Well, my wife, I'd say let's have some tea, a snack, and think it over. But my vote goes to getting the bed put together first. Then the guest room. Yancy and Gen will be here soon."

Bobbi's phone rang. Yancy's cell number came up. "Yes, Dr. Webster here," she said very seriously.

Yancy huffed with laughter. "Hello, Doctor. We're just outside of John Day now. Your fragile medical equipment made it just fine in the Rover. Ryan's asleep in his car seat. He's been out since Wyoming this morning. We're picking up groceries here, getting some lunch, and should be there by two-thirty."

"Great. I can't thank you enough for volunteering to drive my instruments for the new clinic. The movers would never have dealt with it to my satisfaction. I'm going to the clinic tomorrow afternoon."

"See you soon," Yancy said, signing off.

⚜ ⚜ ⚜ ⚜

Erin threw away paper plates from their lunch, while Bobbi and Yancy set up the furniture in the guest bedroom and made the bed. They'd picked up a Pack 'n' Play for two-year-old Ryan tonight and for any future visits.

Gen came around the kitchen island, carrying Ryan's diaper bag. "How's married life treating you?" she asked Erin.

"Well, give me more than forty-eight hours, I might know better, but so far, I love it."

Gen hugged Erin. "We're so happy for you. But, on the other hand, you agreed to come here to Oregon with my best physician. I was hoping she'd stay in Valley View because of you."

Erin shook her head. "I couldn't do that to her, Gen. She had her heart set on coming back home. I wasn't particularly tied to Colorado, so it seemed like a no-brainer to help her set up the new practice. These folks in Ketchum have been traveling over fifty miles for many years, just to see a primary care doctor. They're treating her like royalty. Did you see all the baked goods in the pantry?"

"I saw all those goodies. Muffins, cake, two pies."

"I'm gonna weigh a ton eating it all. You know Bobbi is not into sweets much."

"Don't worry. Yancy has a major sweet tooth. While we're here, you can count on her to help you out." Gen grinned.

A small wail came from the master bedroom. "That's the boy. Let me go check."

"Knock, knock." The Websters opened the door slightly and Fran peeked around it.

"The cavalry has arrived," Bob Webster said in his hearty rancher voice.

"Welcome. It's wonderful to have you come over. Our first guests." Erin hugged them each.

"Guests, hell. I'm moving furniture. Where is it?" Bob looked around the chaotic, box-filled living area.

"We don't have much furniture yet. A small couch and two armchairs," Erin said sheepishly. "We're planning to pick up more in Bend later this winter and have it delivered."

"Well, then let me at the other furniture. I brought my toolbox." He held a bright red, metal box.

"Bobbi and Yancy are putting together beds. Just down the hall."

Fran noticed open boxes of kitchenware. "Do you trust me to put these away where you won't find them until a month from now?" She smirked.

Erin laughed. "I don't care, Fran. Put them where you think items should go. Bobbi and I'll work it out. I trust you to do it right, with your teacher organizational skills."

Fran went to work immediately, pulling pans out of a box.

Gen returned, carrying a tow-headed toddler. "Say hi to Auntie Erin. Hi granny Fran."

"Please, anything but granny! How about Mimi? I've always wanted to be a Mimi."

"Mimi it is," Gen said, shaking her head.

Ryan rubbed his eyes.

Erin took him from Gen. "Hi, big boy. Did you have a nice nap? Do you want something? You slept through Mommie and Momma's lunchtime."

Gen prepared food for Ryan while Erin hooked his booster chair to the dining chair, and Fran busied herself with organizing kitchen utensils and pots.

Gen fed him and they talked.

"How's he doing these days?"

"He finally is sleeping through the night, although his schedule's out of whack with our trip, so who knows what'll happen tonight."

Yancy and Bobbi came into the dining area of the kitchen. "The guest room's all set up, including the Pack 'n' Play," Bobbi said while wiping her hands on her jeans.

"They needed my tools." Bob brushed his nails over his work shirt.

"Dad." Bobbi swatted him playfully. "Thank you. You did come at a crucial moment."

Yancy sat down on the other side of Ryan, picked up a spoon, and fed him some yogurt and fruit.

Erin and Bobbi watched her with amusement, as yogurt began to cover Ryan's face.

"You're doing pretty well there, Momma." Bobbi couldn't help but tease Yancy about the parenting skills she'd acquired in the four months Ryan had been with them.

Gen asked, "What about you two? Making any plans for miniature Erins or Bobbis?"

Bobbi, wide-eyed, immediately said, "One thing at a time, please. First, set up the practice. Then Erin starts her job as chaplain at hospice. Then get the house settled and get to know the neighborhood again. Then. Then, only, will these discussions ensue."

Erin looked at Bobbi. "Oh, and when were you going to tell me these plans?"

Fran looked up from her third open box. "Yes, interesting plans, Bobbi."

Bobbi hugged Erin tightly. "Soon, Elf. Soon." Her heart swelled with love and tenderness. They were just beginning the life she'd never thought she could have. Medicine came first, until Erin came into her life. Now medicine remained important, but she didn't eat, sleep, and live it every day. They enjoyed their date nights, their quiet nights reading, and even riding horses at Triple D Ranch. That reminded her. "Also, we've got to find a place to go horseback riding, now that you're a regular cowpoke."

"Please, that decision can wait a while. My rump hasn't recovered from our last trail ride before Christmas." Everyone laughed, while Erin looked chagrined.

"We have our whole life ahead of us, Elf."

They kissed until Yancy cleared her throat loudly. "Not in front of innocent eyes, please."

For the remainder of the afternoon, Erin cleaned bathrooms, Gen took over Ryan duty, Yancy, Bobbi, and Bob finished the furniture, while Fran cleaned the stocked kitchen.

They finally all sat to enjoy food Fran had prepared and brought over.

Yancy filled their glasses with very good red wine from their collection. "Gen and I brought this Bordeaux we picked up in Paris on our honeymoon, just for a special occasion. Your wedding didn't seem the proper time, so let's give you a good beginning to your new life in Oregon." She raised her glass. All at the table followed her lead. "To Bobbi and Erin. May they live a long life filled with love and laughter."

"To Bobbi and Erin!"

Bobbi then stood, "And here's to my soulmate, my love."

Erin stood and they came together in a crashing kiss, to cheers from the friends and family who loved them.

About the Author

JB "Joey" Marsden recently returned to the family farm where she grew up, after living in more urban areas in New York, Michigan, and Kentucky. She holds a PhD in health systems organization and research, but has fulfilled her dream of being a published author of fiction, after writing many academic tomes that no one enjoyed reading.

Aside from writing, Joey enjoys reading, outdoor activities, and classic movies. Ordained for many years after being an academic, she served several rural churches as an Episcopal priest. Now retired, she can be found most often basking in the quiet of rural living, but both Joey and her wife travel for work and fun both in the U.S. and abroad

Contact info:
Facebook: facebook.com/joeybmarsden
Instagram: joeybmarsden

Check out JB's other book

Reclaiming Yancy – ISBN – 978-1-948232-04-3

Her bossy best friend Roxie criticizes her risky behavior, and warns that she'd better shape up before something serious happens. Her socialite mother loves when she dresses properly, but laments that the clothes hang off her strong yet unhealthily lean body. Colorado rancher Yancy Delaney is a woman grieving past losses, escaping her past by running from any commitment—except to her beloved horses and her work at Valley View, the rural medical organization her family founded.

Enter Dr. Genevieve Lambert, the hot new medical director of Valley View's rural clinics, where Yancy is Board Director. They immediately feel the sparks of attraction, but Gen wants no part of Yancy's seduction game or her reputation for casual one-nighters. And Yancy's missteps and risk-taking may finally be catching up with her, resulting in an injury to herself and a path of broken hearts left in her dust.

Gen and Yancy embark on a journey of romance fraught with rocky rides. Can they overcome their tough trails and find true love?

The Travels of Charlie - ISBN - 978-1-948232-24-1

In 1884, Charlene Dieter needs a new life, away from unwanted male suitors and from Jo, her best friend who has rebuffed her romantic overtures. Charlene finds her new self in "Charlie," the man she always thought she should have been. Charlie decides to start a new life in Illinois, motivated by letters from a cousin of Charlie's deceased dad.

Kitty McIntire, a young woman managing her prairie farm after her father's death, also fends off a suitor, John Cameron. John, however, presses on, despite a rival for Kitty's attentions in cousin Charlie, newly arrived in their small town. Charlie does his best to be a farmer, but sustains injuries that lay him up. Kitty attends him while he recuperates, and they begin to fall in love, when circumstances force Charlie to let Kitty in on his secret.

Charlie and Kitty together face the escalating verbal and physical attacks from John, as he tries to get Kitty and her farm for his own purposes.

Will John come between the love that Charlie has found with Kitty? How can they, two women in a time that men rule, bring John to justice?

Other books by Sapphire Authors

The Four Seasons - ISBN - 978-1-948232-26-5

Music begins the story, and music weaves itself around each changing time period and evolution, Vivaldi's transcendent notes encapsulating the various moods of the Four Seasons.

Irene has taught their intricacies for years, as the music of her life gently coils around her and her longings. As the result of a radio contest, she ends up in Tasmania, crossing over hemispheres and seasons, leaving behind winter for the warm sands of summer.

Helena, mountain woman, humanitarian, and yogurt baron, takes her yearly trek to Tasmania to assess her culture providers, unaware that she will meet her match and love in life.

Individually and together, these two women blend a musically rich tapestry of passion, eroticism, humor, intrigue, and the simple and complex layers of the human existence.

Twisted Deception - ISBN - 978-1-939062-47-5

There are two types of people who can't look you in the eyes: someone trying to hide a lie and someone trying to hide their love.

Addie Blake's life isn't black and white—more like a series of short bursts of color that sustain her until the next eruption. She isn't a ladder-climber in the corporate world. Instead, she works long hours at the office and even at home, something her mechanic girlfriend, Drake Hogan, can't stand. If Addie can't focus on Drake, then Drake finds arm candy that will. After a long week of late nights and a series of text-messaged demands, each one a bigger bomb than the last, Addie has had enough of her Motor Girl.

Greyson Hollister inhabits a world where everything is either black and white, or money green. She's a polished, certified workaholic. As head of Integrated Financial, she has built the ladder others want to climb. Now she intends to attend a business mixer to confront a rumormonger and kill merger rumors involving her company.

Detective Nancy Hill, the lead detective on the Elevator Rapist task force, has just been called in to investigate an attack at Integrated Financial. She can't quite put her finger on it, but something doesn't add up with this latest assault, and Greyson Hollister isn't exactly lending a helping hand.

A storm's brewing on the horizon. Can Addie and Greyson weather it, or will it blow them over?

Printed in February 2019
by Rotomail Italia S.p.A., Vignate (MI) - Italy